Praise for

WHISKEY AND INK

Whiskey and Ink is emotive, sometimes sexual, and as with its predecessor, packed with mystery.

—**Rosie Wylor-Owen**
USA Today **Bestselling Author**

Fia Drake is the kind of heroine who punches you in the gut and you gladly ask for more. *Whiskey and Ink*, the second installment of the Fia Drake, Soul Hunter series, delivers that gut punch from beginning all the way to the end, which leaves you begging for book three.

—**Theda Vallee**
Author, *Stir Until Petrified*

WHISKEY AND INK

Other Books by
D. GABRIELLE JENSEN

Fia Drake, Soul Hunter Series

Drummers and Demons
(Book 1)

WHISKEY AND INK

Fia Drake, Soul Hunter Series
Book Two

D. Gabrielle Jensen

BALANCE OF SEVEN

Dallas

Whiskey and Ink

For information, contact:
Balance of Seven, www.balanceofseven.com
Publisher: dyfreeman@balanceofseven.com
Managing Editor: tntinker@balanceofseven.com

Cover Design by Adam E. Mathews, Pikuled People Art
adammathews@gmail.com

Developmental Editing, Copyediting, and Formatting by TNT Editing
www.theodorentinker.com/TNTEditing

Publisher's Cataloging-in-Publication Data

Names: Jensen, D. Gabrielle. | Jensen, Desiree Gabrielle, 1980- .
Title: Whiskey and ink / D. Gabrielle Jensen.
Description: Dallas, TX : Balance of Seven, 2021. | Series: Fia Drake, soul hunter; book 2. | Summary: The life of Fia Drake, soul hunter, has revolved around independence. Now that independence is being threatened. She'd rather just skip town, but between the tarot revelation of a traitor and the drummer in her bed, she'll have to face the hunt, armed with whiskey and a blessed tattoo.
Identifiers: LCCN 2021931430 | ISBN 9781947012134 (pbk.) | ISBN 9781947012141 (ebook)
Subjects: LCSH: Interpersonal relations – Fiction. | Intimacy -- Fiction. | Mythology – Fiction. | Rock musicians -- Fiction. | Solitude – Fiction. | Tattooing -- Fiction. | Denver (Colo.) -- Fiction. | BISAC: FICTION / Fantasy / Action & Adventure. | FICTION / Fantasy / Dark Fantasy. | FICTION / Fantasy / Urban.
Classification: LCC PS36010.E57 W45 2021 (print) | PS3610.E57 (ebook) | DDC 813 J46W--dc23
LC record available at https://lccn.loc.gov/2021931430

25 24 23 22 21   1 2 3 4 5

One

Fia Drake leaned back against the straight, square arm of her black leather couch, her bruised, scarred, and tattooed arms folded across her bare chest. Her eyes were trained on the glass coffee table that had miraculously escaped demolition when a demon smashed through her balcony door.

Though at the time, she hadn't known that's what it was.

When she was sixteen, a priest had tracked her to the warehouse where she had been living with a handful of other homeless teens and left a crossbow on the sofa she had used for her living space. Zeke, the boy in the tepee next to her couch, had wrapped the bow in an old coffee bean sack.

That weapon—and the sack—had traveled with her until just a week ago, when she thought the bow had been crushed in an explosion. Now the bow rested, once again, on the sack in the middle of her glass-top coffee table.

Fia had lost track of time staring at the weapon, as if waiting for it to transform into a bird or a bouquet of flowers, when Max Hawkins's warm-brandy baritone cut into her thoughts.

"Imagine my surprise at waking up alone in a strange bed. It's a lovely bed, don't get me wrong, but—what is that?"

"A crossbow," Fia replied without turning to face him, her voice completely void of snark.

He nodded, rounding the sofa to sit beside her. "Okay." He sat quietly for a moment, then asked, "Is it yours?"

Fia shrugged. "It looks like mine."

"But?"

"But it shouldn't be. It should be a mangled heap beneath a couple tons of limestone."

"Oh."

Fia stood and stepped away, crossing to the kitchen. She pulled two glasses from the cabinet and held one up for him to see. "Water?"

"Sure?"

She filled both glasses and carried them back to the couch. She handed one to him, rested the other on the table beside the weapon, and retraced her steps to retrieve her discarded t-shirt from the dark wood floor. Near the front door, she found Max's boxer shorts and brought both items back to the couch.

She slipped the t-shirt over her dark copper hair, catching a quick glimpse of their reflection in the glass of the balcony door. She savored the view of Max's nude body— the sharp lines of his muscles, the intricate lines of his tattoos—before handing him the shorts. "Leather," she offered as he took them from her.

"Thanks." He made an elaborate show of peeling his bare skin from the leather sofa and slipped into the deep blue cotton garment. "Why—" He stopped, chewing thoughtfully at his top lip before starting over. "Why do you think it should have succumbed to such a terrible fate?"

She sighed from deep in her gut and shook her head, pressing the heels of her hands into her eyes. A memory flooded into the red darkness.

The crowd of baseball fans gathered in the street was in chaos. Sitting on the concrete, his back against the iron grate along the bottom of the raised sidewalk, a man clutched frantically at a gaping wound in his shoulder. Flesh and muscle had been torn free of the limb, and the wound was larger than he could cover with his hand.

A rough, calloused hand gripped Fia's shoulder, and she jumped, turning to see Max had caught up with her. "Max! What the—get out of here! Or you know what, make yourself useful and see if you can help that guy."

"On it." He pulled his shirt off over his head and utilized a small hole in the side to rip it into a bandage. Fia turned away, toward another scream.

Fia dropped her hands, shaking off the memory. "Max, are you religious? I don't mean 'do you go to church?' I mean, do you buy what they sell there?"

He blinked, scratching his head. "I haven't been to church since high school. But I guess I'm open to suggestions. Why?"

"Perfect. I think you deserve a story, but if you were deeply rooted in either answer, I think it would be harder for you to accept what I'm going to tell you."

She studied the sharp angles of his long face, not really looking for anything as much as just stalling. She took a healthy drink from her glass of water before setting it back on the table with a flat clink.

"I'm just not sure where to start."

"I find the beginning to be a good place."

"Yeah," she huffed. She wasn't even sure where the

beginning was. He deserved something, but how much? "Well, in the beginning, there was darkness. From the darkness, the Mother emerged, and she was called Gaia."

Max's eyes widened, and he chuckled. "Maybe not that far back."

Fia shrugged, an exaggerated dismissal. "Fine, but you're missing out on some quality storytelling. Okay, the crossbow. I guess we'll start there."

She finished her water and rose from her seat, returning to the kitchen. This time, she pulled a tall, square bottle of amber liquid from another cabinet. She filled her empty glass with the whiskey and held the bottle up in a silent offer.

Max joined her in the kitchen. "It's that kind of story?"

"It's that kind of story."

He, too, emptied his glass before handing it to her. She refilled it and, bottle in hand, rounded the island counter to sit on one of the steel stools. She jumped as cold steel touched her bare butt. He took a seat on one of the other stools and sipped at his whiskey before motioning for her to start her story.

"Max, I am . . ." She scratched her head. "Remember that guy at the bar downtown?"

"The zombie guy?"

"The zombie guy. Except he wasn't a zombie. He—it—wasn't even human." A question spread over Max's face, but he remained silent, letting her talk. "What do you know about ancient religions, mythology?"

"You mean, like Greeks, Olympus, that sort of thing?"

"Any of them, really. But yeah, Greeks."

"Not a lot. The standard, I guess: gods, beasts, mazes, Hercules, Wonder Woman."

Fia laughed. "There's a little more to it than that. I learned all that same stuff too, in school. I don't remember learning a lot about the original gods, though. Do you?" He shook his head. "In the beginning, there was darkness . . ."

"You mentioned that."

"Yeah, but now it's relevant. As to be expected, there are some discrepancies in the stories, but basically, there were beings created before the commonly taught pantheon. Titans, furies, and muses were all created before Zeus and his crew."

"Yeah, I remember something about that. Very surface-level stuff. Mostly just that they existed. Not too much about who or what they were or where they came from."

"As it was broken down for me, each belief system kind of functions on the same principles. There is a being at the top of the heap who creates everything under them from nothing. In this story, it's Gaia. Gaia created her siblings— Nyx, Eros—and she created the Titans and some other beings on the same level of their hierarchy."

Fia sipped at her drink. This story made her head swim, and telling it was worse.

"In the world I was raised in, Gaia was God, and the Titans were equated to a race of what we call demons." Fia paused, frowning. "Species? Race?" Max shrugged, and Fia dropped it. "Anyway. Basically, these demons were the first beings. Then there were angels, which would be the same tier as Zeus and his ilk. After the angels, mortals—humans and animals—were created."

"I remember this chapter."

"So, the demons were first, and I guess, like any eldest child, they were grumpy about the angels, so they took off and colonized their own island—Hell, the underworld—and lived happily ever after."

"Until the humans came."

"You do know this story."

"I know this plot formula."

"A group of angels were pissed because Mom favored the mortals over the immortals. So they left to live with their older siblings, which didn't sit well but was tolerable, I guess. Granted, this is coming from the human perspective of someone who definitely wasn't there."

"Of course."

Fia drained her glass and refilled it, offering to refill Max's as well. He took a drink and pushed his glass toward her.

"There's some bit about some beings with one hundred arms becoming jailers of the Titans. I'm not sure how they figure in here, but I guess the demons of this story were turned into prison guards on their little island when Gaia or whoever started sending wicked humans there.

"Which is where my story starts, indirectly. There was a demon, Irzelen, who decided enough was enough and turned all his souls loose. Just happened, he was in charge of the violent ones: murderers, rapists, abusers. He decided the single best way to destroy humanity wasn't to send them to the underworld after death; it was to send the underworld to them when they were still alive."

"Yikes."

Max's face flickered with shock. Fia was at least a little relieved by this reaction. Max had taken everything—from a mythical creature in her living room to something he probably still thought was a zombie—so easily, she had wondered if he was capable of being shocked by anything. She knew it was possible she would finally say something to break him—though she couldn't imagine what, after all he had seen—and he'd run for the hills, but so far, she hadn't gotten much reaction from him at all. That he showed even a slight shock regarding the incident that had helped establish the world she grew up in was encouraging.

"Yeah, yikes."

"Where do you fit into all this?"

She puffed a small laugh through her nose. "Oh, I guess I never finished that. Max, I hunt these souls to send them back."

"Oh." He took a deep swallow of whiskey, which she guessed meant her confession had struck a nerve he hadn't expected to have struck. "That sounds dangerous."

"I guess it can be. I try to stay off the radar as much as possible."

She swallowed hard on the memory of not one but two of her recent bounties gripping her by the throat with the intent to kill.

"That's where the crossbow comes in. Long-distance hunting. It's not a dead-or-alive situation. The only way to neutralize my targets—to reclaim the fugitive souls—is to sever the connection to the hosts, which means killing the hosts. I guess that's like zombies, yeah?"

"Usually, the best way to kill a zombie is to cut off its head, or at least destroy its brain. Some lore suggests that's why they eat healthy, living brains: to keep their own rotting, diseased brains viable . . ."

Max shrunk into himself, a soft blush touching his cheeks. "That wasn't what you—sorry, please continue."

Fia smiled. "So I spent some time as a kid learning to shoot through the brainstem—or at least into the spine—from a distance."

"Then what happens?"

She shrugged. "I've never stuck around to find out. I have these collars that look super simple but aren't, really."

She watched his brow furrow—a look of interest, not

concern—as she explained the collars and how they worked. She relayed then-Sister Agnes's warning about being as far away as possible when the cleaners showed up to handle the corpse.

"I was told it was safer for everyone if I was gone. Believe me, I've been tempted to stay. But I guess when something works, you stick with it."

"Who do you think shows up?"

"I had only ever given a passing thought to a group of priests, or maybe bishops, in full ceremonial robes, gliding in from somewhere off screen. It was all quite theatrical. But realistically, I guess average people, like me. Maybe cab drivers? I can see how something like that would provide them with the ability to be on call for an exorcism at a moment's notice."

"Cops," Max said with a nod. "What about people who work in the sewers? Oh! Or . . . I assume you make a pretty decent living doing this? Your exorcists probably do too. What about someone posing as a transient? They are both everywhere and invisible."

"Sewers?" She laughed. "I guess it's possible."

"Fia, you just told me the mortal earth is teeming with malevolent souls that escaped from Hell. And in case you forgot, the first time I was here, a phoenix shattered your balcony door. I'd say just about anything is possible." He took another drink. "Tell me about the crossbow."

"It was given to me when I first started doing this. And then, about a week ago, I followed a couple of those zombie things, like the one outside the bar, to a hidden little sulfur reserve up north. I had a couple people with me: this priest—the guy who gave me the bow in the first place, Father Scott—and a nun about my age, Rebecca. We got trapped inside. I climbed out through an opening in the ceiling, but I couldn't pack the weapon with me, so I left it with them. Before I could get them out, the whole thing blew. Or caved in. Or both, really. I got thrown, dislocated my shoulder—"

"Fia!" There was the shock she had been looking for.

"I'm fine." She shrugged her bruised shoulder toward him. "A little scuffed but still good. I also spent some time as a kid learning how to relocate my shoulders. And my thumbs. I can dislocate them too. We were trained for a lot of contingencies, but I haven't actually encountered many of them. I don't get close enough to be put in restraints, so I really haven't had the need for dislocating my thumbs—"

"That sounds horrible."

Fia shrugged. "Probably, but it was survival."

"You were a kid."

"They say that's the best time to learn anything."

"They mean foreign languages and swimming, not setting your own joints." Concerned horror mixed with anger dug deep trenches in Max's handsome face. It was a look Fia tried to avoid as much as possible.

The truth was, she knew how all this sounded. She hadn't as a kid, but she had only let a couple of small details slip to Zeke, and he had given her a very similar look. He had told her what she was describing was abuse and she should call the police, report Agnes and the others. She hadn't told him much of anything after that, and she hadn't told anyone else any of it. She felt the tips of her ears burn, feeling a little angry about feeling a lot embarrassed.

"Don't look at me like that. It's ancient history. Besides, I just finished telling you two people were crushed under a small mountain, and you're worried about my childhood?"

"Shit, Fia, I'm sorry. Are you okay? I mean, besides the physical?"

"I thought so. I didn't really know either of them. Not well. There was a weird connection with the priest, Father Scott, because of the bounties. Rebecca seemed like a sweet girl—ambitious, all about her mission to fight the forces of evil—but I hadn't had a chance to really do much bonding with her. So it was weird. Kind of a numb feeling. The acceptance that a human life had ended—indirectly because of something I had done, a choice I had made—but without the emotional attachment."

"You're sure they didn't get out somehow?"

"Max, it was a mess. There was this little bump—I don't know, maybe the size of a garden shed on the outside—and then it was gone. Almost completely flat. I tried to dig in, threw aside what I could, but there was just too much. I guess there is a way. They could have been trapped in some little pocket. I did leave them tucked into a crevice in the wall; maybe that was enough to protect them. But then, how long before they suffocated? No, I was sure they hadn't made it out.

"But now . . ." She looked back at the weapon on the table. "I think it would have taken a miracle."

"You live in a world of demons and condemned souls. Is a miracle really that far off?" Max slipped off his stool and drained the whiskey from his glass. "I want to show you something. Sit tight." He crossed the condo to the front door. Flipping the locks, he left, still dressed in nothing but his underwear.

Fia poured herself another glass of whiskey, swirling it around while she waited for him to return. She climbed down from her stool and carried the drink to the floor-to-ceiling glass door leading to her balcony. The balcony had been one of the biggest selling points when she bought the condo. It stretched the full length of the converted warehouse. She had hung a screen over the corner of the space facing the street and had, on more than one occasion, slept on one of the lounge chairs she kept out there in the summer.

She stepped out onto the concrete platform and rested her glass on the railing, gazing out over the city. The view from here included the lights of downtown, and she found it relaxing. She lost herself in her whiskey and the view and didn't hear Max return. He stepped close enough that she could feel him without him touching her.

Before she could turn to face him, she heard a sound. A soft hum. Not fully electrical but unlike anything else she had ever heard before.

Unlike anything else, that was, except a feather hidden away in a safe in her bathroom.

"Where did you get it?" she asked softly, without looking to see what he held.

"How did you know?" Max reached around her, pressing himself into her back, and laid a feather on the balcony railing. It was pure white, bright enough to emit its own light in the glow of the half moon and stretched from the tip of her middle finger to the crook of her elbow.

"I could hear it. Can't you?"

"I can. I thought I was crazy. But you can hear it?" He didn't let her answer. "I'm sorry, Fia. I took it while I was cleaning up the glass from the door. It was in the mess. I couldn't help it. It just . . . drew me to it. The glow, the hum . . . Fia, what is this?"

She released a deep sigh. "That is a feather. Now ask me where it came from."

"Where did it come from?"

"I don't know, but I have an idea how to find out."

Two

ia woke the next morning eager to get started on her plan.
The sheets on the other side of the king-size bed were thrown back where Max had gotten up before her. She crawled out, setting her bare feet on the yarn rug beside the bed, and padded into the bathroom in search for him, then out to the main room of the condo.

She found Max, fully dressed, standing at the stove. The aroma of sausage and coffee filled her senses, making her mouth water.

"Good morning," he chirped, pouring her a cup of coffee.

She considered his clothes, then her own underwear. Deciding she was underdressed, she picked her shirt up from the floor where Max had dropped it after relieving her of it when they went back to bed. After slipping it over her head, she climbed atop a stool to enjoy her drink. "You could have woken me. Did you leave?"

"Yeah, sorry. I know I shouldn't have left the door

unlocked, but I noticed there was a supermarket . . ." He waved his hand vaguely in the direction he had gone. "And I was starving, so I thought you might be too."

"No, that's fine—yeah, it smells great. I guess I need some groceries." She drank greedily from her cup, watching Max at the stove.

He held up a pair of eggs for her to see. "Scrambled?"

"Sure."

A few minutes later, he placed a plate in front of her, joining her with his own. "What are you going to do about the . . . ?" He nodded toward the coffee table, where the crossbow still lay. Fia hadn't said any more after her initial idea struck.

The truth was, she wasn't sure herself what she was going to do. Not completely. She had remembered a snare gun she had bought early on, when it seemed like fancy hunting toys might come in handy.

She had used it to catch a squirrel.

Fia shrugged. "I'm working on a trap . . ." She tapped a finger against her temple. "But I need a job first."

"Are you going to wait for the cab driver to stop for his exorcism?"

"Whoever shows up, yeah." After a moment, she spoke again, asking him about his plans, pushing the focus off herself.

"I need to pick my gear up from the studio. I was in kind of a hurry to get here last night."

"You came straight here?"

Max nodded. Something twisted in Fia's gut, and she chose to drown it, emptying what was left of her coffee.

They finished eating in silence. The energy Fia felt from Max suggested that, for him, it was a peaceful silence, but she felt tense, even a little panicked. She wasn't sure what to make of Max coming to see her before doing anything else, even taking his gear home.

Once they were done, Max gathered up the plates, rounding the island bar to set both in the sink. He must have sensed her tenson because once he was rid of the plates, he looked across the bar, his gaze so intense, Fia couldn't help but meet it. His face was soft, concerned, and he kept his voice low.

"Did I say something wrong? You clammed up kind of suddenly."

She studied his deep eyes for a moment. They were kind and warm, the light from the balcony door reflecting off gold flecks, making them dance.

More than that, they were safe. While Fia had never been one to shy away from eye contact, the men she usually brought home with her avoided it, as if refusing to look into her eyes made it easier to stay distant, get off, and get out. Max almost left her no other choice but to look into his eyes.

He felt safe.

She breathed a sigh from deep in her gut and shook her head. "I was a little, I guess, freaked out that you came here first, without going home. But I'm okay. Honestly, I'm fine. You know what I do puts you at risk, though, right?"

He nodded. "If I promise to stay out of trouble, can I stay? I mean, not today, gear and stuff, but maybe tomorrow?"

She smiled. "You can stay. You don't have to clean—"

"If I hadn't made the mess, there wouldn't be anything *to* clean." He stopped short and turned to look at her, his eyes wide with mock panic. "Unless you want me to leave. Was that a hint?"

Fia shook her head. She had nothing to do until the next

bounty came in, and she told him as much. His face lit up with a toothy grin.

"Do you want to do something? Like real people do?"

"Like a date?"

His cheeks flushed pink. "No, not like—unless you want—no, not a date. Date is pretty formal. Picnic."

"We just ate, and you want to have a picnic?"

"After I take my stuff home."

Having a picnic, like normal people, sounded almost nice. Fia couldn't remember the last time she had had a picnic. They had done it a few times when she lived in the convent, whenever they came into the city for Free Museum Day. Somehow, her time on the streets had dulled the romance of outdoor dining.

"I think—"

"Sorry," Max interrupted, "that's not what this is—we're just—this is casual, right? No strings. Dates have strings—"

"Max, hush. I was going to say I think a picnic sounds—"

Again, she was interrupted, this time by a *cha-ching* from her phone. "Damn it."

"I don't think that's an adjective." Max nodded at her phone. "What's that?"

"A soul with terrible timing."

"Huh?"

"It's a motion sensor. I have a drop box out in K-Town; it's where the priest—it's where Father Scott used to leave my bounties." She watched confusion wrinkle its way across Max's forehead. "Yeah, I don't know either. I got one after—but if I got a new handler, I'm back at square one getting to know them. At least they know about the box."

"Pretty hands-off, then?"

"Do you want to come?"

Max screwed up his face, visibly disappointed. "I kind of do. But I really do have stuff . . ."

"Of course."

He shoved out his lower lip in an exaggerated pout. "Maybe next time?"

Fia nodded and climbed down from her stool. She circled around the bar to help Max finish cleaning up the kitchen.

Much like the bounty Fia had received for Kristina Masterson, the new packet contained almost nothing compared to what Fia had been used to from Father Scott. Also like Kristina Masterson's packet, this one had arrived at the eleventh hour, and Fia had almost no time to track Abe Mackey, a personal trainer in his midthirties who had steamed two of his clients like lobsters in the saunas of gyms in two different neighborhoods. She had to give him a gold star for covering his tracks, at least.

Now, she was up at the crack of dawn because Abe Mackey liked to run through City Park. She was perched on the lowest sturdy limb of a tree, armed with the little pistol-grip crossbow she had picked up to replace the one that had supposedly been crushed in the explosion. She didn't like the little ones as much; they were less accurate at a distance, but at least they were handy for climbing trees.

Fia heard footfalls on the concrete to her left. Turning her head, she confirmed the man coming toward her was who she was looking for. Running along the sidewalk that wrapped around the park was a short, stocky man with deeply tanned skin and a deep widow's peak of short-shorn brown hair, just like in the photo she had been given. She waited for him to pass her, more trusting of the little crossbow's six-inch bolt reaching its target from the back. Once he was a few feet away, she set up the shot and squeezed the trigger. The bowstring snapped like a rubber band, and Abe Mackey pitched forward onto his knees, before falling face-first onto the concrete.

Fia swung herself down from the tree and took three bounding steps to her target. Her hands moved independently of one another, one removing the bolt from the man's neck while the other flicked open the high-tech collar, reforming it into a circle. The collar was made of titanium and collapsed down to the size of a paperback novel to fit in her satchel. When she had first gotten the bag, she had packed it full with a camera, extra bowstrings, and snacks for long stakeouts. Now, she barely carried anything but the collar, leaving room for two or three, if she wanted to keep them handy.

Along the inside of the titanium collar was a small copper rod about the length of Fia's pinkie and as big around as a pencil, with a GPS tracker that called . . .

Well, that was the question to be answered today. As she had told Max, she had never stuck around to find out who was coming in on her heels. She had filed it away as maintaining mutual anonymity and left it there. But today, she was setting a trap.

She slipped the rod into the wound left by her bolt and snapped the collar closed. The rod would continue to stimulate the host's nervous system, fooling the parasitic soul into believing it was still alive. Then she flipped a switch near the locking latch, and a green light flickered to life.

Grabbing the corpse by the legs, she dragged it off the path behind a nearby shrub and then took cover behind her tree to wait.

What came next had never once crossed her imagination. She hadn't been lying when she told Max she imagined a small collection of bishops in full robes gliding in as if on rails. The reality turned out to be both astounding and far more logical than any mortal answer.

The air between her and Abe Mackey's corpse shimmered and wavered, like the midsummer horizon across the desert. An electric hum, louder than the hum of the feather—*feathers*—rang more in her skull than her ears. Her breath caught in her throat as she watched a humanlike shape form from nothing. It was huge—seven feet tall or better, she guessed—and as it came more into focus, she could see its nude flesh was pearlescent blue. It had a square jaw at the base of a large bald head, a fat, bulbous nose, and sharp cheekbones.

"Okay," she sighed. "That's kind of impressive."

Wings—whiter even than the feathers—fluttered as if shaking free after being restrained. Even slack against the being's back, she could tell they were enormous. She watched the being for a moment, temporarily forgetting why she had stayed. When she finally did remember, she frantically reached into her satchel, hoping she hadn't missed her opportunity.

As what she guessed was an angel reached for the body she had concealed behind the shrub, she produced the snare gun from inside her bag. She had brought it expecting to snare a priest or a cab driver, and she hoped it would still work on this being.

The weighted net ensnared his wings, but she had not

anticipated his ability to shimmer out of it. He disappeared, net and all, and reappeared only a few inches in front of her. He dropped the net at her feet and snarled, "What is the meaning of this, mortal?" He practically spat the word *mortal* in her face.

"Where is Father Scott?" She surprised herself with her own presence of mind, that she could ask this giant divine being anything, let alone anything so direct.

"If that is your meaning, mortal, then you are a fool."

He started to shimmer from view—more and more of the scenery behind him became clear—and then in a blink, he once again became fully corporeal. He dipped to one knee, bowing his head, his wings folded tightly against his back.

Fia turned to see what was behind her that had made the being's tone change so drastically. Standing even taller than the angel on the ground—who kneeling was still nearly as tall as Fia was—was another of his kind, this one wearing Father Scott's round, flushed cheeks and beak-like nose. In what felt more like a compulsion than an active decision, Fia also genuflected. The angel wearing Father Scott's face placed a finger beneath the first angel's chin, guiding him back to his feet and waving for him to finish what he had come here to do.

He lifted Fia from the ground with the same gesture.

A flood of questions ran through her brain, all at once, and she rubbed the heels of her hands over her forehead, trying in vain to corral at least one of them. "You're in one piece, then?" she blurted finally.

The angel wearing Father Scott's face offered her a deep nod, the same gesture of respect he had given her in his human form.

"Are you—did you die?"

"I assure you, I am very much alive. Sister Rebecca is as well, I'm sure you will be relieved to know."

"Absolutely, yes." She grabbed haphazardly at another of the racing thoughts. "So, I scaled the inner wall of a portal to Hell and scraped a good three layers of skin off my back when you could have just saved me with my feet on the floor?"

"It is not quite that simple, Miss Drake."

"Of course it isn't. Nothing is." She turned to look over her shoulder at the place where she had felled her target, only to find a patch of flattened grass. "You're an angel," she said, returning her attention to the front.

"Yes."

"And alive."

"Yes."

"You're still an asshole."

"Noted."

"Okay, but why leave me weird cryptic messages? Why didn't you just tell me?"

"Messages?"

"The feather you left on my car. And the one in my apartment. If you wanted me to know, you could have just told me."

"I assure you, I did not intentionally leave you any messages. What sort of feather?"

She reached out toward his gently slacked wing, though not close enough to touch it. "Like these. About this long . . ." She held her arm out, showing him her scarred forearm. "And bright enough white to glow on its own. In the dark. And it hums. And how do you keep from humming in human form? Because you're about to make my head pop."

"They molt." He gave his shoulders a barely detectable shrug; the wings moved with them, stirring dirt and dead pine needles for several feet in all directions. "As for the humming, I apologize." Despite his words, the humming grew louder, and Fia felt all her hair prickle away from her skin. In a blink, the priest she had known for only a few days stood before her, as if the angel had dissolved, leaving behind this (still giant) human in its place.

At least the humming had stopped.

"Now, Miss Drake, I think you have something that belongs to me."

"The feathers?"

"The Sherpa." His voice carried an undeniable note of annoyance.

"Oh, yeah."

"It's been two weeks!"

"It's been a long two weeks. Yeah, I'll take you to it." She led him to where she had parked her International Scout, and they climbed in. "Did I mention I met a demon? *The* demon, to be precise. It's been a long two weeks."

"No, Miss Drake, you did not mention anything of the sort."

"I know. It was—never mind. Let's go get your tank." Fia pulled out of the parking area and headed for the main street in this part of town. "I guess you want to hear about my meeting with the demon?" He said nothing, his silence heavy in the small space. "A few days after . . . I got another job—hey, was that you? Because the polite thing would have been to say, 'Hey, Fia, we're not crushed under twenty tons of limestone, and by the way, here's your next assignment.'"

Father Scott twisted his face, wrinkling his nose. "No, I have not delivered any new bounties to you since the accident."

"I wondered. These were different: sparse, really vague. I had to do a lot of legwork on my own, and I ended up losing the first one." She let the words hang for a moment before pursuing a new thought. "Do all hunters have an angel?"

"There are a few of us veiled among mortals, keeping track of everything."

"Is that a yes? Is that why my jobs from you have so much information? You have that omniscient presence and know a lot more than a mortal handler would?" He remained silent long enough that Fia accepted he wasn't going to answer her. "I'll take *that* as a yes.

"Okay, so the demon, then. I got this bounty for this woman, but I got it super late, and then there was barely any information, so I lost the soul. But as I'm standing there watching this woman just kind of . . . dissolve, this guy shows up. This guy is huge, right? So, he tells me those things in the cave were actually demons. Someone summoned them to deal with me, I guess. Must have really pissed someone off, somewhere along the way."

"I can't imagine."

"I'm going to ignore that. Anyway, I think maybe it was this creepy priest. He's in that little cathedral downtown? On Broadway."

Father Scott took a moment to process the information. "Miss Drake, I think you may be right in that theory. Father Armando Ariaz is a very dangerous man. There has been talk he is involved with some unholy dealings."

"Dealings? Yeah, I kind of figured out he's a bad dude when he offered to choke me out."

"Miss Drake!"

"Hey, didn't we already establish we were dropping the *Miss* business? I mean, you did die in a cave for me. Or because of me. Whatever. Either way, Fia, please." Father Scott didn't respond. "Anyway, I've had a couple of run-ins with this . . . you said Ariaz?"

"Yes, Armando Ariaz. Do be careful, Fia. If he is in fact the one who summoned the demons to target you, I question his restraint. He may not hesitate to hurt you severely or even try to kill you."

"I appreciate your use of the word *try*. Because I'll tell you right now, he won't succeed."

They put another block behind them before the priest spoke again. "Uhlpir."

"Pardon?"

"My true name. Uhlpir. But I must ask that you continue to call me Scott."

"Scott? Or Father Scott?"

"Perhaps *Father*, in mixed company."

"Cool. Uhlpir." Fia let the name roll around in her brain for a minute. "I dig it. I think I'd pick it instead. If it were my name."

"*Little Flame* fits you."

They had reached one of a handful of garages in the downtown area, and she pulled in behind the Renault Sherpa she had left there two weeks before. Scott unpacked himself from her passenger seat, and she let him get around the Sherpa's rear end before backing up to give him room to do the same.

When they pulled up to the exit station, Scott leaned out through the open window and glared at her.

"What?" she shouted, leaning out her own window. "I wasn't coming back for it. You were dead, and I have my own hunk of steel. I didn't need a baby tank. Just pay the fee, and I'll get you back."

THREE

A dozen or so miles outside the city, Fia followed Scott's decommissioned military vehicle off the interstate at an unmarked exit. They followed a small paved road another mile into the trees, before taking a fork to the left. This put them on a packed-gravel road that wound back into the trees to a structure Fia had yet to figure out a name for. Immediately visible as they approached was a two-story log cabin that stretched, Fia estimated, nearly one hundred feet, end to end. *House* didn't quite seem to cover it.

Scott pulled his SUV around the side of the house, into the trees, and came back to meet Fia at the ascending garage door. Inside the garage were a pair of light-colored 1980s sedans and a small passenger van, the kind that ferried people to and from the airport, painted dark green. She recognized one of the cars—a gold-toned land yacht that had taken her and her fellow orphans on many trips from the convent into the city.

She followed Scott through to the commercial-grade kitchen she had seen when she was here before. It gleamed with sanitary brightness, even without the overhead lights. Every surface that wasn't white was brushed stainless steel. Countertops she had originally thought were solid granite were actually lighter, cheaper concrete polished to match the real granite of the floor.

As Fia watched Scott move across the kitchen to pour himself a glass of water from the tap, she tried to remember what he had looked like as an angel. Or what the other one had looked like, for that matter. The best she could recall, they had been huge. Scott's—Uhlpir's—wings had been enough, relaxed, to obscure her vision of anything that might have been behind him.

She tried then to bring to mind an image of the demon, Irzelen. Again, his size stuck out. And the fibrous sheen of his wings, more like a fly's than feathered like the angels'. His blue-black exoskeleton was visible in her memory, but the facial features were completely absent.

"Hey, did you put some kind of angelic whammy on me?"

Scott turned, extending a glass of water to her. "I beg your pardon?"

She took the glass and felt her brow furrow as a thought passed through. "You *do* know you're an angel, right? It's not one of those dissociative multiple personality things where your human form is unaware of your other form, is it?"

Scott laughed, genuinely. "Yes, I do know, but I must ask you not to speak about it freely. You are, at present, the only mortal who knows."

"Not even Agnes?" He shook his head. "Cool." Fia didn't try to hide her pleasure in knowing something the elder nun didn't, after a lifetime of being kept on a need-to-know basis.

She took a drink from the glass and made a face.

"Spring water," Scott said. "It tastes different from the water in the city."

"Yeah, I remember—I just wasn't expecting it." She took another drink. "What now?"

"Lunch is in little over an hour and a half. I think we should talk a little more before then."

"Lunch? I'm staying for lunch?"

"You drove all the way up here, so you might as well. Meet the kids. And Sisters Annabel and Theresa."

"You're sneaky. Kids? Rebecca mentioned there were some little ones here, besides the hunters?"

"Yes. Four. And four hunters."

"Eight kids, five nuns, and you? All living here?" Scott nodded. "That's a full house. Okay, what did you want to talk about?"

"Follow me, if you don't mind?"

Fia gestured for him to lead the way and followed him through a door that led out of the kitchen into a back garden area and the trees beyond.

Scott waved a hand to his right as they stepped through the doorway. "That path leads to the courtyard and the garden Sister Rebecca helps the children tend. In growing season, nearly all the house's produce comes from their garden."

Fia flashed on memories of blistered fingers and dirt she thought would never come out from beneath her fingernails. She was perfectly happy with the produce section of the supermarket.

She followed the priest through the trees to a small clearing. It was clear from the area's appearance that the teens came out here regularly. Fia knew the drill on that as well. Living in the convent, Fia and the others had firmly agreed on one thing: Agnes had the place bugged. The elder nun had always seemed to know everything they were doing before they even did it. When Fia thought about what they had gotten away with, she was certain Agnes had simply let them do it, possibly so she would have rope to hang them with later.

"I think we can talk freely out here," Scott announced, taking a seat on a large rock.

Assembled strategically around the clearing, the rock was accompanied by a log that came nearly to Fia's knees and another smaller log a few feet away. She spotted but ignored a stack of rag rugs tucked even deeper in the trees and took a seat on the larger log, facing Scott's rock.

"Please," Scott added once Fia had settled, "tell me more about your encounter with the demon."

"Okay, I got a bounty while you were—but it was really sparse and really late. By the time I got to her, it was too late." Fia swallowed hard on the image of the woman kneeling on all fours on the concrete, pulling handfuls of hair and chunks of scalp free from her head, begging Fia to help her. "Man, did you know they're alive?"

"They? You mean the hosts?"

"Yeah. This woman—" Fia shuddered. "And then this guy shows up. Honestly, I was so distracted by the woman that he might have rolled up in a tank and still startled me when he spoke. But that hum—the souls hum, a little, but I'm so used to it, I don't notice at all anymore. You guys, though—"

She shook her head. "So anyway, he starts talking about the spectacle of someone actively decaying at my feet, and then these little demons"—she waved her hand slightly above her knee—"about like so, with super sharp claws and this black stuff—like a beetle—all segmented and clicky all over their bodies—they start eating the woman. He said they eat everything organic. They leave stuff like fake nails, polyester, plastics; they can't digest that stuff. But I'm sure you know about them, right?"

Scott nodded, encouraging her to continue.

"He, Irzelen, the demon—is that what you call him? I mean, do you recognize that name? Zari used it before, but she said it was just one name mortals use for him. Do angels call him Irzelen too?"

"Ms. Dacius taught you a great deal, indeed. Yes, Irzelen is his true name."

"Why did Zari have to teach me this stuff? Doesn't Agnes know?"

"The Reverend Mother's teachings advised against the use of the demons' names. 'To give it a name is to give it power.' Whether she knows Irzelen's true name, I do not know."

"Yeah, I remember something about that power-in-a-name stuff. Zari believed naming an opponent leveled the playing field, so to speak."

"Also a valid viewpoint."

"Is there anything to any of it?"

"With all you have seen, you remain skeptical?"

"I am skeptical because of what I've seen. Did you know? About the hosts?"

"I did."

"Did Agnes?"

"That is something you would need to ask her."

"You knew and kept it to yourself. You didn't think that might be important information?"

"In my station as a mortal priest, I would not have access to that information. I could not presume to correct an expert demonologist in their teaching."

"I mean me. You could have told me."

"I could not. You would have wanted to know how I knew. I could not tell you that without revealing my identity."

"You could have lied." The statement carried more venom than Fia had intended, but she let it. The longer this conversation went on, the more lies she uncovered. Or at least omissions, which she thought were just as bad as lies in their current situation.

Scott remained silent. Fia held her gaze on him for another long moment, challenging him to say anything in response to her questions. When she finally decided he wasn't going to, she pressed on.

"The demon told me something else you might have already known." She paused, but again, Scott didn't respond. "He said those things in the cave were demons as well. They are lower-level demons, I guess, and they shouldn't be able to shift into human form, much less maintain it, which is why they kind of look like drunk zombies."

Scott rose from his perch and stepped deeper into the trees. The light through the canopy shone on his back, and Fia thought she could see a wing-shaped void in the dust motes surrounding him. With his back to her, he spoke softly, his voice tinged with something she couldn't quite identify: regret, maybe, or anger or some combination of the two.

"I suspected that may have been what we were dealing with." He turned back to her. "I had hoped my suspicions were unfounded, but Fia, you are in danger."

"Of course. 'Fia, you're in danger,' but let's go ahead and follow these things that are actively pursuing you into an underground hell pit."

"I recall you leading the charge into the cave."

"I don't recall you trying to stop me."

"Would you have listened?"

No. You know you wouldn't have. Aloud, she replied, "You didn't know that."

"I think we both know I did."

Fia rubbed her hands over her face. "Fine. So none of that matters now, I guess. These things, though. Do you know where they might have come from?"

"I do not, unfortunately. A couple of factors stand in the way of that. While I can access your thoughts and communicate with you telepathically—"

"Whoa, we're going to put a pin in that because we definitely need to circle back to telepathic communication."

"Immortals, like Irzelen and I, are strongly advised against invading the minds of mortals without express permission or dire need—"

"Someone summoned demons to *deal with me*; you don't think that's dire?"

"And while it is ill-advised for me to access a human's thoughts without permission, it is impossible for me to access the thoughts of another immortal without permission."

"Irzelen mentioned something about that. He can't find who's in control—or not in control, technically—of the demons because of a shadow?"

Scott nodded, returning to his rock. "That is upsetting."

"What do you mean?"

"A summoning can be reversed, willingly, but I am afraid if the summoner carries a demon shadow, they will not be allowed to release the thrall of their own volition. Death will be the only way to cut the tie."

"Yuck. I was hoping there would be another way."

"It is highly unlikely."

"Swell." She glanced at her phone. "Do you think we should get back? I remember how mealtimes work around here. Ten minutes early is five minutes late."

"Yes, you are probably correct."

Fia pulled herself off her log and took the lead back to the house. In the kitchen, she washed rich, black soil and sticky pine sap from her palms, sharing the sink with Scott.

"Do they ever bother you anymore?" Scott asked.

"They?"

He gestured to her hands.

"The scars? Not really. Just when someone calls attention to them."

Scott dried his hands on a towel, handing it to her when he was finished. "I will show you to the dining room."

"You're not staying?"

"I will be along shortly. I need to take care of something in my office."

"Sure."

FOUR

"Miss Drake, perhaps the young hunters would benefit from hearing some of what you have learned in the performance of your duties," Scott urged.

After lunch, Sister Cecilia—who, along with Agnes, had been in the convent when Fia was there—had ushered four young children—Levi, Lisa, Callie, and Alex—from the room, on their way into the city for one of Cecilia's customary culture trips. That had left Fia with Scott and Agnes, along with Sisters Rebecca, Annabel, and Theresa, and the hunters, Mercy, Tianna, Kaleb, and Xavier.

"'Performance of my . . .' Yeah, sure, I guess. What do you want to know?"

"What is something you would have wanted to know, had it been offered to you at their age?" Sister Annabel asked.

Though all that was visible of Annabel was her face surrounded by the white of her wimple, Fia thought she looked like she had been built from a kit labeled "Midwestern Farmer's Daughter." Deep, denim-blue eyes shone brightly above the round apples of her flushed cheeks, which were sprinkled with cinnamon freckles. She was small, close in height to Fia herself and Rebecca. Despite the soft, round features of her face, though, she wore a stern, sober expression.

Fia considered Annabel's question a moment before answering. *You would have given anything to know those hosts were still alive and you were putting them out of excruciating misery. Tell them that.* Trying not to blurt it out the way she had to Scott, Fia did her best to tell the room of onlookers about the hosts.

"Fiammetta," Agnes replied once she had finished, "how did you come to find this out?"

"The hard way," Fia answered. "I had a job, after—after the incident at the cave; you all know about that, right?" Everyone nodded. "Okay, good. That's a lot of story we don't need to retell. I had a job after that, a woman, a lawyer—"

Eyes all around the table widened with shock, the rapt audience growing appalled by what Fia told them about Kristina Masterson. Fia took a deep breath, pushing down a knot in her stomach before she laid out the worst of the details: the woman's state of decay had been so advanced, she bled from her pores while begging for help.

"It really threw me off. It's one thing to stab a dude in the neck when he's actively trying to kill you—"

One of the hunters—Mercy, a small girl with dark hair tied up in a practical braid—squeaked. "Wait, wait. You had to *stab* a guy?"

Fia sighed, twisting her neck to get rid of the sensation of a man's hands squeezing off her breath. "Twice. In the last month." Worried expressions made a wave around the table. "No, no, no, this is not normal. I've had a bad month."

She shuddered, moving ahead as quickly as she could to avoid someone dragging her back. "So I froze. I was watching this woman not just die but actively decay right in front of me, and this man . . ." She stopped, not sure where to go next.

She must have been quiet for too long because the second of the two nuns she had only just met—a model-beautiful woman with bright mahogany eyes and sharp features—urged her on. "This man what, Miss Drake?"

Fia shook her head. "Sorry, Sister. Theresa, is it? Please, we are all together in this weird world. Can we maybe be a little less formal? I definitely don't need to be 'Miss' every time someone addresses me. Fia is fine."

Sister Annabel nodded. "I agree with Fia. Nothing about our lives is what anyone would call normal. Perhaps some of the conventions we are accustomed to, Sister Theresa, might be set aside."

Fia watched Theresa's face, waiting for her to argue or concede. When Theresa bowed her chin to Annabel and then to Fia, Fia picked her story up again.

"He looked like a human, a *big* human." She waved a hand at Scott. "I think he might have been taller than Father Scott and definitely broader. But it was his eyes that gave him away. They were yellow, but real glittery, like topaz, and they had slit pupils like a snake."

She stopped to look around. Brows were furrowed, jaws were slack, but eight sets of eyes were trained on her, unwavering. In her pause, Sister Rebecca returned from the kitchen, where she had disappeared earlier with the lunch dishes.

"My apologies, Fia, old habits. I could not simply carry the plates to the kitchen and leave them for later. And after

I washed them, I couldn't not clean up the rest. Please continue your story? I heard a little, outside the door, about a snake?"

"No, not a real snake. I was telling them . . . well, I was telling them I met the demon."

"The demon? Not *a* demon? *The* demon?"

"Yeah, I guess. We call him Irzelen. I guess he was at the helm when . . ." She waved her hand vaguely to suggest everything. "All of this started."

"Did he tell you his name?" Annabel asked, the crease in her forehead deepening.

"I knew it before."

"Fiammetta, that is not something you were told here. Where did you learn this information?" Agnes's voice was stern and rough, and Fia cringed. For a moment, she was nine years old again, being berated for any one of her petty nine-year-old crimes. She bit back the urge to rebel, to challenge Agnes for years of secrecy. This wasn't the time or the place, she told herself.

"I met another hunter after I left here. She was raised and learned to hunt in a different culture. They didn't think naming the demon was taboo." Fia stood from her chair to stretch her neck and back. "I'm sorry, everyone. I'm not used to sitting like this. Does anyone mind if we take this to a new venue? Outside, maybe?"

Agnes rose to join her. "I think that is a marvelous idea."

"Really?" Fia tried to stop her astonishment before it crossed her lips but failed. She couldn't remember the last time Agnes had so openly praised her for anything.

"Yes, Fiammetta, I think a change of venue and some fresh air would be quite beneficial."

"Yeah, okay. Lead the way." She gestured for Agnes to walk ahead of her. The others joined the parade until Fia brought up the rear.

Outside, Agnes led them to the area Scott had told Fia about earlier: Rebecca's garden. A stone path led from the door at the back of the foyer left to a small courtyard. Creamy white limestone and deep red bricks were laid in a spiral pattern. Fia estimated the whole bricked area measured twenty feet across, with the vegetable garden closest to the small raised border and flowering bushes behind that. The garden looked like it had been set up with the strategic precision of an expedition into space. Vining plants like grapes, squash, and cucumbers originated from tall pots at the back of the circle, creating an archway over another small path that led to a shed Fia could barely see through the trees.

In front of the vines were berry bushes, and each new row of vegetables, as they got closer to the house, was a shorter plant. Fia reached out and plucked a handful of dark red raspberries from their bush and took a seat on one of the stone benches near the edge of the courtyard.

The teens took up space on the ground, joined by Annabel and Rebecca, while Agnes and Theresa took the other bench. Scott stood behind them, his hands clasped at his waist.

Just as everyone had settled, Sister Cecilia stepped through the trees on the other side of the courtyard, from the direction of the kitchen. "I apologize for the interruption, but Sister Rebecca, could I get your help for a moment?"

Rebecca regained her feet and bowed slightly to Fia. "We'll have to catch up on our own time, I guess. I would like to hear what you are telling the others, but duty calls."

Fia waved her hand, giving Rebecca a pass. "Just let me know when."

She watched Rebecca scuttle off behind Cecilia before returning her focus to the others. "Now, where was I?"

FIVE

ou had just told us that you met *the* demon," Annabel offered. "The one responsible for releasing the souls."

"What I want to know," interjected another of the hunters, who had bushy brown curls and dark eyes. "Is why, after centuries, did he approach you?"

"Tianna, is it? It wasn't random, and I'm not sure it had anything to do with me, not directly. He suggested we might have a mutual problem, one he couldn't solve."

"What kind of problem would you share with a *demon*?" Mercy asked, the crevice returning between her eyebrows.

Fia scanned the faces looking back at her. "I think the answer to that question is something better left for later. Above all else, it is something Rebecca should hear. It actually has to do with our incident in the cave a few weeks ago."

"Father Scott told us a little about that," Annabel said. "You had followed a target into a cave, and the cave exploded?"

"Yeah, basically. It was several targets, actually, a whole nest—"

"Sister Annabel?" Rebecca interrupted, slipping back into the garden behind Fia. "Excuse me, Fia, but I could use Sister Annabel's help for a minute."

"Apologies, Fia. Please continue without me." Annabel bowed and joined Rebecca, heading off for the kitchen.

Fia watched their robes trail behind them as they left. *They all look the same from behind,* she thought, her mind flashing to the woman she had seen at Ariaz's cathedral. To the others, she quipped, "My audience is dwindling. If one more ducks out, I'm going to take it personally."

She took a quick note of Agnes's expression, and expecting her to miss the humor, Fia plowed ahead before the nun could find an opening. "There was a nest of these things we thought were some kind of possessed hosts that had gotten fouled up. They were all over the place. I saw a couple of them before Father Scott approached me to help him track them down."

She ran through the events leading up to and immediately following the cave explosion, hoping she wasn't directly contradicting anything Scott had already told them.

"Is that what happened to your hand?" Xavier asked. He was the kind of dark Latin European—Italian, maybe, or Spanish—that would feature prominently in an old black-and-white movie. He was tall and lean, with thick black hair that was just long enough to have some play and black-brown eyes.

The others murmured among their ranks. Fia couldn't make out if they all wanted to know or if they were chiding him for his question, though she did hear the word *question* from at least one of them.

She held out her right hand, giving it a twist to show the full extent of her scars. "Nope. I've had these for a while. Shortly after I left, actually, I got in . . . some trouble. I didn't cause it. It found me."

"As it did in those days," Agnes replied.

Fia sighed. "Yeah, I guess." *It still does,* she thought, but she wasn't ready to share that with the group.

"What kind of trouble?" Xavier asked. "Did it happen on a hunt?"

"No, I had given up hunting when I left the convent. I had gotten a normal job."

Is this something you would have wanted to know?

Fia didn't think her experience with Ted was anything the hunters would ever need to know to do their jobs. It was an isolated incident. The odds of them running into something similar in their own experiences were less than slim.

At the same time, she didn't think Xavier would let her off the hook, and she clearly remembered being in their shoes, with adults who simultaneously treated them like toddlers and soldiers, with both extremes on a need-to-know basis.

"I was working in a diner with a couple other girls my age—I was almost seventeen at that point. Everyone who worked there was living on the streets, in some way. It was presented as this kindness the owner was doing for us, hiring street kids no one else would hire, but the reality was, he knew no one would believe us if we went to the cops about his, er . . . side business."

Fever burned through Fia's cheeks, embarrassment mixed with anger. She wasn't actively angry about what happened, but as she replayed the story in her mind, she was back there again. She shifted on the bench, the edge of it suddenly a reminder of Ted's desk, the hard edge pressing into her thighs as he lifted the skirt of that stupid blue dress.

"I do like it when you new girls try to fight back." Ted's voice was rough, gravelly, a product of the same cigarettes that had colored his teeth a rancid yellow brown and probably tainted his breath permanently.

"Instead of letting him sell me like a cheap pot roast, I clobbered him with a stapler and deep-fried his arm. And mine."

She waited for a response. No one moved. She wasn't sure any of them were even still breathing.

"That was the thing that broke you guys? Hey, I'm fine. The guy went to jail; I'm pretty sure he got suicided in lockup before he could even get a trial. It's ancient history." She took a deep breath, convincing herself to put the memories back where she found them. "Unlike the demons in that cave."

"Demons? In the cave?" Rebecca asked, returning to the garden from the direction of the foyer.

"Welcome back. You're just in time. I was about to tell everyone what we really found in the cave."

"Oh?"

Fia took a breath, regrouping her thoughts. "So, this demon guy, Irzelen—he corners me in the garage where I found Kristina Masterson and kind of lets me in on some of his trade secrets. He's got these little piranha demons that form out of the shadows. They're about this big"—she waved her hand out in front of her, just above her knees— "and covered in black chitin like a giant cockroach or beetle, and they eat . . . everything."

She swallowed hard, her memory now filled with the crunching, sucking sounds of the small swarm of demons devouring the corpse of Kristina Masterson. She rubbed her hands over her face, trying to press the memory back into the recesses of her brain.

When she lowered them, Sister Annabel was coming back to the courtyard from the kitchen area. "My apologies, Fia. I hope I haven't missed too much. I had something to take care of inside." She reclaimed her space on the stones and turned an expectant expression toward Fia.

Fia sighed, hoping that was the end of the interruptions. She had never had any aspirations of being a teacher, and now she knew why. "Not at all, Sister. I was just catching Rebecca up."

She was trying to remember where she had been before Xavier threw her back into the world of diner owners pimping out homeless teens when Mercy grabbed her by the hand and pulled her off the bench. "What the—"

"Snake!" Mercy exclaimed, pointing under the bench.

SIX

Fia spun to see what the girl was pointing at. Behind the bench, bright red stripes contrasted against the green of the garden.

"That's a coral snake," announced the other of the two boys, Kaleb.

Fia, calm once again, stepped back toward the bench, crouching to see beneath it.

"Fia! Coral snakes are deadly. Don't get too close," Mercy pleaded.

Annabel stepped around Fia and knelt in front of her. She reached out and pinched the creature just behind its head, pulling it carefully from its hiding place. "You're kind of far from home, friend. How did you get up here?" She let the snake wrap around her arm. "Reverend Mother, would it be all right if I took her into the city to animal control?"

"I think that would be fine, Sister Annabel. You may take the sedan." The younger nun bowed to Agnes and turned toward the kitchen. "As for the rest of us, I think we have had enough excitement for one day. The teens need to get in some training. Dinner is at five, Fiammetta. You may stay, if you would like."

When Fia started this day, she never would have guessed this was where she would end up. She looked around at the other faces, thinking it might be prudent to get to know them a little better. They all seemed to be fighting the same fight.

She shrugged. "Sure. As far as I know, I don't have anything better to do."

She hoped learning the identity of her anonymous employer meant she could stop relying so heavily on the drop box and just get her bounties from him directly. With that in mind, she shot him a quick look to confirm what she had just told Mother Agnes.

He shrugged.

Perfect. You're a lot of help.

Tianna clapped excitedly. "I, for one, would love to hear what you've learned in the field. Maybe some tricks Sister Theresa and Sister Annabel don't know we should know?"

Fia thought for a moment. A lot of what she had learned in the convent had come in handy more than she had expected when she was learning it. She had thought gymnastics training—walking, even doing basic tumbling on the balance beam, and flipping around the bars—had been fun but trivial until she figured out it was faster to jump off buildings than to use the stairs. "Yeah, I guess I could show you something. Sister Theresa, do you mind?"

The nun shook her head. "Not at all, Miss Drake. I agree with Tianna; I am sure you have picked up some tricks I would never think to teach them."

"Okay, then. To the training grounds?"

Sister Theresa took the lead, the teens falling in behind her, and Fia brought up the rear. When they reached the double doors back into the foyer, Theresa branched off to the left. One hundred yards or so, and they reached a barren plot of land, covered in dull yellow straw. As they entered, a shed—or small house, really—stood to the right, a crow's nest resting against the roof.

On the ground before the frame holding up the platform was a log fence, and several yards from that stood five bull's-eye targets. To Fia's left, she saw the gymnastics equipment just as she remembered it—without safety mats. "You will not have mats as hunters," Agnes had explained. Fia had learned to take a fall on the hard ground, and it looked like this batch of teens were learning the same lesson.

Fia took inventory and quickly decided the crow's nest was the best place to start. "Tianna, would you mind coming with me? Everyone else, hang here where you can see the base of the platform."

She led Tianna up the ladder and guided her to the edge. Fia was unsurprised to find a tripod standing against the railing of the platform. She looked down over the top of the tripod to see that, if there had been a weapon there, it would have been pointed at the fifth target.

"Tianna, could you stand here?" She motioned for the teen to stand next to her by the railing. She called over the edge to the others waiting below. "Can you guys hear me okay?" She received nods, and several thumbs went up. "Great. Okay, so here's something I figured out on my very first job. You've already learned a little of it, dismounting from the bars, but think of this as advanced placement. Tianna, when I say go, I want you to head back down to the ground and meet me there. Got it?"

Tianna nodded.

"Cool." Fia positioned herself behind the tripod, as if she were lining up a shot. "Ready? Go." As Tianna took off for the ladder, Fia pantomimed the action of tearing down the invisible weapon, including strapping it around her chest. She glanced back to see Tianna had made it to the third or fourth rung of the ladder.

Fia squatted halfway down and jumped up to the railing. She barely allowed her toes to touch the wood before sailing off the side. At the bottom, she landed on her toes, tucking her knees to her chest and her butt to her heels. Then she counted out loud—"One Mississippi, two Mississippi . . ."—each count coinciding with Tianna's footfalls against the ladder. She counted out five seconds before Tianna reached her side.

"I saved five seconds," Fia told the group. "Which might not sound like much, unless you're trying to get a collar on a host. Then, cliché as it sounds, every second counts. Imagine if that had been a four-story building."

A wave of shocked exclamations rang through the small but attentive crowd. "You would just jump off a four-story building?" Xavier asked.

Fia smiled. "Yep. Right to the ground. Broke a few bones learning how—I'm kidding. No, I do a lot of hunting from the top of parking garages. There are a few that are ten or fifteen stories, but most are around three or four. Sometimes you have to go into the stairwell and drop between levels that way; sometimes you can do it just down the middle, where the parking spaces kind of . . ." She spun her finger in a downward spiral. "Around the center. But if you can shave five seconds off each of four stories, that's twenty seconds overall." She shrugged.

Deciding her tenure as trainer of soul hunters had come to an end, she offered them one final thought.

"The reality is, hard as it might be to believe, this actually gets kind of boring. I'm definitely not going to say I want to be manually strangled every day, but this last month has been different. The seven years before that were a lot of the same. Agnes—Theresa teaches you to hunt from a distance, use your crossbow, shoot from above. There is an underlying message of impending danger in the lessons, assuming they still teach you the way they taught me, but at the end of the day, the techniques you are being taught, the distance, keeps you pretty safe.

"If I could have told fifteen-year-old Fia anything, I think it would have been, it's really not as bad as it seems. Yes, you are technically killing humans, but you are killing humans who are beyond salvation while still being kind of alive. It's a surreal thing to know, but now that I know it, I feel like what I'm doing might mean something. Not on a grand, save-the-world scale, but on a save-this-one-person—and their potential next victim—scale. In a way, I like that idea a lot better."

She put up her hands in a flourish, ready to take a final bow. "And thus concludes my time as your teacher. I return the podium to Sister Theresa."

"Thank you, Miss Drake," Sister Theresa replied with a shallow bow. "Though I think you still have a great deal you could teach our young hunters. Maybe if you hang back and watch some of their training . . . you wouldn't have to teach them in such a formal way."

Fia shrugged. "I guess." She searched the training grounds for a place to sit and watch.

"There is a chair in the storage shed," Sister Theresa offered after a moment.

"Thank you."

"Were you planning to ask or simply sit in the dirt?"

Fia wrinkled her nose. "I probably would have ended up in the dirt."

"I thought as much." The nun produced a ring of keys from within the folds of her robes. "It's the one with the blue ring."

When Fia returned with an aluminum folding chair, she handed the keys back to the nun and found a semi-level plot of real estate. "My apologies, Sister. Did you want one too?"

"No, thank you. I need to be on my feet in case someone needs me."

Fia nodded, turning her attention to the teens.

They were busy behind the log fence, stringing the same old handmade crossbows that Fia had used at their age. "Still having them unstring the bows at the end of the day?"

"Yes. It is good for building their speed. And better for the weapons."

Fia vaguely remembered that part about the weapons. Something about the tensile strength of the strings. "Hm, I kind of forgot about that. Maybe I should go back to that."

"You are shooting with a more technical bow, correct? I believe breaking down the arms on those accomplishes the same goal."

"Yeah, how did you know—"

"Oh, I didn't. I just couldn't imagine jumping off buildings and weaving in and out of city streets with that clunky wooden thing. It just seemed more practical that you would have a more technical, collapsible model."

"Yeah, I suppose."

"Father Scott gave it to you; is that correct?"

"Which time?"

"Pardon?"

"Nothing. Yeah, he gave it to me years ago."

Sister Theresa stepped away from Fia, stopping next to Tianna to help her figure something out with her weapon, and Fia considered sneaking back to the house. As she rose to her feet, Theresa turned back to her. "Are you leaving us, Miss Drake?"

Fia cringed. "Fia, please. No, just had to adjust," she lied. "The edge of the chair was digging into my tailbone."

The nun reclaimed her position next to Fia. "I understand you are involved romantically with a man?"

Fia furrowed her brow. She tried to remember when she might have mentioned Max to either Father Scott or Sister Rebecca, the only ones she had really spent any time talking to before today. "I guess. We have . . ." She let the sentence fall apart, suddenly thirteen years old and facing Sister Cecilia, who had caught her sneaking out of Felix's room in the small hours of the morning.

Theresa must have picked up on Fia's discomfort. After a moment of heavy silence, she spoke again. "My apologies, Fia. I didn't mean to pry. Sister Rebecca mentioned that you were involved. If she was mistaken, then I am as well. I only brought it up because perhaps it would be reassuring to the teens to know they can have intimacy outside their obligations."

"Maybe."

"Please think about it. There truly is only so much we can teach them. You can learn to paint from a book, but a masterpiece must be achieved by doing."

Fia's cheeks grew hotter, a feeling she decided had little to do with the afternoon sun. "I don't know about masterpieces, but if they have questions, send them my way?"

Theresa beamed, a broad grin filled with straight white teeth. "Thank you! I do appreciate it, greatly."

"I guess it's the least I could do."

They fell silent, watching the teens load, shoot, and reload their weapons. Theresa had them running to retrieve their bolts, even as the others were shooting, and Fia was impressed with their intricate dance as they ducked beneath each other's aim to find their way to their targets.

"Agnes never had us doing anything like that. I like it."

"It keeps them aware of their surroundings," Theresa explained.

Fia nodded. "Hey, Sister, I'm going to head back inside. Got a couple things I want to talk to Father Scott about."

"Absolutely. I am glad you chose to join us. We will see you later, for dinner?"

"Maybe. We'll see how the next few minutes go."

"Understandable. If we don't, thank you, and I hope to see you again soon."

Fia forced a smile. "Yeah." If someone had told her, even just yesterday, that she would be back in the mountains, cut off from everything she knew, hanging out with nuns and aspiring hunters, she would have laughed at them. Possibly considered having them committed.

Seven years ago, she had let an anonymous priest drag her back into a world she had wanted so desperately to leave. He had baited her with enough cash to make anyone think twice, but for a teenager living on the streets in one of the harshest winters Fia could remember, it had been impossible to resist.

But they had had an arrangement. He gave her dossiers and cash and left her alone. She took his cash, delivered the fugitives, and left him alone. It had been a good arrangement. She had liked it. A lot.

Now, that same anonymous priest, who was no longer anonymous—*or a priest*—had dragged her even deeper. She had a few things she wanted to get straight with him.

SEVEN

Fia followed the path back to the French doors leading into the immense granite foyer.

The foyer reached to the top of the second floor of the massive safe house. As Fia passed through the heavy glass-paned doors, to her left was the entrance to a library. Walled almost entirely in glass, it looked from the outside like it might be a greenhouse. It, too, reached from the ground level to the roof and included a recessed third level below ground.

Immediately to the right of the doorway was a staircase leading to the nun's residences. Fia glanced at the upper level and changed course. She crested the first set of steps that curved into the main stairs and had just set her foot on the first step when she was interrupted.

"Fiammetta, can I help you with something?"

Fia turned to see Mother Agnes standing in the foyer, where she hadn't been a moment before. *How does she do that? She's like a damned cat.*

"Reverend Mother, I was just taking a peek. What's up there?"

"Nothing of your concern. Our quarters are in the upper level. Save for Sister Cecilia, who resides in the back with the children."

Same old Agnes. Need to know only.

"Okay, then, nothing I need to know." Fia returned to the white stone floor, the only thing in a space otherwise filled with deep red wood that reflected rather than absorbed light. "Where is Father Scott? I wanted to talk to him about a couple of things."

"Father McGregor has gone into the city on business."

"Swell." Fia considered Agnes's earlier invitation to stay for dinner and Theresa's assertion that not only would she be welcomed but her company would be enjoyed.

"Was your time with the hunters productive?"

"I think they thought it was. I'm not sure how you would view it."

The hardened older woman remained silent. She was several inches taller than Fia, bordering on six feet. The difference in their height had always made Fia feel like the nun was looking down on her, literally and figuratively, and she shivered under the woman's cool-steel eyes.

"Was there something I could help you with, Fiammetta?"

"I think I prefer Miss Drake. No, it's specifically a question for Father Scott."

Fia glanced at her phone screen. She had only been out with the hunters for an hour. She didn't know if she could kill another three waiting for dinner. Cecilia was gone; Annabel was gone. Agnes made her feel like she was eight years old again.

"Is Sister Rebecca free?"

"She is in the library, I believe."

"Cool." Fia waited, the feeling of needing to be dismissed nagging at her and preventing her feet from stepping away from the nun.

"If that is all, I have some business to attend to, getting the teens prepared for school." Agnes barely waited for a response before skirting around Fia and ascending the stairs.

Fia shook her head and sighed. "Br." She turned toward the library and made her way inside.

She hadn't seen the inside of the library on her previous visit. The space was impressive. Just beyond the door, a spiral staircase wound up and down from the ground level. Beyond the stairs was a collection of tables and chairs in the same dark wood as practically every other surface in the house. To Fia's right was a desk, and beyond the desk was the first of the stacks Fia had seen. Four sets of shelves, eight feet high, with cards at each end to indicate what could be found on the corresponding bookshelf.

Fia looked around the main floor, glancing into the stacks as she moved toward the stairs. Seeing no sign of the young nun, she looked up the stairs and down, weighing her options. Arbitrarily, she decided to start down.

At the bottom of the stairs, Fia found herself facing another set of library stacks, with a large open space to her right. Moveable walls had been pushed out of the way. A collection of tables and folding chairs had been collapsed and loaded against the walls. A vacuum cleaner stood abandoned nearby.

Fia crossed the space to search between the bookshelves but found nothing. When she turned back to leave the lower level, she started. As if she had been there all along, Rebecca stood behind the vacuum, seconds away from firing it up.

"Sister, I'm glad I found you."

The nun didn't answer.

Fia moved closer, reaching out to touch Rebecca on the arm. The young woman jumped and turned wide, startled eyes toward Fia. She slipped a finger beneath her wimple, pulling free an earbud she had concealed inside.

"Wow, Fia, you scared me half to death."

Fia looked at the little speaker dangling from out of Rebecca's habit and smiled, an amused chuckle escaping without her consent. "I did not expect that. Sorry, Rebecca, I didn't realize you couldn't hear me."

"Did you need something?"

Fia felt her smile fade. "Everyone is so concerned with getting me something or doing something for me. I just thought we could chat. Get to know one another a little better."

Rebecca turned a tentative eye to the vacuum and back to Fia. "I really do have work to do. Perhaps later?"

"I can help. Get me a rag. We'll talk while we clean." A tension built between them, nearly tangible, and Fia took a step back. "Or not. You probably don't get a lot of quiet . . ." She gave the earbud another glance. "A lot of time to yourself, with the little ones around, huh?" Fia's experience with small children was limited to the time she had spent being one. She had no idea what taking care of four really consisted of, but she guessed it was time-consuming, at the least.

"No, please, Fia, don't go." Rebecca looked around the library. "I'm sure I can find—"

"I get it. We'll talk later." Fia turned and headed for the stairs before Rebecca could protest again.

Back in the foyer, Fia looked around. From where she stood, she could see the stairs crested into a dark hallway—*Why is everything in this place so dark?* Below that was the hallway that would lead her to the kitchen. On the left side of that hallway was the dining room, and the bedroom where Fia had stayed on her first visit was on the right.

She worked her way down the hall toward the kitchen. She had accounted for all the nuns, all the kids, and Father Scott, so she felt free to check out the other end of the house. She passed through the big sterile kitchen to a swinging wood door on the other side. Scott had brought her this way to an office, where he had given her a set of flimsy bolts for her crossbow. The projectiles hadn't been intended to kill, or even really injure, her targets. Instead, she had used them to mark one with a GPS tracker, though they hadn't ended up utilizing the information from the tracker.

The back hallway leading to the office was in the shape of an L, for even more security, she guessed. The first part off the kitchen had nothing but another smaller door at the end. She peeked in, expecting to find—and finding—a utility closet containing a couple of vacuums and some oddball cleaning supplies.

To her right from the closet was the other half of the L. She followed it, taking note of several closed doors. She reached for a knob, but remembering her own childhood, when privacy had been a valuable commodity, she drew back.

Along the right side of the hallway were two doors, spaced as far apart as possible. She guessed those were the bedrooms, likely boys in one, girls in the other. On the other side were two swinging doors, separated by one more regular latching door, also closed. Finally, at the end of the hallway were two more doors. Fia knew the one on the left led into the office; the one on the right, she surmised, must be Cecilia's room.

Deciding there was nothing to see without violating the

kids' privacy, Fia turned back. When she got there, she realized the door leading to the kitchen was hung in such a way, she could not check whether the coast was clear on the other side without giving away her position. "Clever."

She pushed through to the kitchen as if she had nothing to hide, though she was grateful to find the room empty. However, her relief was soon squashed. She wanted to leave, and the Fia of a week ago would have walked out without a word. But guilt nagged at her. She cursed under her breath and poured herself a glass of water, sitting at the steel table to drink it while she planned her next step.

From the foyer, she heard a crash as someone slammed open the rear double doors. "Reverend Mother!" Kaleb's voice shattered the stillness of the house. "Reverend Mother, Mother Agnes, we need your help! Mercy's hurt!"

Eight

Kaleb led the pack in from the training grounds, with Sister Theresa bringing up the rear. A few steps ahead of her, Mercy had a cloth pressed against a knot on her head and a trail of blood on her cheek. What Fia could see under the cloth looked like someone had strapped a rotten grapefruit to her head. Fia's skin prickled as her intuition insisted something was wrong beyond just what she could see.

Mother Agnes was halfway to the bottom of the stairs when the parade reached the foyer. "Kaleb," she scolded. "We do not bellow indoors."

"I'm sorry, Reverend Mother, but Mercy's hurt."

"What happened?" Fia asked, stepping into the group at the same time Agnes reached them.

"Fiammetta, please stand back and let me handle the hunters."

Unexpectedly wounded by the elder nun's curt dismissal, Fia took a staggering step backward. Sister Theresa rested a hand on Fia's shoulder. "She's worried, Fia. Don't take it to heart."

"Thank you, Sister, but I've heard that tone my whole life. *Fiammetta, you're in the way.*" She nodded to Mercy as Agnes looked over the goose egg on the girl's head. "What happened?"

"Sister Theresa, what's going on?" Rebecca asked, coming in from the library.

"I'm not really sure," Theresa replied. "We had just started running a circuit when I heard a noise behind me. I only turned long enough to see what it was before Tianna started yelling for me. When I looked back, Mercy was lying on the ground. I think she slipped off the high bar. The other kids said they didn't see what happened either."

As soon as Theresa had finished her statement, Agnes asked her to repeat it. Fia turned to Rebecca. "I'm going to get out of the way. I'll be back; I want to spend some more time with the teens and see what else is going on around here. But I need to clean up from the bounty I neutralized this morning—I just have some stuff to do. Can you . . . ?" She gestured to the crowd.

"I'll let them know. I am glad to see everything came out okay for you, after the explosion. It was good to see you."

"Yeah, I'm glad . . . well, you know." She dipped her head to Rebecca and backed slowly toward the front door, slipping out unnoticed.

Outside, something nagged at her. She pulled the Scout away from the house, into the long drive, and then walked back. She took a low path around the recessed level of the library, past a door she had overlooked from the inside, and climbed up a small, steep hill to emerge at the far side of the training grounds.

"Theresa said Mercy slipped off the high bar," Fia said quietly. She looked around cautiously, hoping everyone would be busy fussing over Mercy for a little longer. She crossed the training grounds to the gymnastics equipment. She didn't know what she expected to find, but she wanted to look around without anyone hovering over her.

She positioned herself beneath the lower of the two uneven bars and jumped, swinging herself up to sit on it so she could get a closer look at the higher bar. "What are you even looking for?" she asked herself. "Do you think someone greased the bars? It was an accident. That's all."

She reached out, keeping herself balanced, and ran her hand over the bar, anyway.

Nothing.

She swung herself back to the ground, keeping her eyes up on the high bar for several more seconds. "Just an accident."

She headed back to the Scout the way she had come, slipping down the hill on her butt and hitting a jog to get back to the car.

Fia's first stop on the way back to the city was her bunker. She wasn't even sure why she still came up here, other than the idea that something had worked for her all along, so why stop?

From within the concrete space, she carried a box up the equivalent of two stories to reach the surface. She pulled a can of accelerant from the box and placed it on the ground at her feet. She placed a box of matches beside the small tin can, then capsized the box, letting the envelope within fall into the firepit that sat twenty feet from the entrance to the bunker.

She poured an unnecessary amount of lighter fluid on

the envelope and backed away five feet before lighting a match and tossing it in the direction of the pit. With a *whoosh*, the envelope became a tiny conflagration, chemically aided flames reaching two and three feet into the air. The whole mess was ash in a matter of seconds.

She returned to the ten-by-fifteen-foot concrete box, buried deep below the earth and concealed by a concrete obelisk made to look like a tree.

Exhausted, she dropped the box to the floor and kicked it back under the desk, hard enough that it bounced back at her. She flipped off the fan and pulled the chain to turn off the light above the door, returning once more to the surface.

Stopped at a traffic light on her way back into the city, Fia checked her phone for messages.

Max.

Playing tomorrow night at the Lounge. If you want to come, text me when you get there. Meet you with a laminate to come in the back. No cover.

He had punctuated it with a tiny picture of a drum and a heart.

Fia sighed, tossing the phone to the side. Backdoor access seemed more advanced than she was ready to be. She'd let him know later.

The route back to her condo took her by a shelter. It was open for a couple of hours in the early afternoon for people to come in for lunch, but they couldn't stay during the day. Between the hours of eight in the morning and five in the evening, anyone using the facility had to be out. And they had to be back by seven in the evening, or they weren't allowed in. Right now, the only people there would be employees and volunteers, getting ready for five o'clock.

As she waited at yet another light, Fia's attention was drawn to a pair of black-clad figures leaving the shelter. One was a priest she had seen coming out of an office in the creepy priest's—Father Ariaz's—small church. He was an older man, probably in his early sixties, with white hair peeling away from his shiny red pate. His cheeks were flushed and round, matching the rest of his physique.

Walking beside him was Sister Annabel.

"What is she doing with him?" Fia asked aloud, even as the angry blat of a car horn alerted her that the light had changed. She waved over her shoulder and pulled through the intersection, trying to watch both the road ahead of her and the pair walking away from her in the opposite direction.

Several blocks still separated Fia from home, but she could barely wait to crawl into bed. Maybe until sometime tomorrow. It had been a long day.

NINE

EJ, the bouncer stationed at the front door of the Lounge, was one Fia recognized from other venues, and he flashed her a quick smile. There were still a handful of people standing in line ahead of her, but he waved her through.

One blonde, overdressed for a dive bar in this part of town, protested as Fia slid by her, but EJ shook his head, unperturbed by her outburst. "Calm down. Everyone will get in."

"I was here first!"

"You can keep yelling at me, and I might decide we're at capacity."

"This dump?"

Her friend put a hand on her arm. "Melanie, chill. I like this band."

Melanie shrugged away from her companion. "She didn't even pay the cover."

Two steps inside the door, Fia turned back and met Melanie's glare. Melanie had an easy six inches on Fia and probably fifty pounds, but when Fia looked at her, she shifted her weight back onto her heels. Without breaking eye contact, Fia handed EJ a five-dollar bill and turned back inside. Once out of sight, Fia couldn't help herself; she stopped to listen. Melanie didn't say another word that Fia could hear.

Fia stepped up to the bar. The bartender, a familiar girl dressed like a rockabilly pinup model with her dyed black hair tied up in a bandana, blew Fia a kiss from bright, glossy red lips. "Jack and Coke for you, sweetie?"

Fia nodded, only slightly unnerved by the bartender's informality. She had only had a few brief encounters with the woman and couldn't remember ever indicating she was interested in anything more than the woman's whiskey.

Kim—bass guitar player for Max's band and the singer's wife—stepped up next to Fia and extended a hand. "Fia, right?"

"Yeah. How did you—"

"I've seen you around, and you've got my drummer pretty twisted up. I'm Kim."

"Yeah, I—"

The bartender slid Fia's drink to her. Fia reached out to pay, but Kim waved her off, handing the pinup girl something that looked like a raffle ticket. "We get a couple of these for every show, and I don't drink," Kim explained. "Max said you turned him down when he offered to let you in the stage door?"

"Seemed a little, I don't know, advanced."

Kim smiled. "Actually, I'm kind of glad to hear that."

"How's that?"

"Max is a . . ." She paused. "Passionate person."

Fia sniffed, amused by Kim's choice of words.

Apparently picking up on the innuendo, Kim laughed. "Well, I don't know anything about that. But he loves hard.

He's the type of guy who's really good at breaking his own heart."

Fia took a second to process this information, suddenly feeling like Kim had ambushed her. Was Kim trying to warn Fia off Max? He's good at breaking his own heart, so he doesn't need your help?

Fia put up her free hand defensively. "I don't know what—"

"Fia, whoa. Look, I'm not here to attack you. Max likes you, and frankly, I like how this new crush looks on him. Might be messing with his ultra-cool drummer aesthetic, but beyond that, he's excited. And it's nice."

"So don't screw it up."

"Well, that wasn't quite what I was saying."

"But now that I mention it . . ."

"You have some trust issues, don't you?" It sounded like a genuine question.

"Maybe." Fia felt a little silly. Maybe Kim really did just want to introduce herself and say hello. Fia took a step back, both figuratively and literally, and held a hand out between them.

Kim lowered her eyes to Fia's extended right hand, and Fia's cheeks burned.

Kim shook Fia's hand, locking gazes with Fia, making a visual effort not to stare at the reptilian scales. "Max already told me about your arm." Fia released a sigh that felt like it started in the heels of her sneakers. "No, not—I think he just didn't want us making a big deal about it. Look, Fia, we got off on the wrong foot, and that's my fault. I just wanted to let you know that I—we—Mitchell, Tracen, and me—we know who you are. And we're all glad Max has found someone he really likes."

Her face twisted thoughtfully. "Are you a hugger? We're all kind of huggers around here."

"I—" Fia flinched at Kim's approach without really meaning to.

"No? That's cool. Just know: you're okay with us." She patted Fia on the arm. "I gotta run. Here." She handed Fia two more of the little carnival tickets. "We'll talk more later, okay?"

Fia nodded, not sure what to say without sounding like she was filling silence or trying to get in the last word. Kim strode off through a curtain that separated the bar area from where the band would be playing.

Fia had turned down Max's invitation to come in through the stage door. And it did seem like a bigger step than she was ready to take. This was the band's first show since they'd gotten home from their tour—she was actually a little surprised they were doing another one so soon—and the first one she had been to on purpose.

She looked around the bar. There weren't very many people yet—it was still early—and she wondered how many were there to drink and how many even knew there was a band playing in the back room. Then she spotted Melanie and her friend.

And Melanie's friend spotted her.

Before Fia could duck out of sight, the girl stopped her. "Hey, sorry about my friend. She started before we got here."

Fia tried to dismiss the conversation, muttering something that she hoped sounded like, "It's fine," but the girl continued.

"I'm Claire; she's Melanie. I think I dragged her out here. She's usually not like that. That's why she's like that. She took a shot of liquid courage before we left the house."

"Just the one?"

"Well, maybe three or four. Anyway, she's usually kind of a shut-in; she even works from home. So I plied her with alcohol and dragged her out to see the band tonight."

"Seems kind of drastic for a shut-in."

"You may be right." Claire took a moment before continuing. "You like the band tonight?"

"Yeah, they're good." Fia didn't know how much she wanted to say to this stranger.

"Drummer's cute."

"Um, yeah, he's—"

"Fia, Max wants to talk to you." Kim peeked through the curtain, tossing Fia a lanyard with a laminated card hanging from it. On the card was a stylized photo of the band and the name Wyldfire above crisp block lettering spelling out *VIP*.

Fia turned back to Claire. "Sorry, I got . . ." She waved the lanyard and passed through the curtain.

"Thanks, that was getting uncomfortable."

"Let me guess. Some girl came out tonight to see us because she thinks Max is cute."

"Yeah, how—"

"That's another thing about this life, Fia. Max says you have a complicated life. He does too. Maybe not to him but to girls." She led Fia to a set of stools at the side of the stage.

Stage, Fia thought, was a generous term. Little more than a quarter of the room's floor was occupied by a waist-high platform. The stools were level with the platform. Kim sat on one and patted another next to her.

"What do you know about Max?"

Fia suddenly felt like she didn't know anything more than his name and his tattoos.

"Sorry," Kim apologized. "I've put you on the spot. I

think maybe what I really want to know is if he's told you anything about why you were able to get your hands on someone all the girls seem to want. You've been to a couple of our shows, yeah? I can't imagine you haven't heard the whispers."

Fia thought about Claire. The pinup behind the bar had said something too, shortly after she first met Max.

That night, she had been trying to forget about the lithe, little drummer through an anonymous tryst that ended with her murdering a man in a filthy restroom. It had been self-defense, she had told herself a dozen times. And he had been taken by a malevolent soul, though she hadn't known that at the time. But she had lured him into the restroom for sex, and when he had attempted to strangle her, she stabbed him in the throat.

Her adrenaline had carried her to a bar and, by complete coincidence, one of Max's shows. *Cute but aloof* had been the bartender's assessment. She had definitely noticed he was single, though, jerk or not. So, sure, Fia had heard comments. Of course there had been comments. There was a lot to comment about.

"Max runs into a cycle. He meets girls at shows because that's his life. He doesn't do much else. None of us do. So, he meets girls who are looking to date a musician because they think he's sexy and it's glamorous. But then they get mad—they always get mad—when other girls make comments like that girl out there." Kim nodded toward the curtain. "Because that girl out there doesn't know who you are. She's just sharing her opinion. And she's entitled to her opinion. How you receive her opinion is going to be the thing that either sets you apart from your predecessors or leaves Max heartbroken again."

Fia hadn't considered any of that before. Max had

hinted, when Fia finally gave him room to talk, that it was hard for him to keep a girlfriend. They hadn't gone into much detail. They hadn't talked much at all. There had been sex. There had been really good sex. And there had been a flaming bird and broken glass. Later, there had been one of those zombie things, and they hadn't talked much that night either. She really hadn't given him much opportunity to share. Though she hadn't taken any of her own opportunities either.

She felt embarrassed, watching Kim watch her as she ran through all this information. Sure. It all made sense. It probably was hard for girls who thought they were getting sexy glitz by dating a professional musician to then have to deal with other girls who had the same ideas.

"How do you and Mitchell do it? I mean, you're pretty, and Mitchell . . ."

If Max got a lot of attention, Fia thought, Mitchell must get twice as much. He wasn't her type, but she knew a lot of girls did go for his type. The type with arms as big as their heads.

Kim gave her a half smile and a shrug. "Yeah, we don't get out much. I mean, at shows and stuff, we hang out in the van or the green room. Sometimes, side stage. I've told Max he's looking for trouble going out into GA with everyone else, but he's a little more, I guess, extroverted than we are."

"My bassist and my girlf—friend having a powwow. Should I be worried?" Max's warm-brandy voice cut through their conversation. He rested a hand on Fia's hip and pressed a hungry kiss into her lips.

Kim grinned. "You know I have to give the new girl all the dirt. Though I'm sure you've already smelled his swamp feet. Look at those things! Why does someone so small need feet like that?"

Fia chuckled, even harder when she saw the deep angles of Max's cheekbones flush red. "Jesus Christ, Kim," he muttered toward his shoes, trying to hide behind his hair. After he had taken a second to recover, he touched his hand to Kim's shoulder. "Mitchell sent me to find you." He leaned in for another kiss from Fia before following Kim through the door at the back of the room.

Fia looked around the room, ultimately deciding to keep the stool Kim had claimed for her. She pulled out her phone, intent on busying herself with popping bubbles until Max and the others took the stage.

The game hadn't even fully loaded when Fia felt eyes on her. She looked up to see Claire standing a few feet away. Meeting Fia's eyes, she stepped closer. Too close.

"Hey, wow. Can I apologize for epically sticking my foot in my mouth? I didn't know when I was going on about that hot drummer that you—"

Fia put up a hand, shaking her head. "No reason you should have known. It's not like I am wearing a sign."

She hoped Claire would be satisfied having made amends and return to Melanie. She hadn't put any real thought into the things Kim had mentioned—other girls, the "romance" of dating a musician—but now it nagged at her, a little. And something Kim hadn't mentioned but now crept into Fia's mind was the time Max had been gone.

Maybe absence really did make the heart grow fonder. He had been gone three weeks, and by the time he came home, he was all she could think about. Not the cave that had imploded and nearly killed her and two others, not the weird zombie creatures that had led her into the cave in the first place. Not even the creepy priest who had been stalking her around the city. Every spare thought had been of Max. Dreams she normally wouldn't remember had been of Max.

She guessed that was probably equally hard for girl-friends of musicians to deal with.

Claire was not finished atoning. "He really is gorgeous. I'm sure you have to listen to that kind of stuff from his fans all the time."

"I really don't—"

"Oh! I did it again! I'm so sorry."

The harder Claire tried to patch things up, the more uncomfortable Fia felt. She found her imagination wandering again, and this time, she saw a hole opening up in the floor, wider and wider, until it swallowed this stranger determined to make right things that hadn't even existed before five minutes ago.

"Hey, look. It's fine. I'm not mad. Let's just let it go?"

"Yeah, sure. I didn't mean—are you guys close? I mean, you came in the front door."

"We have killed zombies together." Maybe that would make her go away.

Claire blinked a couple of times before smiling weakly. "Oh, like a video game. Ha, funny."

"No, like real zombies. You didn't know? They're all over the city."

"Okay, look, you don't have to be mean. I just wanted to apologize."

"And you did."

Claire rolled her eyes and turned away from Fia, who, in turn, rolled her own eyes and returned her attention to her game.

A few rounds later, the energy in the room shifted, and the hair on Fia's arms prickled. There was a hum in the air, nearly inaudible. She guessed she was the only one who really heard it, but she was growing unreasonably accustomed to the sound and the electric feeling that came with it.

The cave blast hadn't gotten all of them. All things considered, maybe the cave blast hadn't gotten any of them.

Fia quickly scanned the room, looking for whichever drunk looked drunker than the other drunks, probably flying solo. She spotted the girl, barely legal to be in the bar, swaying near the stage, a yard or two from where Claire and Melanie had set up camp. While everyone in the room was facing the stage, this new addition was facing Fia directly. She took a few shuffled steps forward, bumping into Melanie along the way.

Melanie swore and pushed the zombie girl, knocking her into the stage. The zombie girl turned and hissed— literally hissed—at Melanie before continuing her pursuit, aimed at Fia.

Fia groaned. "Not tonight, Satan." She climbed down off her stool, remembering the first of these things she had seen, staggering drunkenly around downtown. Ariaz and his no-neck thug had easily gathered him up and redirected him toward Ariaz's church. She met the girl halfway and, taking hold of her arm, led her on the path of least resistance, which unfortunately took them to the back exit of the bar. She hoped Max would still be close by to run interference if anyone gave her trouble, but she didn't have time to get his attention.

Outside, the staff parking area was empty. She spotted Max's little white coupe a few yards away, the drum kit charm that hung from the rearview mirror glinting in the piss yellow of the streetlamps.

She half led, half dragged the creature away from the lights, hoping that would also get her out of sight of any security cameras. Years ago, when she had first started all this, her de facto mentor, Zari, had assured her that the magical energy exuded by the release of a soul all but hexed surveillance equipment, especially digital cameras. Fia, however, still liked to be as ambiguous and invisible as possible. When she hunted, she would wear all black with a hood to cover her rust-colored hair and conceal as much of her face as possible.

Tonight, though, she was dressed for Max.

As much as she dressed for any man.

Instead of her stealthy black, she wore one of her rock t-shirts, worn-out jeans, and sneakers, the standard-issue white laces replaced with purple ones that she'd left untied, their ends tucked inside the shoes. She looked like basically everyone here, save for her hair, but she still couldn't allow that to be the sole source of her anonymity.

Too many people were onto her scent these days, anyway.

So she led the creature away from the lights, searching as she walked for a weapon. Another thing that her all-black hunting wardrobe provided was a hidden pocket with access to a knife she kept sheathed on her thigh. Something else that hadn't come with her tonight.

Fia found a length of rebar discarded in the weeds at the building's foundation. Not the best choice, but she could make it work. Once sure she was out of sight from just about everyone, she turned the woman and pressed her back into the bricks, focusing on her face for the first time.

Really focusing on one of their faces for the first time.

This thing, now gnashing its teeth at Fia's arm as she pinned it to the wall, had never been human. One indication she used to identify the possessed was a haze over their eyes, similar to cataracts, if cataracts were made of smoke. The longer the host was possessed, the worse the haze became. And their pupils would dilate as the body slowly died. Fia guessed this was the reason so many media depictions of possessions gave them black eyes.

Plus, black eyes were kind of creepy.

In the movies.

They were, Fia had just discovered, even worse in real life.

In the movies, black eyes appeared to be regular eyes with dark irises. Sometimes the filmmakers would black in the whites in post-editing as well, but they still mostly looked like human eyes.

What occupied the orbits of this being were not eye-balls.

Sheathed within the human-looking eyelids was black chitin. The same chitin that made up the exoskeleton of Irzelen's little piranha monsters.

Fia considered her options.

Those things had been vaguely humanoid, despite being the size of a terrier. She wondered if they possessed similar anatomy. If covering its mouth would muffle any screaming it might do when she ran the rebar through its throat.

Fia looked around quickly to see if she was still alone with the demon. When she decided she was, she thrust the rebar up through the soft flesh behind its human jaw. Force and momentum drove the rusted metal out through the top of the creature's human skull with a squelch and a crunch.

It fought against Fia's grip, but thankfully, it did it silently. As it thrashed, the veil dissolved, and Fia came face-to-face with the demon beneath.

It was bigger than the little carrion demons. This thing was the size of the human disguise it had worn, but twice as strong. And maybe even stronger as it fought for survival.

At least, Fia thought it was fighting to survive. Not

knowing for sure how its anatomy was arranged, she may have done little more damage than if she had put the iron rod through its foot. Painful, but probably not fatal.

Fia had grown used to the electric charge that came with the demon's presence and barely even noticed it anymore. Until it changed. Soon, what she might have equated to "standing near a transformer" felt more like "being actively electrocuted," and she let go of the creature, instinctively gripping the sides of her head. It didn't help—she really hadn't expected it to—and she collapsed to her knees, every muscle in her body jerking and twitching, refusing to support her weight.

His voice echoed in her head until she thought it would bounce right out the top, taking her skullcap with it.

"I did not mean, bring about the death of my children to break the mortal's thrall. You are not obeying my request."

Her brain ached with the effort of organizing a coherent thought. Between the surge of energy Irzelen had brought with him and the telepathic link he had created, she felt like someone had shaken her like a snow globe. Little bits of thought danced and spun, obscuring the thing she really wanted to focus on.

He reached out a clawed hand, and Fia realized he was in his natural demon form, not masquerading as a human. Not that his human form of nearly seven feet was any less conspicuous than a professional basketball player. He gripped her chin in his claws and lifted her off her knees and off the ground, high enough to look him in the eyes.

Amber eyes with oblong, slit pupils resembling those of a cat.

Or a snake.

They were the only part of him that wasn't black enough to absorb light. He smelled like an electrical fire.

She wrapped both her hands around his wrist, holding on in case he decided to let go. She wasn't interested in falling seven feet to the asphalt. He squeezed her jaw, slowly, firmly, as if she were a balloon he wanted to test, to see how hard he could squeeze before it burst. She thought she could hear the bone creaking beneath his fingers, and the agony brought tears to her eyes. Then, just as suddenly as his attack began, he let her fall to the asphalt, her legs buckling on impact.

The air between the brick buildings grew hot enough to draw all the oxygen from her lungs. The scars on her arm prickled with the memory of another kind of heat. A gust of wind accompanied the cacophony of every bone in his body shifting and crunching as they reformed. The sounds were soon replaced by the crackling of a flame, which was then replaced by a bird.

Where the demon had stood looming over her was now a phoenix, half her size, with feathers of blue and gold—not yellow but real gold, with its soft sheen and faint green hue—and eyes that burned with blue-white flames. It preened a handful of rogue feathers into place with its golden beak, then flapped its elegant wings, rising up from the ground and out of the alley in one seamless motion.

Fia fell the rest of the way to the pavement and watched the air that rippled with heat slow to a stop. At the edge of her vision, she saw black leather high-top sneakers and black jeans moving toward her, quickening with each step.

"Fia! What—are you okay?" Max crouched in front of her, gathering her off the pavement, helping her sit up. "Fia, you're bleeding."

She reached up and touched the side of her face where she had felt the warmth seconds before, then pulled her fingers away to examine them. She stuck her pinkie in the opposite ear, as tightly as she could, and looked up at her gallant knight. "Say something."

"What do you want me to say?"

She breathed a sigh of relief as his voice sounded clearly in the bleeding ear. The demon hadn't caused any real damage. "That's good enough."

"Was that . . . ?" He lowered his voice to barely a whisper. "Was that the same phoenix?"

"God, I hope so."

Ten

Max had offered to drive Fia home after their set was finished, and she had graciously accepted, even though it meant leaving her scooter overnight in an open parking lot. She had come straight in and slept in her clothes, stopping only long enough to kick off her sneakers beside the bed.

She woke with the sun and padded into the condo's expansive bathroom. Amber-colored lights bordered the room, embedded in the wall a few inches above the floor. They worked on a motion sensor and were set to shut off when the overhead light was turned on. Without switching on the light, she stepped up to the inset vanity sink and splashed her face with cool water. She winced as it stung an abrasion on her cheek. She couldn't remember if the wound had come from the demon's claws or her fall to the asphalt.

In the dim glow of the footlights, Fia spread a finger full of antiseptic cream on the angry red scrape, then examined the rest of her face and body for further injuries. Finding none, she brushed her teeth and headed back to the bedroom.

She stripped out of last night's jeans and t-shirt, exchanging them for a soft sports bra and green plaid boxer shorts. She shuffled through the condo across the dark hardwood floor to the kitchen area. The open layout had the kitchen divided from the living room by a bar-top island. Fia guessed someone more domestic would have filled some of the excess space with dining room furniture, maybe used rugs or screens to further differentiate the areas.

She, on the other hand, had four steel stools at the bar—because the ones she had wanted came in a set of four—and a whole lot of empty herringbone walnut wood between the stools and her black leather sofa, with its straight square angles and exposed steel frame. She could probably host a rave in the empty space.

Or put in a workout area. Maybe a heavy bag and a speed bag, like Agnes had had in the convent.

Fia fixed a cup of coffee and a bowl of scrambled eggs, into the latter of which she diced tomatoes and roasted green chilis, and carried it all to the balcony. She stretched her legs out over one of the wooden deck chairs she had set up, resting her coffee cup on the small table between them. When she finished eating her eggs, she placed the bowl next to the cup and leaned her head back against the chair.

She woke again with the sun burning into the pale skin of her face and bare stomach. She gathered her dishes and headed back inside.

After draining the bottom half of her coffee cup, she washed both cup and bowl by hand and went to dress for the day. Jeans that had long ago gotten snagged on a large screw had been torn off above the hole to expose the bottom half of a tattoo made to look like a watercolor painting. She slipped into flip-flops and a black tank top.

Now more fully awake, Fia took another glance in the bathroom mirror, grabbed her phone, and ordered a ride-share to take her back to the lot to pick up her scooter.

When the car—an SUV painted deep blue—pulled up, Fia climbed in the back and gave the woman her destination. "Actually, I'm picking up my car from last night, so I'll have you drop me at the parking lot on the next block."

She turned to watch the city pass by the window when she was hit with an idea.

"How often would you say you pick up an unusual fare? I mean, if you picked up a circus clown, would that stick with you for a while?"

The woman glanced at Fia in the rearview mirror, a deep crease in her forehead. "I guess I would probably remember picking up a clown. Why do you ask?"

"Just making conversation." Fia returned her attention to the window. She had noticed, getting in, that this car did not have the large logo decal for the rideshare service on the door. The one she had seen pick up the nun outside Ariaz's church had probably been the exception rather than the rule.

When they reached the parking lot, Fia thanked the woman, handing her a five-dollar bill, and climbed out. She was relieved to see the glittery red body of her little scooter right where she had left it.

She pulled her helmet from the compartment beneath the seat and secured it over her hair. She pointed the nose of the machine to the south, away from her apartment, and wound her way through a growing jungle of concrete and steel.

The neighborhood around the bar was low, single- and double-level businesses and homes, a crayon box of colors.

The closer she got to downtown, the taller the buildings grew around her, mirrored-glass windows reflecting one another's images. Pulling up to a light, she felt a chill pass over her, despite the intensity of the sun on her skin. Ahead on the next block, she could see a small Catholic cathedral. The Gothic building stood out as an anomaly, surrounded by glass and steel.

Inside, she would find Armando Ariaz leading a double life. In one life, he spoke to a congregation who believed and followed the Holy Bible, the word of their God translated for the masses.

In his other life, he commanded a demon horde, usurped from the pits of Hell.

It's all about balance.

She guided the scooter past the cathedral, hoping the icy feeling in her gut would ease sooner rather than later.

When Fia reached the busy street that divided the commercial areas of downtown from the residences to the south, she turned left toward the distant plains. The state capitol loomed ahead of her on the right.

She put several of the narrow side streets and small businesses between herself and the famous gold dome. Outside one of the tattoo shops she frequented, next to the bright-pink exterior of a kitschy doughnut shop, she caught sight of a sign: *Walk-Ins Welcome.* She had had a flicker of an idea even before Wyldfire left on their tour but had quickly pushed it aside. As she continued past the tattoo shop, the idea came back to her, and she made a quick decision to turn left into a residential area.

On the next block, she turned right, slowing to a stop outside a small but ornate Victorian house that could have been mistaken for gingerbread, if not for the glass commercial-style door in the front. Fia cut the engine, looped the chin strap of her helmet over the handlebars, and strode up the sidewalk.

The bamboo pipe above the shop door greeted her with its warm, husky whistle, and Zari called out from behind a heavy velvet curtain. "Be right with you."

"It's just me, Zari."

Fia passed through the shop toward the glass display case, where a simple old cash register sat. The counter to one side of the register was clear, allowing customers to look at a small collection of ritualistic-looking antiques Zari kept locked inside. To the other side was a small plant, not much more than a sprout, in a clay pot. Behind the counter, Fia passed through a heavy dark-red curtain.

When Zari Dacius relocated from Louisiana to Colorado, she had purchased the small Victorian gingerbread house and, after some paperwork, converted over half the space to set up her crystal shop. The shelves were packed with a mixture of mass-produced tchotchkes that *looked* mystical—"The machine kills the spirit of the crystal," Zari had once explained—and authentic magical items. Even on this residential side street, Zari attracted tourists and serious practitioners alike, and most of them were automatically drawn to the merchandise that was meant for them, eschewing the rest.

Behind the curtain, Zari sat at a large round table made from the slice of a 150-year-old tree. In the kitchen of the apartment, Fia knew she would find a second similar table, made from a different section of the same tree.

Zari had her deck of tarot cards strewn over the entire surface of the table, an amethyst chip in the center of each one. "Just cleansing, *chérie*. Would you like a reading?"

Fia shrugged. It wasn't what she had come here for, but it might answer her question anyway. "If you've got time."

"Fiammetta, for you, always." Zari gestured to a chair across the table from her. "Rest your legs."

Fia obliged. She enjoyed watching Zari's rituals. It was relaxing and deepened Fia's sense that there was a lot more to Zari than merely a woman who had been raised in the voodoo traditions of Haiti. She had thought, since their first meeting, that Zari possessed real magical abilities.

Once she was satisfied with the condition of her cards, Zari urged Fia to focus all her thoughts on them. "Listen to them; let them guide you. Remember, the cards are for clarity, guidance. They do not presume to speak in absolute terms." It was a speech Zari gave to all the customers who came in looking for a card reading, but it was specific to Fia as well.

Zari had read Fia's cards multiple times back when Fia was coming here all the time. Fia had always struggled to see beyond the literal images, despite the efforts Zari had made to help her learn to interpret the messages.

With the first card off the deck, face down, Zari began explaining to Fia the relevance of each. "This first card is your situation, the circumstances you find yourself in. The second represents a challenge, the person or thing that is working against you, either to deepen your situation or change it. The third card is especially meant to guide you. It is meant to advise you regarding overcoming your challenge. You can do that through following the focus of the fourth card. And finally, this, the fifth card, is the potential outcome of all these elements combined."

After laying down the final card, Zari lifted each by the right edge, flipping it to the left to reveal the print of a watercolor painting on the face side.

Fia watched Zari's face darken with each turn of a card. A knot began to form in her stomach, tightening on itself, making Fia feel nauseated. She allowed Zari a few seconds with the cards after turning the last one before speaking.

"Is everything . . . is everything okay?"

"*Chérie*, you are strong. You are capable. But I see devastation ahead. You face a traitor . . ." She tapped a finger against a card featuring a man lying prone, swords like quills protruding from his back. "I cannot help but read the Ten of Swords as it is painted."

"Stabbed in the back?" Fia asked, studying the card.

"*Oui*, likely by the person here." She gestured to another card, the only one of the five that was facing Fia. "The High Priestess, in the reversed position, *chérie*, next to the Ten of Swords . . . well, who better to stab us in our backs than someone close enough to touch us with their sword?"

"Someone close to me? One of the nuns?"

"Nuns, *chérie?*"

"Day before yesterday, I spent the day at . . . it wasn't the convent. They moved. I didn't find out why. But I met a couple new nuns. They said they came here because of me."

"I discourage you from jumping to conclusions, but you have heard that before. *Priestess* doesn't explicitly mean holy woman; please remember that."

"No, I get that. I think. But who else would it be?"

"That, I cannot tell you, Fiammetta. That is for you to determine for yourself."

Fia scrunched up her face. Of course Zari was right. The cards weren't magic; they were guidance. They didn't have actual answers, only suggestions. And Zari didn't know the nuns. But all of what she was saying, about a traitor, someone working to stab Fia in the back—that all went along with what the demon had told her.

"What else do you see?"

"I see only what I think should be obvious—with

someone in your circle plotting against you, you must be wary of deceit, of lies, even of half truths. Things are coming, Fia, that are sure to lead to devastation." Zari tapped a finger on the Tower card in the fifth position, the "Outcome" position. The painting on the card was of a castle perched at the top of a craggy rock. A serpent was poised below the castle, and from the castle's spirals and turrets, jagged bolts of lightning fractured the sky.

"Is there a way around that?"

"There is always a way, *chérie*. The cards are not absolute. But this is a high probability, given all that you have told me already."

"The demons?"

"*Oui*, the demons." The bamboo pipe over the shop door alerted them to a customer entering the shop. Zari rose and walked around the table to Fia. She gripped Fia's head in her hands and kissed the top of it.

"All I ask of you is be cautious. Be wary. Be alert. Be vigilant."

"All things I have under control, Zari."

"Yes." The word was affirmative, but Fia didn't feel like the tone was. "You are welcome to sit with the cards as long as you need, Fia. I must get back to my shop." Zari passed through the heavy curtain, leaving a gap of nearly six inches between the panels.

"May I help you?" Fia heard through the curtain.

The response came in the form of a heavy Scandinavian accent. The woman explained to Zari she was looking for objects to remove a malevolent soul from a human host. The request naturally piqued Fia's interest. She rose to her feet to stand nearer the curtain, hoping to peek through the gap Zari had left.

In trying to keep her own face out of the opening, Fia could barely see the woman Zari was speaking with. She was tall, six foot or better, with platinum-blonde hair cut into a practical bob off her neck.

"I'm afraid I don't have anything to help you with that particular quest," Zari was explaining. "The ritual aids I have here are used more for elemental magic, less for the kind of spiritual rituals you are speaking of."

"I was told this was the best place to find such items. I am looking to find a blade made of quartz."

"*Mais non*, I do not stock weapons. I can give you the name of another—"

"I was told this is the best place. If you are unable to help me, I will be going."

Fia didn't hear Zari respond. The woman moved out of Fia's limited view, and seconds later, she heard the pipe signal her departure.

Fia scurried back to her chair. She focused her attention on the two cards Zari had seemed most concerned about: the Ten of Swords and High Priestess, reversed, so she looked out from her throne to see Fia looking back at her.

Fia had come here with an idea she had wanted to get Zari's opinion on, but now she was focused on the cards and what Zari had said about them.

Stabbed in the back.

By someone close to her.

And everything was likely to go up in flames if Fia wasn't careful.

At least, that was what she had gotten out of it. She looked at the Tower card once more. "You're going to need more than lightning to scare me."

ELEVEN

Fia stepped out of the glass shower enclosure, rubbing a plush black towel over her arms and legs before ruffling it through her short red hair and letting it fall to the floor. Standing naked in front of the brightly lit vanity mirror, she smoothed lotion over her cheeks, her neck, and down over her chest and arms. It had been a full day since she received the messages from Zari's cards. She had let her little scooter wander the streets on the way back to the condo, for long enough she had had to stop for gas.

She had stepped away from the counter, headed for her room, when her phone buzzed and performed a little jig.

Hey. Are you home? showed in the incoming text bubble. She replied with a thumbs up. *Come downstairs. I have a surprise.* It had been less than forty-eight hours since he had rescued her from the pavement.

In a few. Just got out of the shower, she replied. She held onto the device, waiting for his response.

BRT

She pushed the little phone icon to call him instead of continuing in this manner. "Stay put," she said with a laugh. "I'll be down in a minute."

"Fine. Tease." She was sure she could actually hear him pouting.

Fia ended the call and finished up from her shower. After a minute, her phone rang again. "Wear pants," his warm voice instructed.

"I planned on coming down naked, but if you really insist on pants . . ."

"Wear jeans," he corrected. "This is a jeans kind of surprise."

"Yeah, sure. Any other instructions?"

"Maybe a jacket."

Jacket? It was eighty degrees. "Jacket, yeah, okay."

She slipped into a comfortable pair of blue jeans, a black t-shirt, and her battered combat boots, grabbed her hoodie on the way out, and made her way to the elevator.

At street level, Fia found Max at the curb, astraddle a large motorcycle, the kind with a second seat behind the driver, one helmet in his hand and another on the seat between his thighs. She shrugged into her sweatshirt before stepping into the afternoon heat.

"What's this?"

"I think people usually call it a 'motorcycle.' Although, I have heard 'motor bike' or simply 'bike.' Can't say I've ever heard anyone call it a 'motorized bicycle.' Maybe we could start something new."

She pointed ahead of him to the next block and a bank of motorized bicycles for rent. "Oh. Right." His crestfallen response was quickly brightened by a giddy grin and small bounce on the machine's leather seat. "I rented it. Thought we could go for a ride."

She blinked. She was definitely surprised. "Do you even know what you're doing? That thing is huge."

He shrugged. "Yeah. I've always wanted one. I think I'm kind of a motorcycle guy. The hair, the tattoos, the leather, right? Just never had the opportunity to buy one. So every now and then, I rent one from this little shop and ride it up into the mountains. It's quiet. Serene. I like it up there."

He patted the passenger seat and extended the helmet toward her. "Hop on. Come with me."

She climbed up behind him, strapping herself into the helmet. "Do you know where you're going?"

"Vaguely."

"Cool."

He turned the machine on, and they rumbled north, out of the city.

Fia squeezed his hips with her knees, her hands on his firm stomach, and watched the mountain scenery in a way she hadn't before. In all her trips out here, even living in the mountains as a child, she had never seen the trees and foliage this way. She was even surprised at the difference between her scooter in the city and this. There was feeling of freedom back here—maybe even flight—and she spread her arms out to the sides. She could feel Max's laughter through the press of his back against her chest and leaned forward into him.

They leaned into twists and turns, climbing high into the isolation of the peaks, the air cooling as they rode. Several miles out of the city, Max pulled the bike off the road onto an outcropping overlooking the city.

"It all looks so small from up here," Fia said, barely above a whisper. Max said nothing and climbed off the machine, kicking down the kickstand. He hung his helmet on the handlebars and reached out to help Fia down. He lifted the seat where she had been sitting and produced a small cooler. "What's this?"

"The surprise."

"I thought the bike was the surprise."

He shook his head. "We've been doing this—whatever this is—for a while, but we're working from the inside out. We started with the intimate, real shit—sex, killing zombies, that sort of thing—and skipped the courtship part."

"Courtship?"

He smiled—not his usual crooked grin but a shy smile. She even thought she could see a flush of pink in the hollows of his cheeks. "Dates. Getting to know each other."

"What's in the cooler?"

"Barbecue. This hole downtown has the best barbecue, maybe ever."

"This from someone who has been all over the country. Wait. A hole downtown? Can't be Billy Boy's?"

He laughed, breaking the strange tension in the air. "Of course you know it."

"I did a lot of growing up in that neighborhood."

"You never told me where you lived."

"Maybe I'll take you there sometime."

He put his hands in the small of her back and pulled her hips into his own, brown eyes glittering in the late afternoon sun as he studied her face. He lifted one hand to the back of her head and pulled it toward him to kiss the top of it. "I would like that."

He held her like that for a long moment before breaking the embrace and pulling a blanket from the compartment beneath her seat. He spread it out on the ground, kicking a few stray rocks out of the way, and set the small cooler in the center of it, guiding her to sit down with him.

When they were finished eating, he put the cooler aside and pulled her in close to lie on his chest. They lay there awhile longer as the sun dipped below the horizon.

"We should probably get back," he whispered into her hair.

"Probably."

They packed up the picnic and climbed back on the bike, heading back into the city. At the first red light off the interstate, Max shouted back to Fia over the sound of the engine. "Am I dropping you at home, or . . . ?"

"I want to show you something." She pointed ahead. "Left at the next light."

Max followed her instructions, guiding the bike into the left-turn lane. They rumbled past the amusement part, working north toward an old industrial area that hadn't fared as well as Fia's current neighborhood.

In all her travels around the city over the years, Fia had somehow managed to avoid this area. Most of what had been here when Fia was a teen was gone. Save for the cheatgrass and milkweed, about the only things she still recognized were the street signs. She guided Max into a Park-n-Ride lot adjacent to the light rail tracks.

There was one car in the lot besides them.

Fia climbed off the bike and crossed to the center of the asphalt slab. She looked around to get her bearings. The building was gone, to make way for the addition to the train routes, but the memories were indelible.

Seven years earlier . . .

"I'm Zeke." He reached out a spidery arm to shake her hand.

"Fia."

"Nice to meet you, Fia. You can stay here. If you want. There are some rules, but I think you'll do okay."

"Rules? What kind of rules?" She had run away to avoid so many rules.

"Don't steal, but don't give anyone a reason to want to steal. Don't get into fights. Don't bring drugs in here. There are a few rugs over there." He waved a hand to a pile of rugs in one corner. "Grab one to sleep on if you want. You can have this space next to mine."

He ducked into his tepee and returned with a foam to-go box. "Here. Don't get used to it, but you look hungry." She flipped open the lid and found a chicken leg and what looked like a cup of smoked chopped pork. "I already ate most of it, but you can have that."

"Thank you." She picked up the drumstick and nibbled at it.

"Billy Boy's BBQ. It's a few blocks from here, between here and sixteenth. It's a tiny shack, blink-and-you'll-miss-it sort of place. Health department says Billy has to throw out whatever's not used by a certain time, so if you're there at that time, you can get a box to go."

"Why are you telling me all this? Doesn't me knowing mean less for you?"

"Because someone told me when I first got here. And you'll tell someone else in a few months. If you're still here." He ducked back into the tepee, this time without returning.

Fia held her arms out to her sides and turned back to face Max, still atop his steel steed. "This is where I lived."

Max climbed off the bike and moved to join her.

"Of course, when I was here," she continued, "there were walls and . . . most of a roof." She stamped her foot against the pavement. "This was concrete, not asphalt." She waved a hand toward a lone thistle off in the distance. "That guy, though? That's Frank. He's always been here."

Max looked around at the landscape, his eyes lingering on various empty spaces before moving on.

"You're trying to imagine it, and I haven't even given you the fifty-cent tour. Follow me to the parlor, Mr. Hawkins."

She led him to the edge of the lot farthest from the platform. "Here is where we kept our piles of shit. No, not literal feces. At one point, the warehouse—or *factory*, I guess—was used to process coffee. So there were all these leftover burlap sacks. We filled them—and other things, like garbage sacks, grocery sacks—with scraps of fabric, scraps of insulation, and paper trash. Once a week, everyone went out into the city and picked up litter, brought it back here. Stuffed it in the walls, tossed it in the trash-can fire. Kept things comfortable. Or we thought it did."

Max walked the edge of the lot, running his hand along an imaginary wall. "You're right; it is warmer down here." He waved the same hand near his knees.

Fia raised an eyebrow and led him back to the center. "We all congregated closer to the middle. Most of the time, there were about fifteen of us. There were some people, like the twins, who stayed here only when they didn't have anywhere else. Parker was good at finding places for them to stay."

She turned to face Max, studying his handsome face. The streetlight was behind him, casting him in heavy shadows. The darkened hollows of his cheeks made the chiseled edges of his cheekbones appear even sharper. His mahogany eyes looked black and sad. He had taken condemned souls and demons in perfect stride. It was the rest of Fia's life that seemed to trouble him.

"Don't look at me like that. It's all ancient history."

Max skirted around her to the other edge of the lot. "What was here?"

Fia followed him. "Boards and boxes. More garbage. In a little farther was Trina's little cardboard apartment. It was an engineering marvel, really. Built entirely from boxes and a little bit of duct tape."

She took a few strides toward the entrance to the lot. "There was a big wooden box here, filled with blankets and rugs. More rugs than blankets, honestly. It was—is a weird agreement between concertgoers and the homeless population. But I guess you've seen that."

Max's face shifted to confusion. "Seen what?"

"Really? Before a show, people go buy cheap blankets and rugs to sit on while waiting in line. Then they dump them before going inside. Leave them in a pile by a garbage can outside the venue."

"That's cool." He meant it. "No, I didn't realize people did that."

"Yep. And we would go by, gather them up, and bring them back here. I think that's how I really got into the alt-rock and metal world. Those were the best shows to find stuff. That's why I figured you had seen people doing it."

She shrugged and pointed back to where they had started the tour. "A couple, maybe three weeks after I left the convent—I guess I'd been here about a week—I found a sofa on the street. Someone had left it out for the garbage pickup, but I bribed some help to get it here and made a home out of it. The frame was pretty hollow, so I stashed stuff inside. It probably had fleas, but it was better than sleeping on a bath mat."

She took a deep breath, debating whether she wanted to continue.

Max made her decision for her. He pulled her by the hand, turning her to face him, and pulled her into his chest.

"Don't apologize," Fia said.

"I didn't?"

"You were going to." When he didn't respond, she pulled back to arm's length. "Your apology now doesn't change anything . . . that happened then. I pulled myself out of it; I'm better. I'm good. Hell, I'm terrific." She paused, giving him an opportunity to reply, before continuing. "It's this, as much as the souls and—it's this that makes me . . ."

She broke free of his hands and started back toward the bike. "I can walk from here if—"

"Fia, what did I do wrong?"

"You didn't do anything, Max. I brought you here. Apparently, there are more souls in my life than just fugitives. Just brought up some memories."

"You're not walking home." Max joined Fia beside the motorcycle, handing her the helmet she had been wearing. She took it and waited for him to get on before climbing on behind him.

When he reached the block occupied almost entirely by her building, she tapped him on the shoulder and gestured for him to pull into the garage. On the third level, he slipped into the space next to the Scout and cut the engine.

"Would you like to stay the night?" she asked gently.

He blinked at her a couple of times before smiling. "We're okay, then?"

She nodded. "I'm okay, if you are." She led him into the apartment, kicking out of her boots by the door, and crossing to the balcony. Outside, she stretched out on one of the wooden deck chairs and waited for him to catch up.

Max padded through the sliding glass door in black socks and looked around. She waved at the second chair. "Have a seat."

The railing of the balcony was glass, with only a steel cap to obscure the view of the city stretching out before them. They sat in heavy silence for several minutes before Max broke it.

"Fia, maybe I should go——"

She jumped up from the chair and hurried back inside to her bedroom, picking up a black shopping bag from the corner of her bed. She passed through the second glass door leading from her room back to the balcony, leaving it open behind her.

"I got you something. Sorry I didn't wrap it." She dropped the bag unceremoniously into his lap and sat at his feet to watch him open it.

"What's this?"

"Why do people ask that? Just open it, and you'll find out."

Max reached in and pulled out what was inside, holding it up for inspection. The black t-shirt, advertising a rock band from the 1980s, was a replica of a shirt he had torn to make a bandage for a man injured in a demon attack. She had bought two, uncertain which size he would prefer, but had returned the second after sneaking a peek at one of his others.

"I know it's not authentic, but I made a teenager really uncomfortable when I asked him what size he wore, so I hope you like it."

He chuckled and laid the shirt on his chest. "It's perfect. Thank you. And the other one wasn't authentic either." He leaned forward, dropping his feet off either side of the lounge chair to get closer to her. "Fia, I'm glad you showed me where you came from. I get the feeling that wasn't easy for you."

"It's been a long time, and it wasn't one of the brightest periods of my life."

He reached out, taking both her hands in his own. "If you want to scare me away, you're going to have to come up with something better than homeless teen in an abandoned warehouse."

Fia pulled away and found her feet. "I don't *want* to scare you away. I'm just not sure sticking around is in your best interest. Max, people die around me."

"You said that priest and the nun ended up okay?"

"They did. But not just them. And they shouldn't have." She had told Max the same lie Scott had told everyone else to explain the miracle escape. "But others too. I'm just not sure it's safe to get close to me."

"Don't you think that should be my choice?"

She sighed. "I don't know. All I know is, I don't want any more innocent blood on my hands."

Max stepped up behind her, wrapping his arms around her waist, pressing her body against his. He was slender and wiry, the knobby ends of bones visible in his wrists, deep hollows defining his collarbones. But for all that, he was surprisingly strong, and as he enveloped Fia in his long, spidery arms, she felt vulnerable and protected at the same time.

"What if I promise to move away when the bleeding starts? Go bleed in private? Then you won't get any on you."

Fia turned, breaking his embrace, and faced him, her jaw slack and her eyes wide with shock. The face looking back at her wore a smile that wrinkled the corners of his dark eyes.

"Fia, I'll be fine. I think I've proven I can both be helpful and stay out of the way. And I'll take your lead. If you tell me to hide in a closet, I'll hide in a closet. But I like you, and I think you like me too. Why do you want to deny yourself free music, questionable humor, and great sex?"

"Well, I don't know about 'great.'"

"Oh, but you see, I've been in the room when I made you scream. I'm pretty sure you know all about 'great.'"

Fia laughed, still apprehensive, but she appreciated his attempts to quell her anxiety.

Max stepped back, his face drawn, somber. "I think maybe I should go." Surprised, Fia started to protest. He turned away to pick up her gift where he had left it on the chair. "It's been a perfect day. I'll call you tomorrow?"

She sighed and nodded. He pulled her into him, pressing a kiss hard against her lips. "Good night, Fia Drake."

TWELVE

The next morning, Fia let herself sleep in, pulling herself from under the covers into the darkness of her room around ten o'clock. She ran through a quick shower, dressed in her usual uniform of jeans and a tank top—today she chose one in a dark olive green—and left the apartment, on her way to the safe house. She had decided—between all Max had seen and the walk-ins sign outside the tattoo shop—that she wanted to discuss the possibility of getting Max a ritual tattoo.

As Fia approached the parking spaces she had claimed for herself, she felt the air in the garage change, shimmering with the electricity she was starting to recognize as the presence of one of the divine.

"Is this going to be a thing now, Uhlpir?" Fia turned to face the angel behind her.

The angel's head reached almost to the ceiling, and he looked like a bird still getting his footing after a long flight, his stance tentative, his wings still slightly unfurled. Even in their semi-relaxed position, the wings cast a deep shadow across the floor of the garage. The being met Fia's gaze, and the image of the angel glittered away, replaced by that of the priest.

"Apologies. I didn't expect to find you out here. I was heading toward your apartment."

"Oh? What for?"

"To touch base with you, see if you had heard or seen anything worth noting."

He left the words hanging in the air, and she wondered if he was referring to something specific, maybe her encounter at Max's show. When he didn't offer any more, she picked up the slack. "That's convenient because I was on my way to talk to you about something too."

"What's that?"

She waved a hand toward the International Scout. "Get in. I think I should include Agnes in this as well."

"You're in luck, then. The Reverend Mother is in the city this morning. A meeting at one of the high schools. I was on my way from here to meet up with her."

"Beats driving out to the middle of nowhere. Where do we meet her?" She pulled the Scout up to the gate of the parking garage and punched her code into the keypad. "Which way am I turning?"

"Left, south, toward the Tech Center."

"Really? She's shipping one of the kids clear down there?"

"There's a diner down there. That's where I was going after I spoke with you."

Fia wound through the series of one-way streets on her way to the interstate. The air in the car was heavy with the weight of an impending conversation. She hated the feeling, especially when the tension was as unnecessary as it was now.

A few weeks ago, the only person she would have needed to run her idea by would have been Max. And she was certain he would go for it. But now Fia felt compelled to consult Agnes, as if the reintroduction of the nun into her life had dragged her backward in time. And consulting Agnes felt like a wild card.

Fia and Scott made it all the way to the south side of the city in silence, Scott only speaking to give directions. Fia eased the SUV into the parking lot of a corporate chain restaurant. "You could have just told me this was where we were going." She huffed, cutting the engine. "Is she here?"

Scott waved a long hand toward an unoccupied gold car a few spots from where they were parked. "Looks like she is already waiting inside." He climbed out of the car and started for the building.

Fia sighed.

She followed Scott into the diner, where she found herself enveloped in the aromas of breakfast. Bacon, coffee, and a hint of cinnamon invaded her senses. She spotted the elder nun sitting alone at a table near the center of the room, already reading from a menu.

The woman looked up as Fia and Scott approached, an expression of surprise washing over her face. "Fiammetta, I was not aware you would be joining us." From the look of the table, Fia guessed Agnes had already ordered a water for Scott before they arrived.

"I stopped off to touch base with her on my way here, Reverend Mother, and she told me she had something she wanted to speak with both of us about, so I asked her to come along. I hope that's not a problem."

"No, I don't suppose it is. We'll have to get the young man to bring us another menu."

Fia shook her head, reaching for one of the remaining chairs. "I don't really need one. These places are all the same. Breakfast is meat, more meat, and a side of cake."

By the time Fia had finished her sentence, Agnes was flagging down their server. "Oh," the young man said, looking at Fia. "You have a new arrival. Can I get you anything to drink?"

"Coffee," Fia replied. "And water."

"And another menu, please," Agnes said, almost over the end of Fia's request.

Fia waved her hand in defeat. "And a menu."

The young man nodded and scuttled off toward the host stand at the front door, returning moments later with a menu for Fia. She flipped it open, searching for any surprises she might find, as well as whatever clever name they had put on a simple helping of bacon and eggs.

By the time their server—his name tag read *Trey*—had returned with Fia's coffee and water, everyone was ready to order. Fia knew from experience that Agnes thought it inappropriate to begin a conversation, especially a serious one, in a restaurant before the meal had been delivered.

And conversation should pause whenever the server checked in to fill drinks or anything else.

So Fia waited quietly for her chance to bring up her idea. She didn't have to wait long, though. When Trey was safely out of earshot, Agnes turned to Fia. "You wanted to speak with me about something?"

"Straight to the point, then."

Fia realized, in that moment, she had a little catching up to do before she could present her idea to Agnes. Given the current situation, Fia knew she hadn't told Scott about Max, but she wasn't certain she would need to either. She took a deep breath, making a mental note to leave out some of the juicier details, and launched into her story.

"I have been spending some time with this guy," she began. She laid out the events Max had been present for. "And the final straw was a couple nights ago. One of the demons came into the bar where his band—Max's band—was playing. I know it's not effective against demons, only the souls of mortals, but if this guy is going to stick around—or probably even if he's not; at this point, I think he's already at risk for just being associated with me—he's going to need some protection."

"Fia, what are you trying so hard not to say?" Scott asked.

"Yeah, well, I was thinking—these tattoos we got—do they have to be done the way we did them? With the thorns and stuff?"

"Fiammetta, are you inquiring about getting this young man a protective marking? Are you sure that is prudent? You indicated you have only known him a few weeks."

"He's a little like a bad penny. Except I guess I kind of like having him around. But he has managed to entangle himself into this whole ancient, divine mess. I guess, more than anything, I don't want to risk his name popping up in one of my bounty packets. So I was wondering if it had to be done the way we did it."

"The ritual is the most important part," Scott replied. "I believe it would suffice if I were to accompany Max to a modern machine-tattooing shop."

"No offense, Father, but I'm not really looking for *suffice*. If I'm going to ask him to do this—"

"You have not asked him?"

"He's a tattoo guy, has several already. I didn't want to get his hopes up in case I couldn't follow through. But I think I want the whole shebang: the Indian guy, the chanting in a basement, all of it."

The table fell silent for what Fia felt was an eternity. Then Agnes spoke.

"I think that is an excellent idea, Fiammetta."

"You do?"

"Yes. And as it happens, we have a fakir coming in for the teens before they are away from where we can keep an eye on them for several hours each day. Do you think you could bring Max to the safe house Saturday afternoon?"

"That fast? Yeah, yes, I think I can. The guy will be here anyway, so this isn't just for me?"

"Correct, this is not for you at all, Fiammetta."

"I know, I meant—never mind, yes. I mean, no, I don't think that will be a problem at all."

Fia was a magnet for the kinds of trouble she was trying to keep Max out of, so no Max until at least Friday. She thought she could handle that. She wasn't sure about him, but he wasn't going to get a choice. She decided radio silence was the best option. He wouldn't accept *Don't call or stop by for the next two days, for your own safety* as an explanation. If there was one thing Max Hawkins was, it was stubbornly chivalrous. He accepted her strength and capabilities, but he couldn't resist the mantle of knight in scuffed leather sneakers.

She would just have to duck him.

They finalized some of the details and finished their breakfasts—she guessed Agnes viewed this meal more as a brunch—in relative silence. Trey returned once with a coffeepot and pitcher of water, leaving the check behind. Eschewing everything she had been taught, Fia stood and reached across Scott's plate to retrieve the little folio from between him and Agnes.

"Fiammetta—"

"Stow it, Reverend Mother. I crashed your party; the least I can do is buy your meal. I've got it to spare."

Fia had always assumed the money she got from her bounties had come from some private, secret account in the Vatican. Maybe that was a more elaborate story than was actually feasible, but she hadn't much questioned where her anonymous benefactor was getting all the cash he passed along to her. Now, she couldn't help but wonder if that part of her bounties was an anomaly as well. She had already decided the copious amounts of information Scott left her was not normal, likely obtained through divine magical channels. Why wouldn't the money come from the same place?

Fia glanced over the ticket, made a visual fuss over calculating the tip, and slipped a crisp fifty-dollar bill into the folio. She closed it, holding it tightly until Trey returned. "Keep the change," she told him.

"Fiammetta, how much was that bill?"

Fia smiled at the nun. "Enough that fifty covered all of it plus tip." *Everything else around here is "need to know." This can be too.*

Agnes stared sternly at Fia, an expression that would have made ten-year-old Fia confess. Twenty-four-year-old Fia only smiled genuinely, challenging her elder to back down. Agnes wasn't going to win this battle.

"Very well," Agnes finally conceded. "If that is the case, Father McGregor, Fiammetta, I must be going. I have a meeting with the administration of one of the schools the teens will be attending."

Scott rose from his chair, guiding Agnes from her own. As he moved to reclaim his seat, Fia rose too. "I think I should be going too. I have some work to do. Do you need a ride back to—you didn't have a car in the garage."

Scott winked, shrugging his shoulders as if flapping invisible wings. Fia laughed. "Oh. I guess if I could, I would too. Beats driving in this traffic."

Thirteen

As Fia stepped out of a shop in Lower Downtown, something caught her attention. A black sedan parked across the street wouldn't ordinarily draw attention, but she had seen this car before. There was a rideshare company logo adhered to the passenger door, and the driver was waiting inside.

She crossed the street behind the car to hopefully avoid being seen, planning to ambush the man in the driver's seat. She just hoped the door would be unlocked when she got there.

She grabbed the door handle and popped it open, climbing into the passenger seat before the car's owner could protest. "Hi. Don't panic; I just have a couple questions for you."

He looked her over, his eyes pausing a couple of times in their journey—once at her breasts and the second time near her hips—and one corner of his mouth quirked up into a predatory smile. "Well, hello there, sweetheart. How can I help you?" He shifted in his seat, turning his hips toward her as far as the center console would allow.

"Slow down there, tiger. I literally just want to ask you a couple of questions about a fare you picked up a couple days ago."

His demeanor shifted, his smirk fading to a disappointed frown, the air in the car growing heavy. "You don't look like a cop."

Fia laughed. "Why would you think . . . ? No, no, I'm not a cop." She considered her options for a second. "Bounty hunter." She slipped a twenty-dollar bill from her jeans and waved it in front of him. "Give me your name, and if what you tell me helps me catch who I'm looking for, there's more where this comes from."

He reached for the bill, and she snatched it back just before his fingers closed around it. "Name and info first."

"Yeah, whatever. For twenty bucks free and clear, what do I care? Name's Travis. What'd ya want to know?"

"Gonna need a last name, Travis."

"Mitchum. What do you want?"

"You picked up a nun, over by that little cathedral."

"Yeah. Don't do that too often. You're looking for her?"

"She's not a real nun," Fia improvised. She had no idea if the woman she was looking for was a real nun, although the intimacy between her and Father Ariaz suggested her commitment to her vows might be shaky, at best.

"Ah."

"Did you get a name, Travis?"

As his brow furrowed, Fia studied his face. Dark skin offset icy-blue eyes that were really the only thing remarkable about him. She committed those eyes to memory, not sure if she would need to remember this face later. She eyed him another second, trying to determine if she was going to get the truth out of him. She was pretty sure he was just in it for the money and might give up his own mother for the right price.

He must have been sizing her up, too, because it took him a long pause before he spoke. "Don't you know her name?"

"Trying to figure out which alias she's been using."

Her story was getting more complicated the longer she sat here. She considered cutting bait before she got in too deep with Travis Mitchum. She didn't want to have to remember lies made up on the fly later.

"Makes enough sense," Travis replied. "I think the name on her app was Amy, maybe. Doesn't sound much like a nun name, now that I think about it."

Now it was Fia's turn to crease her forehead. She had thought she was going to catch the mole, but there was no one in the safe house she could easily connect to the name Amy.

"Amy. Amy?" She repeated the name, rolling it around in her mouth, searching for something she recognized that might have sounded like Amy in his memory. "Annie?"

"Hell, maybe. Sorry, didn't know there was going to be a test."

"Don't you have a record?" She nodded to the phone on the dashboard mount.

"Nah, it resets at the end of the day. I can tell you when I picked her up and where I dropped her off, but even the cops gotta go to corporate for more than that."

"Where did you take her?"

"A parking garage down south."

"Garage?"

"Yeah, said that was where she left her car. Nuns have cars?"

"Do you think they just walk everywhere? They have to get around somehow. Did you stick around to see the car?"

He perked up at the question. "Actually, yes. I didn't want to just drive around aimlessly waiting for another fare, so I cut the engine across the street from the garage. I think it was her; the windows were really dark, but the timing was right. About five, seven minutes after she got out, a car came out. Some big 80s land yacht. Creamy, beige, something light."

"Didn't follow her, did you? No, of course you didn't." Fia sighed deeply and tried to think of anything else he might have noticed about her. That she, a bounty hunter, shouldn't already know. "Just making sure I got the right person—about how old would you say she was?"

"Midtwenties. Honestly, if she hadn't been dressed up like someone who beat me with a ruler as a kid, I might have hit on her."

"Swell." Fia handed him the twenty. "Thanks for your help. I'll be in touch." She probably wouldn't be.

She climbed out of the car and bumped the door closed behind her with her hip. She looked up and down the street, considering what to do next. The Scout was parked around the corner, but she had some things to think about and thought a walk would help.

"Light-colored sedan. There were two of those in the garage at the safe house. But that woman who picked up Ariaz down by the capitol—what was she driving?"

She barely registered a handful of concerned glances as she spoke openly to no one in particular. She wished she had one of those little ear things. No one noticed people talking to themselves with those.

A few blocks up, she ducked into a convenience store in search of a bottle of water. As she passed by the store window, she saw him.

The thug she had met with the creepy priest stood on the opposite side of the street, facing the store, his hands deep in the pouch of his sweatshirt. He appeared to be tailing her from the other side of the street. Had she really been that deep in her own head that she hadn't noticed him? Someone that size should be hard to miss.

She abandoned her quest and tore back out the front door. "Hey!" she shouted before darting into the street. She had barely taken the time to check traffic, thankful she was on a one-way street, and she was halfway into the far lane before the walk signal started to flash in her favor.

He had turned when she shouted and taken a set of stairs two at a time down into an underground walkway. "Damn it!" she swore as she caught her toe on the curb, stumbling enough to slow her pursuit but not enough to fall. "Hey! Come back here! Why are you following me?"

She eschewed the stairs, opting instead to swing herself between street level and the upper level of the pathway around the building's circumference. She hadn't seen which direction he went and took a gamble, turning to her right, only to find a dead end around what she thought was the next corner. A heavy steel door marked *Authorized Personnel Only* was set a foot and a half in from the main wall and locked tight.

She punched the door.

Certain she had lost the big guy when she went the wrong way, she turned back the way she had come. Frustrated and defeated, she walked, head down, back toward the stairs. As she came around the corner, something caught her in the gut, knocking the wind from her lungs.

The big man had been waiting for her around the corner of the building. He had blocked her passage with a broad swing of one massive arm across her middle.

She coughed, the impact of the blow making it hard for her to breathe. "What the hell?" she spat.

He responded by swinging his tree trunk of an arm again, this time aiming a fist the size of her face, at her face. *You're lucky he's so big,* she thought, deftly ducking the punch and landing one of her own into his pelvis, a hand's width south of his navel. She hadn't really aimed the blow but commended herself for its placement.

He gasped, clearly relieved she hadn't aimed better, and took a second to recover. That second was all she needed, and she drove her shoulder into his gut, pushing him off-balance and into the wall behind him. Once she had him pinned, she started swinging punches at his sides. She couldn't overpower him; she was too small. But she could move faster, and she did exactly that, delivering rapid-fire strikes to his abdomen, treating him like the speed bag Agnes had had in the basement of the convent.

Before he could gather himself enough to push her off him, she darted away and up the stairs to street level.

Fia looked back to where she had left Travis. The street parking was clearing out between lunch and dinner crowds, and his black sedan had gone with them.

She dialed up another driver—the app told her he was dropping off another fare—and planted herself a couple of blocks away on a side street.

When the green compact pulled up, she climbed in and gave the driver directions to Zari's crystal shop.

"I will be with you—"

"Armando Ariaz?"

The priest looked up from his desk, the color draining from his deeply tanned face. "Father McGregor. I don't believe we've met, but your reputation precedes you."

"Father Ariaz."

Scott spoke softly, calmly, hoping his docility would mask his anger. He had followed and watched over Fia, closer than any mortal had in her life, for seven years. He had watched over her more closely than he had any other before her. He had taken her under his wing, except in the one moment she hadn't needed him to, and in that moment, she had thought he died for her. Few before her had seen his true form, and she had worked that out on her own, with help from the man she had taken up with.

Scott really hadn't planted a feather from his own wings for her to find. That was the truth. He had pushed her off the subject, not knowing how the truth would affect her. The truth was, he'd been on Earth too long, cut off, exiled. The longer he was away from his true place, the weaker his connection to it—his wings—grew. That he was shedding feathers without knowing it meant his wings were growing weaker than he realized.

He was bound to Earth until this problem was contained. Two millennia was a blink in the eyes of eternals like him, like Irzelen, like the condemned souls. But it had gone on long enough, in mortal time, that the eternals were being sent to fix it, or else.

If he lost his connection completely, he would be Earth-bound for eternity, without his wings, without his power. He didn't like that idea, at all, and the feathers Fia possessed concerned him a little.

Scott took a seat across the desk from the other man.

"I understand you had a visit with a parishioner of mine, Fia Drake?" Father Ariaz feigned confusion. Scott played along. "Abrupt young woman, red hair and an attitude to match? 'Though she be but little, she is fierce.'"

"Ah, yes. I think I remember her. She came in to look at the church. Said she spends a lot of time in this part of the city and had always admired the architecture."

"Interesting. I wouldn't have taken Miss Drake for a lover of art. I must admit, her account of the meeting was a little more . . . colorful."

"Oh?" The mask of confusion was growing transparent, but Ariaz maintained it, baiting Scott to break his own façade.

Dressed from head to toe in fully traditional cleric's clothes, his shoulder-length hair tied back away from his face, Scott turned away from the smaller man and locked the office door.

"Father McGregor, I must insist—"

"Drop the act, Armando. I think you know why I'm here."

"I'm afraid I don't—"

Scott was across the room, lifting Armando Ariaz from his chair before he could finish the statement.

"Listen to me very closely."

The air in the room began to move, almost imperceptibly, a slight vibration, like air near an industrial electric transformer. The buzz was less a sound and more illusionary. The sound came from the energy in the air vibrating through human organs and bones, turning the tiny bones of the inner ear into a tuning fork. Scott maintained his grip on Ariaz's robe, holding him close enough to feel hot breath on his skin.

"You revealed yourself. You are no longer playing from

behind the curtain. I take that as a challenge. I take that to say you are fair, open for retaliation, and believe me when I say, it will come."

A look of arrogant amusement washed over the smaller priest's face, and he chuckled joylessly. "You are nothing but empty threats. You are good. You wear the white hat atop the white horse. You may wish to punish me, but you won't lift a finger to do it."

Before Ariaz could take another breath, Scott had pinched it off, closing the palm of one hand over his trachea, squeezing tightly enough to make Ariaz's eyes flash with involuntary panic. "You know nothing of what I would do. I could crush your windpipe before you have a chance to blink."

"Do it," Ariaz said once Scott loosened his hold, sounding as though he were speaking through gravel and broken glass. The panic was gone from his eyes. "Kill me, priest. Murder me in your rage. Watch the life drain from my eyes, feel my body go slack within your grasp. Become one of the condemned souls you have devoted your life to hunting. Join them in your rage."

Scott squeezed the other man's throat harder, quickly, before releasing him. Earth-bound was punishment enough; he wasn't going to lose his wings over this pathetic sycophant. Ariaz had bowed to Irzelen, taken up the demon's quest for mayhem. Death would be a blessing for this man who would never be free and who longed for Hell. Hell may not have been what he had wanted as a child, but it was almost certainly what he desired today, as an adult.

No, killing him was not an option. Not for the reasons Ariaz assumed, but he couldn't know the real reason. So Scott released him and stepped away. Maybe he could use these crumbling wings to his advantage, after all. Armando Ariaz may need to stumble across a feather of his own.

"I knew you didn't have the balls. Empty threats."

"I won't kill you. But I won't stand in Fia's way if you push her to that point. Watch your step."

Ariaz smiled, this time with a look of malice and morbidity, the desire for death Scott had assumed existed mixing with arrogance, and Scott liked that. Arrogance was the quickest path to mistakes, and Scott hoped those would come sooner rather than later.

Ariaz let the smile fade and returned to his chair. "I trust you can see your way out."

"Remember what I said. I won't hesitate to let her put a knife in your heart. I may even provide the knife." Scott turned, letting himself out of the office.

FOURTEEN

The wooden instrument over the door signaled Fia's arrival. Zari stood at the checkout counter, busy with a ledger. She looked up at the sound and greeted Fia with her deeply sweet Caribbean accent.

"*Ma chérie*, how good to see you! Twice in two days. I hope this is going to become a habit."

Zari swept around the counter and pulled Fia into her chest, kissing the top of her head. She pushed Fia back out to arm's length and studied her face. "You are burdened, *chérie*. Are you still focused on the cards I gave you?"

Fia released a heavy sigh and nodded. "I wanted to talk with you a little more about it. If you have time?"

"*Mais oui*, for you, there is always time. Come, sit with me. Have you eaten? Would you like some tea?"

"Tea sounds nice."

Zari flipped a sign on the front door and locked the deadbolt before leading Fia to her apartment.

In the small apartment's kitchen, Zari pulled a glass jar from the icebox—a real, authentic icebox—and poured from the spigot into two tall glasses. The liquid was deep amber in color, like the rich honey she used to sweeten it. The woman had sugar in her pantry—Fia had seen it—but she sweetened nearly everything with raw honey she got from a local apiary.

Fia waved the glass beneath her nose. It smelled the way tropical flowers looked—dark, heavy, and sweet.

It tasted like it smelled.

Fia pulled on half the glass before reconnecting with their conversation. Zari's eyes were fixed firmly on Fia's face as she waited patiently. Fia reached for the pitcher and refilled her glass. "Tell me more about the High Priestess."

Zari smiled, a sad expression that made Fia's heart sink. It bordered on a look of pity. Fia hated pity, but if there was one person she especially didn't want it from, it was Zari.

"Have you given any more thought to what I told you, Fiammetta? That you should not take the cards at face value? That they are meant more to be felt than they are to be seen?"

"I have. And I still don't understand."

Zari rose from her chair and pushed through the curtain leading back to the shop. Fia was considering getting up to follow the woman when she returned, carrying a deck of cards.

"These are different cards, Fia. The same tarot but different illustrations."

She set the deck on the table next to Fia and picked up a plate of cookies from the counter. She set those next to the cards. "The bee master who gives me the honey also grows dandelion and lavender. For his bees, of course. A section of his crop had gone dry, so he finished preparing it and gave me some."

Fia inspected a cookie, sniffing it before taking a

cautious nibble from the edge. "So this is a lavender-and-dandelion cookie?"

"*Oui*. The recipe is basic shortbread, but I added the dried flowers. Perfectly edible. Delicious, *mais non?*"

Fia took a larger bite, mulling it around in her cheeks to get the full flavor. "Yeah, it's different but tasty."

"Have another."

Zari pulled the card deck closer and began sorting through it, searching for something in particular—Fia guessed the High Priestess card. "Ah, here she is." She rested the card on the table, facing Fia so she would have the same view as before.

This deck was newer and more intricate than the others. Instead of a holy woman on a throne, Fia found herself looking at a woman with long silver hair, sitting in the curve of a crescent moon. The woman's expression was somber, serious, and wise. The head of her scepter glowed white, and craggy fingers of lightning extended out from the glow.

"Do you see anything different in her now?" Zari turned the card, showing Fia the upside-down image.

From the new angle, Fia could see more clearly the shadows created by the folds of the High Priestess's dress. She stared at it, so hard, she thought her eyes might fall out of her skull. As she watched, the shadows seemed to shift, the way the shadows in the garage had shifted . . .

"A mortal has taken control of my demon soldiers and placed them in unnatural circumstances. I cannot reclaim them without being stripped of my immortality. I request your aid, as they were seized to target you. I believe returning them to me is of equal benefit to us both."

"I guess that makes enough sense," Fia muttered.

"I'm sorry, *chérie?* I could not hear you."

Fia shook her head. "Nothing. Well, not nothing. I was

thinking she looks strong and powerful and remembering something the demon told me."

"Fiammetta, I am concerned you may have skipped a chapter or two in the story."

"Geez, sorry. I guess I'm having a little trouble keeping track of what happened when." Fia rubbed hard at her temples. "After the first time I came to see you, to ask about getting a new handler? I got something. I'm not sure what. It was a bounty, but I'm not sure it wasn't a trap or bait for a trap." She laid her initial encounter with Irzelen out on the table for Zari, catching her up with that part of the story.

When Fia was finished, Zari clucked her tongue against her teeth. "What you are telling me, then, is that the creatures you followed into the cave were leading you there by intelligent design?"

Fia shrugged. "I don't know if they knew what they were doing or if their human master has them on remote control. Apparently, immortal wardens of Hell are cagey and prefer to recruit mortal thugs who can puzzle things out for themselves."

"How's that, *chérie?*"

Now Fia laughed. "Sorry, Zari. I just meant, I think he, Irzelen, told me what he thought I would need to know to figure out the rest of the details on my own. He said he couldn't break the bond between mortal summoner and demon because of *divine law*. Scott—Father Scott—suggested that probably meant Irzelen wants—or needs—me to kill the summoner."

Zari's face twisted slightly, but not in the way Fia had expected. On some level, Fia thought, Zari had been expecting this news.

"I urge caution in this matter, Fia. But I believe your

priest is likely correct. The bond between summoner and demon can be severed if the summoner releases the demon with intention. I don't foresee, however, that that will be the case here. If you are not able to convince them to forfeit their control of the demons, you may be forced to kill them."

Fia studied Zari's face for a long moment. "Have you ever had to—have you ever killed someone who wasn't a host?"

"Not in the way you mean, *chérie*, but I have enough innocent blood on my hands to paint the walls of this kitchen."

Fia suddenly remembered the look of pity she hated and made an effort to wipe it off her own face.

"How do I find this person, Zari?"

Zari rested a finger against the tarot card. "Have you come any closer to deciphering who this might be?"

"Other than the person who summoned an army of demons to target me? No. I haven't the foggiest. There's a priest, Father Ariaz, I think Scott said. He's a piece of work, for sure, and connected to everything—"

"How do you know this?"

"I saw him. Kind of. There was a guy . . ." She told Zari about the man she had presumed to be a staggering drunk that Ariaz and Muscle had gathered up off the street. "And that no-neck thug was there when the cave blew. I'm pretty sure he blocked us in."

"How did he know you would be going there? Based on what you told me, I didn't think you knew you were going until you got there."

"Yeah, I don't know. We have our trackers; maybe they do too? Maybe he followed us after picking up the other one off the street."

"Perhaps. Perhaps someone alerted him to your plans?"

"It was just me, Father Scott, and that nun I mentioned, Rebecca."

Zari cocked an eyebrow. "I know that trust is a difficult thing for you, Fiammetta. You trust your priest. What about the nun?"

"The others trust her."

"Do you?"

"She hasn't given me a reason not to, if that's what you mean. She's been around, though. She was in the convent . . ."

"What happened to the convent, *chérie?* Why are they no longer there?"

"Adding that to the list of questions I need to ask next time I'm around them."

"Your young Sister Rebecca—she has been with Sister Agnes for a long time? And the elder will vouch for her?"

"I asked, but I got the impression I was encroaching. She took her vows to repay a debt."

"Ah. Hm. There was another nun there when you were a child, of whom you were fond. Cecilia?"

"She's still there. Mother Lou and Sister Bernadette moved on, but Agnes and Cecilia still know me. You're not suggesting—"

"I am not suggesting anything, Fiammetta. I am asking you to evaluate the situation like a predator, not prey. Tell me more about the priest."

"Scott?"

"Ariaz."

"He's a super creep. I caught wind of him—he was lurking in the shadows after one of my jobs. I tried to chase after him, but he jumped in a car. The woman in the car . . ."

"*Oui?*"

"There was a woman who picked him up that night. We were in this area, actually."

"Don't see a lot of holy men in this area, I will agree. Rabbis, occasionally, but not priests."

"That's what I thought. But this woman—I think I saw her with him again. I think she might be a nun. And I think they might be—I know this is going to sound strange, but I think they're lovers."

Zari flinched visibly at this revelation. "That is peculiar, to be sure. Why do you think this, *chérie?*"

"She was coming out of his church awhile back, carrying her wimple in her hand. She put it back on before getting in her rideshare—I caught up to the driver earlier today. He said he thought her name was Annie. Annie could be short for Annabel, right?"

"Ah. I see now why you are battling with this card. Perhaps we should draw another?"

"What for? Isn't that like manipulating the cards?"

Without answering, Zari slipped the High Priestess back into the center of the deck. She gave the cards a couple of quick shuffles and laid them on the table. She lifted half the deck off the top and moved it to the bottom.

"I want you to focus on that High Priestess, *chérie*. Think about what you saw in her face, in her eyes, in her gown. Think about the people you suspect may be working against you. Focus your mind on each of them, one at a time. Inhale deeply as you bring them to mind. Hold the breath as you study them. Study their face. Study their energy. Then exhale and release them from your thoughts."

Zari fell silent, letting Fia run through the ritual she had prescribed. She started with Ariaz, his deep-toned skin, the sharp lines of his high cheekbones and narrow nose, his black-brown eyes.

Exhale.

The next face belonged to Annabel, her denim-blue eyes and pink cheeks, her Midwestern farmer's daughter disposition.

Exhale.

Rebecca's amber eyes and the warm tone of her diamond-shaped face followed.

Exhale.

One by one, she brought forth faces, then pushed them from her mind. The last face to surface belonged to Max. *You know you have to consider him.* Deep brown eyes, the sharp angle of his jaw, the crooked smile curling his full lips floated through her mind.

Exhale.

"I think that's everyone," she announced.

Zari replied with a deep nod. She slipped a single card from the top of the deck, resting it on the table between them. "I want you to think about what you see. I want you to think about each of those faces you just studied. Use your gut, Fia. Tell me if anyone stands out when we see what is on this card. *Oui?*"

Fia nodded.

Zari turned the card. Fia's breath caught in her throat.

FIFTEEN

Gazing back at them from the face of the card was a pair of youths, a young man and young woman, each holding a chalice. They poured from their chalices into a clay pitcher. From the pitcher rose the apparition of a caduceus.

"What do you see, Fiammetta?"

"Is this meant to implicate someone?"

"No, Fia, not if that is not the message you receive from the cards. And traditionally, the Two of Cups is an incredibly positive card. The youths are each adding their own strengths, pouring from their own cups, to create an even stronger bond. What do you see?"

Fia gulped at her tea, which she had all but forgotten until now. "Max."

Zari tilted her head. "I can't say I recall mention of a Max."

"He's a . . . guy. He's gotten himself tangled up in my mess, and I'm not completely sure I want him untangled."

A sly smile crossed Zari's face. "Is he friend or lover, *chérie*?"

Fia laughed, a nervous sound that had little at all to do with amusement. "Lover. At least, he started out as lover. Tryst, actually. But he's insinuated himself into the role of friend."

"Those are the best kinds." Zari stood, gripped Fia's cheeks in her hands, and pressed a loving kiss hard against her forehead. "You do not deserve to be lonely, Fiammetta. I do not think we are closer to figuring out who the High Priestess is, but we have figured out who she is not, *mais non?*"

"Yeah. I think so. I mean, cards, right? Not an actual decree from the gods, but . . ."

"Sit with it awhile longer. The answer will come to you when you are ready to receive it. I must get my shop reopened, *chérie*. You will be all right?" Fia knew she meant on a larger scale.

Fia nodded. Zari and her floor-length skirt swished from the room, leaving Fia alone.

Fia nibbled her way through a third cookie and drained the contents of her glass. She called out to the front, "Hey, Zari?" and stuck her head through the velvet curtain separating the spaces. "Can I take some of this tea with me?"

"I'm not sure I have—"

"I have a bottle in the car."

"Then please do. I am pleased you like it."

Fia passed through the shop to the front door. Outside, she climbed into the SUV, stretching her torso across the driver and passenger seats to dig underneath, producing dust bunnies, a few dried leaves, and a large insulated plastic bottle. Crawling back out, she gave the door a bump with her hip and returned to the kitchen through the shop. She gave the bottle a quick rinse, dropped eight or ten ice cubes into the bottom and poured the sweet amber liquid over them. They cracked and whined their protest as she screwed the lid back on.

When she passed through for the final time, Zari had disappeared. "Thanks, Zari," Fia called into the emptiness.

"I will see you soon, *ma cherie.*"

Fia opened the door of the International Scout and wedged the bottle into the cupholder in the center. Just as she moved to take her place behind the steering wheel, something metal caught the sun.

A scuffed silver coat hook glinted at her from the passenger seat.

Sixteen

Gingerly, Fia lifted the metal hook from the seat, bringing it closer to her face to examine it, though she wasn't sure why.

It was a coat hook. More to the point, it had been removed from the door of a stall in a public restroom.

It had been forcibly removed from the door of a stall in a public restroom and driven into the neck of a man dead set on choking the life out of the anonymous woman who had led him into the stall in the first place.

Fia released a startled cry and stuffed the weapon of opportunity into the center console. She scanned the neighborhood, but whoever had left her this overt message had choreographed everything to avoid being seen.

The question was, how had they known she would go back inside after coming out of Zari's shop? The hair on her arms stood on end. She was being watched.

They—whoever *they* were—would have stayed close to watch her reaction. She scanned the windows with a view of the inside of her car. There weren't many. Only one had the curtains open, and there was a *For Sale* sign in the yard.

They could be watching through those thin, gauzy curtains, and you'd never know.

She considered going back inside, asking Zari how well she knew her neighbors, but in the end, she decided she didn't need Zari worrying about her safety. She turned the key and pulled calmly away from the curb.

Minutes later, she pulled around the corner onto the top level of her own garage and slammed on the brakes. Inches from the Scout's front grill stood a man dressed head to toe in black. He even had his hood drawn up in the August heat. He'd stepped out from behind the support column, directly into her path.

She leaned on the horn, filling the concrete box with sound. "What the hell?" When he didn't move, didn't respond to the blaring horn, she furrowed her brow and set the parking brake, climbing out of the car to confront him. "Are you looking for me?"

Nothing.

"Hey, what's your problem, mister?"

As soon as she was within arm's reach, he did just that, squeezing a thick hand over her throat and pushing her into the wall, lifting her feet several inches off the ground. The momentum of the strike knocked his hood back far enough she could see his eyes in the shadowed space.

They were the color of late, post-dawn clouds, a soft blue streaked with white and an even lighter blue, all clouded over widely dilated pupils. He breathed stale, mildewed breath into her face and stank of damp, dead leaves.

You've got to be kidding me.

She kicked out with both feet, connecting but not well. She brought up her left arm and slammed the back of it—

fist clenched, muscles rigid—into the inside of his arm, causing him to lose his grip. She fell to the ground and, without hesitating, found her feet and lunged past him, back into the open car door. She slammed it on his hand as he reached for her, several bones crunching with the force. It didn't slow him down. He ripped it free, stripping off several layers of skin and tissue.

"Damn," Fia swore as she reached into the center console, where she kept a spare bolt. With it in hand, she crawled between the bucket seats into the back, over the bench seat, and into the cargo space.

One thing about her old-model Scout was, it didn't have all the fancy extras. Where a newer model SUV would have had a toolbox built into the floorboards, Fia had the regular kind, locked in place with bungee cords. But what was inside was anything but regular. She grabbed one of the two containment collars she found inside and climbed out through the tailgate.

He was on her in a flash, but she was ready for him. She let him grab for her and used his momentum to throw him over her back to the concrete on the other side. She stepped on his throat, leaning her weight forward into her foot, and could feel his Adam's apple crush beneath it. He growled out her name as everything gave way with a squelching crunch.

Pulling the body up by its shoulders, she drove the bolt into the soft indent at the base of the skull, before snapping the collar into place.

It wouldn't be long before the angel showed up to gather the soul, but Fia didn't want to take any chances. She hauled him into the back of the Scout, leaving the tailgate open as she drove to her regular parking space and eased between the scooter and the wall.

Once parked, she dragged the corpse back out of the

car, letting it fall to the ground, and rolled it under the SUV. "There. That should take care of that for a few minutes." She sat heavily on the bumper and let her head fall back against the car.

In seven years, she didn't think she had ever heard one of them call her by name. She didn't know what it meant, but she was certain it wasn't a good thing.

She considered that maybe the host had recognized her, that he had spoken around the soul. She didn't recognize him. He didn't look like the type she would have picked up and brought home, but there had been enough of them, she could believe she didn't recognize all of them. She couldn't think of anywhere else she might have bumped into this guy that he would have known her name. She tried to avoid that as much as possible too.

The other possibility was that the souls were learning who she was. She had recently lost a soul in a public restroom. She hadn't given Brent Newman her name, but maybe the soul had heard Rylan say it.

The air shimmered like asphalt on a desert highway, and the angel formed from nothing, barely acknowledging Fia as she gestured for him to look beneath the car and stepped back against the wall, out of the way. She wasn't sure what she was expecting, but she was pretty sure she couldn't have imagined what came next if she had been given one hundred years to try.

The being pulled the corpse out from beneath the Scout and crouched down beside it. Tiny lightning bolts, little more than a static charge in a dark room, extended from his index finger to the lock on the collar, and the whole mechanism popped open. As soon as the copper rod was free of the wound in the neck, the body crumbled away, like a sandcastle in the wind.

With a quick gesture, the being trapped a whiff of smoke in a ball between its hands. One of the little piranha demons seemed to form out of the shadows in the garage, and the angel passed the smoke off to it.

The little demon inhaled the smoke through a comb of thin, sharp teeth with a hiss and melted back into the shadows.

With impressively little ceremony, the angel also vanished, taking its electric charge with it. Fia rubbed at her arms, trying to smooth the hairs back into place. Her phone buzzed in her pocket, but she ignored it, staring at the empty concrete. Seconds before, it had contained divine creatures and a human corpse.

Now, there was a futuristic titanium-and-copper containment collar and a whole lot of nothing. She picked up the collar, turning it in her hands before tossing it into the back of the SUV and gave the tailgate a shove.

The angel had given the soul to one of Irzelen's demons. Or a demon. "I guess they don't all belong to him." She wondered if Scott—if Uhlpir could clear any of this up.

"Of course," she muttered into the shadows, "if he can, that means he kept it from you. More secrets." She was tired of secrets. Especially when they could make a difference in her odds of survival. She rubbed hard at her temples and turned for her apartment.

Inside, she dropped her keys and phone onto the counter and headed straight for the balcony, forgetting about whatever had made her phone buzz before. She stretched out on the lounger, her head pounding with new information. More than anything, she couldn't help but wonder why it was all coming to light now.

Not just that she had been at this for seven, almost eight, years and was figuring out all these things she had never known, never been told. But in the grand scheme of things, why was this all coming out now? After a couple thousand years.

She had a direct connection to divinity. She shared a secret with an angel, something she suspected was not a product of her own clever ideas.

"He let me catch him," she said aloud. "He trapped me in my own trap." She banged her head back against the chair. "I thought I was setting a trap to catch him, but that stupid goddamned crossbow was his trap." She thought about that for a second. "But which time?"

She chewed on what to do next. "Let's recap," she said, continuing to think aloud. "You've met an angel—two angels—a demon who apparently can't just set humans on fire, so he tried to recruit you to figure out who hijacked an army of his demon thugs. Which clearly means you pissed off one somebody more than usual."

She sighed, holding her temples. "But I'm nobody."

Struck by an idea, she found her feet and headed back inside. She grabbed her things off the counter, stuffed her phone into her pocket, and returned to the garage.

Fia pulled the scooter into the parking lot of the small cathedral and cut the engine, looking up at the ornate decorations along the roof through the windshield. What were the chances he would even talk to her, let alone tell her what she wanted to know? The only way to find out, she decided, was to go in and try.

She climbed off the scooter and headed toward the side door, which led to meeting rooms and offices behind the main sanctuary. Half expecting it to be locked, she tried the handle and was pleased when it clicked open. She moved through it into the cool shadows of the church.

Inside, she looked around, unsure which direction to go first. She had arbitrarily chosen the left hallway, going deeper into the church, when a young woman shuffled toward her, her attention focused on a sheet of paper in her hands.

Fia stepped in front of her. "Excuse me."

The woman started, looking up at Fia with wide eyes. "I'm sorry. Can I help you with something?"

"I'm looking for one of your priests. Father Ariaz, I believe, is his name."

"Yes, he is here. I can see if he's available. Can I give him your name?"

"Don't interrupt if he's with someone, but he'll want to see me."

Fia hesitated, wondering in what capacity this woman worked for the priest. Was she just a secretary, or did she know who he really was? She waited for Fia to finish, unmoving.

"Fia. Drake."

"Certainly, Ms. Drake. I will let him know you're here." She shuffled off in the same direction she had been headed in the first place, leaving Fia to study the crown molding.

A few minutes later, the woman returned. "Ms. Drake? Father Ariaz will see you. Follow me?"

Fia fell in behind the woman. They passed through one door into a reception area Fia guessed belonged to her escort, who held open the inner door, ushering Fia through.

The priest stood against the outside of his desk, hands at his sides and feet crossed in front of him. The woman left the door open and resumed whatever mission she had been on before Fia distracted her. Ariaz stepped around Fia and pushed the door closed.

"What can I help you with, Ms. Drake?"

She met his eyes and held his gaze without responding. She was waiting for him to drop the façade that she knew was only in place for the secretary. By now, Fia was relatively certain she was just that, a secretary, and nothing more. She had no idea who—or what—she was working for.

When Ariaz didn't break character, Fia took a challenging step closer to him, encroaching on his personal space as much as she dared, the memory of the last time still fresh in the fading bruises he'd left. At least this time she was ready for him. She planted her feet in a fighter's stance, her left foot slightly forward of the right, and she turned her shoulders enough that it would be hard for him to grab her throat again.

No pretense. He knew why she was here, and she knew he knew. There was no point in hiding it. Maybe if she didn't, he wouldn't either.

"You look defensive, Ms. Drake. Have I done something—"

"Stow it. I'm looking for answers, and I think either you have some or you can tell me where to find them."

He shifted back onto his heels, relaxing instead of defending. Fia cocked an eyebrow.

"I see. And you have come to me because your own Father McGregor and the Reverend Mother are not forthcoming?"

"As far as I know, they don't have the answers I am looking for."

"How are you so certain?"

Damn. That was a good question. She quickly put a few words together, but they sounded foolish in this context. She was certain because they were the people who had been around the longest. The only other person she trusted fully was Zari. If she couldn't trust them to answer her questions to the best of their ability—

She knew they—she knew Agnes had kept things from her. She didn't think the nun had ever outright lied to her, but how could Fia be sure?

Ultimately, Fia decided Ariaz was going to believe whatever he wanted to anyway. "They just don't."

It was his turn to raise an eyebrow. He half shook his head, a gesture that read, *Have it your way,* before turning and retreating behind his desk. He lowered himself slowly, deliberately, into the cushioned chair, moved a few things from the center of the desk to the sides and leaned forward on his elbows. He smiled at Fia with only his lips, baring teeth without extending the smile to the rest of his face. The look of a feral cat watching a squirrel.

The look made the scaled flesh of Fia's right arm crawl. It was predatory, but not in the way she expected. She refused to let him see her discomfort.

He let the smile fade. "Tell me, Ms. Drake. What answers do you seek?"

She kept her eyes on him a moment longer before moving to one of the chairs facing him from the other side of the desk. "I had a visitor before I came over here. In fact, that's what prompted this visit. Believe me, I considered several other options first."

"A visitor?"

"One of the possessed. What I want to know from you, Ariaz, is how to summon the demon. You do know, don't you?"

He leaned back in the chair, genuine astonishment passing over the deep angles of his face. "I have, regrettably, not met the demon. I envy you a bit for having stood toe to toe with him and survived to talk about it. As I understand it, this is not something many mortals can say. I cannot say I would connect you to him, had I the means, but I do not, so whether I would is a moot point, yes?"

Fia frowned. He was telling the truth. "Then I guess we're done here." She rose from the chair and started for the door.

Ariaz jumped up, nearly capsizing his chair, and stretched his strides to beat her to the door, slamming it closed as she pulled it open. He closed in on her, pushing her to step away, until he had her pinned against the wall. He reached out, gliding a hand down her arm, and lifted her hand, turning her arm back and forth to look at her scars.

"I think I remember hearing about how you got these. Pushed some guy into a deep fryer, is that right?"

"Did they tell you why I did it?"

"Can't say I heard that part."

She hooked a finger, urging him to lean into her. She could feel his breath on the skin of her neck as she whispered into his ear.

"He was selling little girls for sex and tried to get me involved. I literally cooked a man alive because he was a plain-vanilla pervert; what do you think I could do to someone like you?"

He shifted his weight back away from her, not truly stepping away but giving her room to breathe. She lifted herself away from the wall and took the opportunity, driving an uppercut punch into his ribs to punctuate her threat. As he doubled over, coughing, she pushed by him, turning to open the door. He snarled a swear at her as she crossed the threshold.

"Toodle-oo, Father." She waved her fingers at him with feigned reticence as he snatched at her uselessly. "I'm sure I'll be seeing you again. Probably sooner rather than later."

She pulled the door closed behind her as she left the office, nodding to the secretary as she crossed back toward the hallway. "I'll see myself out."

In the hallway, she hesitated. "Out" was to the left, toward the door to the street. Right took her deeper into the building. She wasn't sure what she thought she might find if she turned right, but she decided to try it.

The hallway was dark, darker the farther she traveled back into the church. She passed a handful of rooms, single doors leading to offices and classrooms, double doors leading to conference rooms. She found her way into an empty industrial kitchen before a voice broke her thoughts.

"Miss Drake? Is there something I can help you with?"

Fia turned and saw the secretary looking at her from the kitchen doorway. "I'm sorry?"

"Is there something else we can do for you?"

"No. No, I'm good. I just got turned around."

She pushed past the mousy woman, back out into the hallway. As she approached the office, she ducked off the carpet runner, pretending to tie her shoe. A hundred feet away, Father Ariaz was greeting another man in cleric's clothes. After the last few days, she was hesitant to assume a priest's collar automatically meant priest.

She heard Ariaz's gravelly drawl creep through the hallway, soaking into the wood of the walls. "To what do I owe this surprise?"

"Could we speak in your office?"

Fia recognized him. It was the man she had seen with Annabel in the city. Further, it was the man she had seen lurking outside this same office a few weeks earlier.

She wanted to know who he was, why he looked like a trapped animal, but the secretary was only a few steps behind her and didn't seem too keen on letting Fia range freely through the church.

Fia finished with her laces and moved, as slowly as she dared, toward the exit, hoping to at least pick up a name as she passed the office.

Nothing.

The two men had already moved inside, closing the door behind them. Maybe even more intriguing, though, was the thug—all three hundred pounds of him—had been stuffed into one of the little armchairs in the outer office. His attention was intently focused on picking the skin from his stubby fingers, and Fia used that opportunity to slip by unnoticed.

Outside, she remembered the ignored messages on her phone.

Max.

"Shit," she muttered, stuffing the phone into the side of her bra. Ignoring him was going to be hard, but she had already figured out he wouldn't let her do it any other way. If she told him he needed to stay away for his own safety, he'd play that chivalric knight card. Her only recourse was to get out of town.

Seventeen

Fia pulled the Scout off the small paved road onto a gravel drive mostly concealed by thick forest. The drive led her another mile back into the trees to the expansive cabin. She stopped on the far edge of the clearing that surrounded the house and pulled out her phone.

On a job. Can't talk. Catch up with you in a couple of days.

She sent the text to Max, hoping that would keep him at bay until she was able to bring him up here too.

She leaned over the center console to peer out the passenger window at the front door of the safe house. Once again, she brought up her phone, this time hoping she had a strong enough signal to complete a call. She pulled up Scott's number in her phone book.

"This is Father McGregor," he answered.

"Really? You don't have me saved as a contact? I should at least be in your top five speed-dial numbers: God, Gabriel, Agnes, me—whatever. Hey, I'm sitting in the driveway, but I had a moment of panic that I might get my knuckles bruised if I showed up unannounced. Can I come in?"

The line fell silent long enough, Fia was wondering if the call had disconnected when Scott replied. "Yes, I will meet you at the garage door."

As if to punctuate his statement, the wide door of the garage began to rise slowly, revealing one of the sedans and the passenger van.

Fia cut the engine of the Scout and made her way inside. Nearly seven imposing feet of long-haired angel-priest stood in the doorway that led into the house by way of the sterile-looking commercial-grade kitchen. He stepped aside, motioning Fia through the door ahead of him.

"Please. To what do we owe this visit?" He closed the garage doors behind them.

"I had to get away from Max." Scott cocked an eyebrow, and Fia realized how her statement must have come across. "No, not like that. Actually, we probably should discuss the whys concerning my extreme attempt to avoid him."

"Oh?"

She took another look at her phone. She had missed a response from Max. *Pleading face. Sobbing face. Thumbs up.* She decided that meant he had accepted her dodge.

She looked at the time. "Shit, I'm interrupting dinner."

"Not for me. I actually just got back from the city myself."

Fia nodded, unsure what she was supposed to say in response. "I can put something together if you'd like?"

"I'm not inept. I simply don't spend much time in the role of chef."

"I didn't mean—you said you don't cook much. I figured you either hadn't had a lot of opportunities, surrounded by these worker bees, or you didn't enjoy it."

"You don't strike me as particularly domestic either."

"Probably not, but I can cook." She opened the door to the freezer and searched around a little before closing it again. "I don't have to thaw anything to make sandwiches."

Scott chuckled. "That's fine. There should be a sandwich tray of meats and cheeses in the refrigerator."

Fia brought the tray, a bottle each of mayonnaise and mustard, a loaf of bread, and a pair of knives to the large steel table to join Scott.

"So, tell me why you are ducking the man you wish to protect."

"To protect him. After I left you this morning, I ran into—did I mention that creepy priest, Ariaz, has a hired muscle? Big guy—about your height, actually, but two of you across—no neck, wears a black sweatshirt in ninety-degree heat.

"Anyway, I ran into him downtown. We got into a scuffle. I wailed on him like a speed bag and ran before he could recover. But he was definitely following me. I went to the priest to find out what he might tell me, and he came on to me. I assumed his vows were shaky, but that was a little blatant, if you ask me. I guess he's decided since I know he's not on the up and up, he no longer has to put up the front for me."

She decided to leave out the detail of finding the coat hook in her car. She hadn't said anything about the incident with Brent Newman, although she was sure Scott—or Uhlpir—already knew. But because she hadn't said anything, she didn't know for sure if he knew, and she didn't want to have to explain the significance of an otherwise innocuous piece of hardware.

Later. She'd get into all that later.

"So," Fia continued, "after getting attacked and then hit on in a way that was still all too familiar—and that's just the humans—I decided it was in both our best interests to put some space between us until he's got his tattoo."

Scott took large bites of the sandwich he had assembled without saying anything in response. Fia thought she would give anything to know what he was thinking.

He finally spoke once he had finished eating. "I think you are probably correct. If you choose to stay here, there is the bedroom you may occupy, and I am certain the teens will be more than thrilled for the chance to learn more from you."

"The teens. How is Mercy?" Fia asked.

"She is fine. Mild concussion, but she's taking things easy."

"And does she remember what happened? Why she fell?" Fia hadn't found any signs of sabotage on the bars, but something still nagged at her.

"No. Just lost her grip, it seems. That's her best guess too."

Fia finished her sandwich and briefly considered building another before pushing her plate away. "What happens around here after dinner?"

"Not a lot. The teens are finished with their training for the day and free to relax. The younger children have some activities with Sister Cecilia before bed. Calm activities to get them ready to go to sleep."

"I remember a little of that. Reading, drawing, anything that could be done without moving much more than hands and arms."

"Precisely. Sister Annabel works with her in that area. Annabel guides them in some meditation, simple bits designed for younger minds."

"Do the teens get in on any of that?"

"Some. They have been going to Sister Annabel directly."

"I learned a few tricks from Zari they might be interested in. Self-hypnosis. Good if you get knocked out or drugged or something. They can piece together lost bits of their own memories without needing someone else to guide them through it. I might even see if Mercy could remember any more about what happened."

"I think that would be a good idea. Do you think it is something they can learn in a day?"

"Yes and no. I can teach them how in an afternoon, but they'll have to practice on their own to get good at it."

"Logically."

"Should I clear it with Agnes, or do you think I should just ask them if they want to?"

"You seem to harbor some . . . I don't want to call it animosity, but there is definitely a tension between you and the Reverend Mother."

Fia shrugged. "You're the second person to bring that up. She's the one with animosity. When Mercy got hurt, she dismissed me like a child. Told me I was in the way."

Scott nodded, though Fia didn't think it was a response so much as an acknowledgment. He had heard her and would now consider her words. "Perhaps she simply wanted to spare you from . . ."

As he spoke, his words grew slower and further apart, as if he were making up the sentence word by word.

"Thanks for trying, but there's really no way you can finish that sentence that is going to sound like Agnes wants me hanging around here."

"Agnes is from a different way of thinking. You are brash, outspoken, not what you are expected to be."

"I hunt fugitive souls. From Hell. Actual Hell. Am I supposed to do that while curtseying? Should I raise my pinkie when shooting my crossbow? She didn't teach us any of that. Why does she expect it of me?"

"She just expects a little more discipline."

"Mother Agnes and her obedient little soldiers. That's the way it's always been. Get only the information you need in the moment you need it, don't ask questions, don't break rank. So I broke rank. And I think she knows she can't do anything about me, but she can limit my time with the hunters. Or keep me away from them altogether. Why would she want a bad influence like me around them?"

"Have you ever wondered what effect your leaving had on your peers?"

"Now you're going to get in on it too?"

"Fia, no, that's not what I—I really just wanted to know if you had wondered."

"I'm sure they got punished because I wasn't there to catch it myself. I'm sure I sent the whole place spiraling into chaos."

"Do you know what happened at the convent the morning Agnes discovered you were missing?"

Fia raised an eyebrow. "What happened?"

"Rebecca arrived. To a house of chaos. To a house searching for a lost teen. A search led by Mother Agnes."

"Only because Mother Lou told her to."

"She was quite upset at your choice to run away."

Fia shrugged. "That probably sucked for Rebecca, though. Walking in on that mess."

"Perhaps it's something you should speak with her about."

The door that led from the kitchen to the hallway swung open as Sister Rebecca pushed through it, her arms loaded with dishes. "Fia! Hello. When did you get here? You missed dinner." The nun gave her armload of dishes a small hoist for emphasis.

"Sc—Father Scott and I had sandwiches."

"Oh, did you come up here with him from the city, then?"

"Fia came on her own. Arrived only a few minutes behind me, in fact."

Not far behind Rebecca, Tianna pushed through the door with a second load of dishes. "Fia!" She nearly dropped her load in the sink so she could double back to the table. She looped her long arms around Fia's shoulders, squeezing her before Fia could protest. "I was worried you wouldn't come back after what happened."

Fia turned to Scott. "See? I didn't make it up. Tianna noticed Agnes's sunny disposition too."

"Tianna," Rebecca called over her shoulder, interrupting Fia, "there will be time for chatting after the dishes are washed and put away."

Tianna jerked her head toward the sink and the nun. "I gotta . . ."

"Hey, you know what?" Fia slipped off the stool to stand in front of Tianna, her nose barely level with the girl's shoulder. "I'll help. I'll wash, you dry, and Sister Rebecca can put them away. Sound good? Rebecca?"

"It is important that the teens learn discipline."

"There's that word again," Fia half snarled. "This place is so rigid. Just let them be kids." When Rebecca didn't respond, Fia turned to Scott. "Hey, is that room I stayed in before open?"

"You are staying?"

"I was hoping to. Until I can move around the city without creating collateral damage."

"You didn't bring a change of clothes."

"In the car. I didn't want to pack them inside if I couldn't stay. But I'd like to."

Eighteen

Fia dropped the backpack she had brought with her on the bed. With every intention of meeting with the teens in their recreation room, she sat down beside the bag and stretched her neck and back. Her ribs hurt where the big man had hit her. She lifted her shirt to inspect the area. Finding no outwardly visible bruising, she poked a finger gently at the area. He had hit her—or she had hit him—hard, but nothing felt more damaged than just sore.

It had been a long day.

Her body ached; she was pretty sure everywhere. Even her toes and fingers ached. She took off her shoes, tucked her socks inside them, and rubbed hard at her feet, bending and pulling at her toes to stretch them. With a deep yawn, she fell back against the bed, savoring the soft mattress beneath her.

As soon as she felt her eyes close, she sat up. "Nope. You came up here to talk to people, not sleep. Up and at 'em." She fished flip-flops from inside the backpack and wiggled her toes around the strap. Over her tank and cold arms, she slipped an old long-sleeved t-shirt emblazoned with the name of a popular song and the silhouette of a woman behind the letters.

She slipped out into the hallway and looked around. She realized she had failed to figure out where the teens would be after dinner and decided to head toward the library.

At the top of the stairs, she listened for voices. If they were sitting around reading or playing board games, she likely wouldn't hear anything, but she listened anyway. After a few minutes, she finally did catch a sound, but it wasn't coming from anywhere in the cavernous library. She turned around to find Mother Agnes standing in the doorway.

"Reverend Mother."

"Fiammetta, Father McGregor told me you hoped to be staying with us until the fakir arrives and you can bring Max for his ritual. Is that what you had in mind?"

"If that's okay. I don't think it's safe for him to be hanging around me, and I'm not sure I can avoid him."

"You are serious, then?"

Fia shrugged. She wasn't at all comfortable discussing the intricacies of her relationship with Max with a nun, and especially not this nun. But she didn't have an answer for the specific question Agnes had asked either.

"We spend a lot of leisure time in the same places. We run into each other a lot without meaning to. A couple of times we've run into each other, we were joined by demons. I just thought it would be better for both of us if that couldn't happen."

Agnes remained quiet, her steel eyes fixed on Fia. The same look that always made Fia feel so small. She decided to change the subject.

"I was hoping to talk a little more with the teens. Do they still have personal quiet time after dinner?"

Agnes turned, motioning for Fia to follow her. "This way, back in their quarters. I believe the young ones are with them as well; Sisters Cecilia and Annabel are tending to some business for me."

Fia followed Agnes's black figure back down the dark hallway, through the kitchen, to a room behind the garage. Except for the door from the kitchen, which could just as easily have been mistaken for a pantry, there was almost no sign this part of the house existed. Outside, it nestled so deeply into the trees, behind the edge of the garage, that one had to be looking for it to really notice it.

Agnes pushed open one of the two doors facing the bedrooms and waved for Fia to pass through.

"Fia!" Mercy hopped up from the floor where she and one of the younger children—a dark-skinned boy with thick, curly hair named Levi—were playing a card game. She hugged Fia and beckoned her to sit with them. "Play with us?"

"Maybe next round. It looks like you are elbow deep in this one."

"No, that's the great thing about this game. Anyone can join anytime."

"It's a ridiculous game," Kaleb muttered from behind his book. "The rules were made up by a five-year-old."

"Who asked you?" Mercy shot back. "Please, Fia?"

Fia shrugged. "If that's how it works, sure. Deal me in." She let Mercy explain the rules—Kaleb was right; it did sound like it had been made up by a child—and she let the game run a couple of loops around the table before speaking again. "What happened out on the training course the other day?"

"I'm not really sure. I've never fallen off the bars like

that. But I got the stars knocked out of me, so I don't even know if I could remember if I wanted to."

Fia looked around the room. Xavier was playing a handheld video game that Fia thought would never have been allowed in the convent. Kaleb was reading alone, curled up in an armchair. Tianna was sitting in a far corner, reading quietly to the other kids.

"Hey, I was talking to Father Scott about teaching you all a few more tricks I've learned since I left."

"That would be awesome," Mercy replied. "Like what?"

"One thing I was thinking would help right now is self-hypnosis. The woman who mentored me after I left—Zari—taught me how. It helps you draw forward memories you sometimes don't realize you have. Maybe it will help with the brain fog."

Kaleb groaned without looking up from his book. "Sounds like a load of bullshit."

"What's your problem, Kaleb?" Mercy demanded. "You've been negative all day." She turned her attention back to Fia. "Sorry. Kaleb's been a jerk today. Pissing all over everything I say."

"Not just you," Xavier added without looking up from his game.

"Ignore him," Mercy said to Fia. "Tell me more about the hypnosis."

The next afternoon, Fia sat with the hunters in one of the classrooms in the lower level of the library. Three of them—Xavier, Mercy, and Tianna—sat at their desks, facing Fia. Kaleb had pulled his desk away from the others and sat sideways, leaning against the wall, his legs kicked out to the side. He seemed to have the same chip on his shoulder as the night before.

"Kaleb," Fia said, watching his posture. "If you don't want to be here—"

"Reverend Mother said I gotta be here. She didn't say I gotta like it."

Fia shrugged. "Whatever. At least be quiet so the others can concentrate. You got headphones? I won't say anything if you want to put them in and ignore us."

"Just get this over with so we can get out of here."

"To what? The same shit, different day? You really itching to get back out in the dust and heat and shoot at targets for the next three hours? Remember, I've been where you are. I've spent endless hours running the same drills. I know you would rather be in here doing anything different."

Kaleb replied by rolling his eyes and slouching deeper into his seat.

Fia turned to the others. "Okay, I guess. Who wants to try first?"

Mercy was the first to volunteer. She sat cross-legged on the floor facing Fia. It hadn't taken long for the girl to fall into what appeared to be a deep, restful sleep, despite her rigid posture. Her lips moved quickly, as if she were telling a story, but the words were inaudible.

After a minute, maybe two, Mercy blinked her eyes slowly and looked around the room.

Fia waited, watching her eagerly until she decided the girl wasn't going to say anything. "Well?" she asked with a laugh. "Tell me what happened."

"I'm really not sure. I don't think I saw anything important. Or helpful? I think I remember some movement in the trees, but it might have just been something blowing in the wind."

"Trust your instincts, Mercy."

"Who could have been out there? We were all on the ground, Sister Annabel had taken that snake to the city, Sister Cecilia had the little ones, and everyone else was inside."

Fia didn't say anything. She didn't want to influence the teens into remembering something that wasn't real.

"Tianna, do you want to try?"

The blonde girl shrugged. "I don't know what I can offer. I didn't even see her fall. Just saw her on the ground."

"If you decide you want to try it, even just to learn how, let me know. Mercy seems to have a pretty good handle on it too. It's really just about concentrating, accessing more of your brain than you normally do."

"Maybe later."

Someone knocked on the door before giving it a gentle push. Annabel's face appeared in the space. "Fia? Reverend Mother would like to see the teens back upstairs. She has some things she wants to talk to them about concerning the start of school."

"Oh, yeah. Hey, when is that?" Fia asked.

"Monday," Xavier said.

"Wow. Yeah, sorry. I'm sure you guys have a ton to do to get ready."

Annabel stepped out of the way to let the teens skirt around her. She stepped into the room after they were gone. The hair on Fia's arms bristled as the nun pulled the door closed and stepped into Fia's space.

"I wanted to talk to you—"

"Hey," Fia said, trying to brush off the discomfort of having Annabel so close. She edged around the woman, pulling her phone from her pocket. "What time is it, anyway?"

"Half past three."

"Dinner is at five? I need to run something—have you seen Father Scott?"

"It is. And I think he is in his office."

Feeling less trapped, Fia slipped her phone back into her pocket and turned her focus onto the nun. "I haven't had a chance to ask you: how did everything work out with the snake?"

"Pardon?"

"The snake, animal control. The last time I was up here, you rescued me from that snake and took it to the city."

"Right, yes. It turned out fine. They were surprised she was up here so high. But they took her out of the city, I think. Released her. Snakes are solitary creatures, so she'll be fine."

"Great."

Fia hoped her voice didn't sound as unsure as she felt. The truth was, she really didn't care about the snake, but something in Annabel's familiarity with the creature made Fia's skin crawl.

Maybe it was just the memory of the snake itself.

She'd never given a lot of thought to snakes. There weren't too many in the city, and they had been too high at the convent to have snakes there. But now she was thinking about them and quickly deciding she didn't want to think about them anymore than she had to.

She shuddered.

"Snakes really aren't the bad creatures people think they are," Annabel asserted. "I mean, coral snakes are poisonous, obviously, but most simply help to control the pest population."

"Thanks. But I think I'll keep my distance. How do you know so much about them?"

"Kind of part and parcel of growing up in the desert.

You learn which ones are helpful, which ones can kill you, and how to respect them both."

"Did animal control have any idea how it got up here?"

"They said someone must have brought *her* up here." Annabel put a heavy emphasis on *her*, and Fia inferred that the nun was at least annoyed, if not angered, by Fia's resistance to referring to the snake the same way. "It's possible she got into someone's car by accident. Apologies, Fia, but I need to get back upstairs." Sister Annabel turned and let herself out of the classroom, leaving Fia alone with her thoughts.

Which she quickly filed away for later. She followed along behind the nun, closing the classroom door behind her.

When she crested the stairs to the main floor of the library, she saw Sister Rebecca sitting at the large desk just inside the doorway. She stepped up to the desk and leaned against it.

"Hi."

"Fia." Rebecca barely looked away from the computer screen in front of her to nod a greeting, leaving it to hang heavily in the air.

"Do you have a minute?"

Rebecca sighed and turned her swiveling stool to face Fia directly. "How can I help you?"

"I was talking with Annabel downstairs. About that snake. She seemed very attached to it but said it didn't belong here." Fia gestured to the library stacks. "Got any books about snakes? Or do you know anything about coral snakes?"

"You are welcome to look around. Books about animals are over there." Rebecca pointed toward one of the far shelves.

"Do you think someone might have brought that snake here intentionally?"

That got Rebecca's attention, and the nun looked Fia fully in the eyes. "Are you suggesting that Sister Annabel had something to do with that? She said animal control told her it had likely come in someone's car."

"Yeah, she told me that too."

"Fia, we do not have the luxury of suspecting one another here. The snake's presence was an accident, just as Mercy's fall was. It will not do anyone any good to start looking for monsters where there are none. Especially now that *you* have made contact with a real monster." Rebecca put extra emphasis on *you*, as if something specifically about Fia having met Irzelen bothered her more than the rest.

"I didn't mean—" Fia looked around the cavernous space, not sure what she hoped to find, other than an escape route. "Do you know where I could find Sister Theresa?"

"She has had some time to herself today because the teens have been otherwise occupied. It is possible she is in her quarters. Or possibly in the garden." Rebecca nodded and swiveled her stool back to face the computer screen. Fia watched the nun for another moment, studying the similarity of one black habit to another.

Fia turned and left the library. She stopped in the foyer, looking first down the hallway toward the room she was occupying, then out the small windows of the French doors leading to the garden and training grounds. She had only used finding Sister Theresa as an excuse to leave Rebecca, but she thought maybe she should check in with her anyway.

As she passed beneath the canopy of trees that formed an entry to the garden, a hand locked around her arm, hauling on it hard enough that she lost her footing.

NINETEEN

"What the hell?" Fia barked, jerking her arm free of her attacker's grip. "Kaleb! What are you doing?"

"Sh, follow me." He waved his hand toward the trees behind the kitchen.

"What—"

"Please, Fia, just come with me."

She sighed and motioned for him to lead the way. "Shouldn't you be in the Reverend Mother's office?"

Kaleb huffed. "They're sending us off to public school to *socialize*, to learn to behave like real people in the real world."

"Yeah, I went through all of it, remember?"

"Did they split you up?"

"They did. It sucked, for a while. But I think we all got used to it and made friends. I know I did."

"Do you wish you hadn't left?"

"Left? The convent? Hell no." They reached the same clearing Scott had brought Fia to, to discuss his angel identity. "I thought this place looked a little suspicious."

"Huh?"

Fia waved a hand at the conveniently placed logs and boulder. "You guys put all that there, didn't you?"

"Yeah. I'm not saying Mother Agnes has the place bugged, but she always seems to know what's going on."

"I think Sister Rebecca has a little to do with that too."

"What do you mean?"

"She's cool, I guess. But a little icy. I see a lot of Agnes's influence in her."

Kaleb shrugged. "I guess so, yeah. She is kind of a junior Agnes, isn't she?"

"So why the kidnapping?"

"I wanted to apologize for being a jerk."

"That's a good start. What did I do to deserve that? Or Mercy? Or whoever it was you were lashing out at?"

"Honestly, the Reverend Mother. Something's going on, and she won't be straight with us."

"But I will, so why bring it down on me?"

"I don't need to be hypnotized. I saw what happened to Mercy."

Fia cocked an eyebrow. "Tell me more?"

Kaleb took a deep breath and launched into a rapid-fire story. Fia guessed he thought if he talked fast enough, she couldn't interrupt or argue with him.

"I didn't *actually* see what happened, but I saw a habit in the trees at the edge of the training grounds. She was moving down the hill. It was a few seconds after Mercy went down. We had just started our circuit when she fell. Tianna and Sister Theresa ran to her; I froze like a jerk. She was down for a minute—I don't know, minute and a half—before I noticed something moving to the right, in the trees. When I looked, I saw the black, her habit, but I really couldn't even tell how tall she was. The trees are so thick."

"Yeah. Who—you don't know."

"I don't even think the other hunters believe me. I don't know why they should. I'm throwing one of the nuns under the bus, right? But Fia, I know what I saw."

"It couldn't have been a bear or—"

"No, it was definitely a human. Maybe it wasn't a nun. Maybe it was just someone in all black. I'm sorry. I wish I had seen her face. You don't believe me either."

All black? Like a black hooded sweatshirt? Kaleb insisted it was a woman he had seen, but he also hadn't seen enough to even be positive it was a nun and not just someone in black.

"Kaleb, I believe you. I don't think I'm ready to explain why; I still need to do some digging. But I believe you."

"You believe me, but we can't tell anyone."

Fia sighed. She knew how he felt. She had been in that same spot, knowing something she couldn't talk about without putting someone else in danger. Or sounding crazy.

"I know where you're coming from." She couldn't tell Kaleb about the priest or seeing Annabel in the city, but she thought maybe she did have a story for him.

"It's not exactly the same, but can I tell you a story? You asked if I regretted leaving the convent. And for the most part, I don't. But there is at least one person—two, actually, though one of them might have done what he did—"

She shook her head. "I met another kid after I left. He was a runaway too." She told Kaleb about the warehouse and Zeke, all that she thought might help him feel better about what he knew and why she didn't think they should say anything.

"And he got shot. It was a ricochet, I think. Or at least the guy wasn't aiming for Zeke. But—" Her voice cracked. She took in a lungful of air, closed her eyes, and held her breath for a five count, before letting it go. "He died. I watched him die. Because . . . shit."

"Because you didn't tell him what was going on."

"Damn it, Kaleb, that wasn't the point of telling you that."

"But you did. And I think we should say something."

"Please, just sit on it for a couple more days. I know you think it will help, but just let it sit for a couple more days. I want to watch a little more, see if anything else pops up."

"And if another one of us gets hurt?"

"I won't let that happen." She knew she couldn't make that promise. She couldn't have made it to Zeke if he had known, and she couldn't make it to Kaleb. But she intended to do all she could to keep it.

"Who do you think it was?"

"I can't tell you yet."

"Because you don't want to, or . . . ?"

"Honestly, I just can't. I don't know yet."

"I guess that's fair."

"We should get back to the house."

"Wouldn't want anyone to think we're doing anything weird."

"Right. Definitely wouldn't want that." Suddenly, Fia's adulthood slapped her in the face. "Kaleb, is there something—"

"Gross! No! I was making a joke." He worked his face for a second, clearly deciding whether he could talk openly with her. "Can I tell you a secret?"

"Please."

"I think . . . I mean I don't know because I don't have any experience really outside this place, but I think I might have a crush on Xavier."

"Oh." Fia blinked and blinked again. "Oh? Hey, Kaleb, can I tell you something else about me?"

"Sure?"

"I went into high school thinking I liked the only boy in the convent with me. His name was Felix. I don't know where you and Xavier stand, but Felix and I . . . let's call it 'experimented' . . . before we started public school. Then I met someone at school and realized Felix was more realistically the result of an abundance of hormones and a lack of choices. We were friends, sort of, though I think that was from lack of options too. But when I got presented with other options, I didn't have the same feelings for Felix that I thought I had."

"So, stop acting like a jerk about being split up and be open to meeting new people?"

"I really think that's Agnes's goal with this whole public-school experiment."

"I guess I can try that for a while."

"I recommend it." Fia reached out and slapped the teen on the back. "Let's get back to the house."

"Tell me about the teens." Fia had sent Kaleb to Agnes's office, armed with a lie that she had cornered him about his attitude. Back in the house, she had found Sister Rebecca alone in the kitchen, without her customary teenaged sous-chef, and offered to help her clean vegetables.

"What do you want to know?"

"Well, I spent my whole life in that convent. But I only left there seven years ago. They're fourteen, and they weren't there when I left. Where did they come from?" She thought for a moment before continuing. "Furthermore, the little ones. Levi, is that his name? He's the oldest, right?"

"He is. Seven. As of March. Callie is six; the twins are five."

"Twins? Lisa and Alex are twins? Oh. Cool. So, I can see why I never met the kiddos. But the teens—where did they come from?"

"They were in a group home about five years ago. Father Donovan ran it. But they ran out of money and had to close down. He brought these four here, knowing Reverend Mother was looking for new hunters."

"So they didn't grow up in this world?"

Rebecca shook her head. "No, they've only been here for five years."

"Five? So, were the twins in that same group? Callie and Levi?"

Rebecca took a deep, shuddering breath. Fia was wondering if she had said something to make the nun cry when Rebecca spoke again. "Levi was born here. Well, not here, in the convent. Callie was left with us when she was an infant."

Fia wanted to press, to ask more questions, but the tension coming off Rebecca was palpable, so she finished with her basket of vegetables in silence.

Once they were finished, Fia asked if there was anything else she could do to help Rebecca with dinner. "I have it all under control. You've done enough. Thank you." The nun, roughly Fia's size, became a blur of black fabric moving around the shiny silver-and-white space.

Fia considered saying something before she left but decided against it, slipping quietly through the swinging door into the hallway. Rebecca would have dinner ready for everyone in less than an hour. Fia listened to her sneakers squeaking against the hardwood floor until it gave way to the granite of the foyer. She looked around the vaulted space, taking in all the details she could.

The convent had consisted of two stories, though nowhere near as elaborate as this. The hallways had been just as dark, but also dank and cold. Even in the summer. The walls had been brick instead of wood, and there hadn't been anywhere indoors with as much natural light as here in the foyer.

At the back of the foyer, left of the French doors, was a pair of steps that led to a landing before the stairs turned to the second floor. Fia sat on the landing quietly and traced the veins in the granite with her finger.

She had lost track of how long she had been sitting there like that when Sister Annabel came in through the back doors. "Fia? Is everything okay?"

"Huh? Oh, yeah. Great. I guess. I just had some time . . . nothing to do for a while, waiting for dinner." Thinking about what Kaleb had told her, Fia patted the floor beside her. "Sit. Talk with me. Tell me about Annabel."

"I-I don't really have—"

"Sure, sorry. I guess I've kind of forgotten how much you nuns really do. As a kid, it seemed like they were always busy, but we never really saw them doing anything, you know? Sister Bernadette cooked and tended the garden. We saw her do those things. And Cecilia took us on field trips. But we never really knew what they did, otherwise. I guess I still don't."

"I wasn't going to put you off, Fia. I was going to say I don't have anything to tell you about myself."

"Yeah." Fia felt her face fall. "Maybe I'll just go . . ."

She wasn't sure how she wanted to finish that sentence. She wanted to spend more time, talk to the nuns more, talk to the hunters more. The kids were not a problem, and she thought she had pinpointed why, if they had only been part of this life for a short time. But the nuns—she wanted to get to know them better, but they didn't seem to want to share.

"Fia, please . . ." Annabel sat down on the step beside Fia. "I didn't mean to upset you."

"You didn't. Well, you did, but not for the reasons you think. When I was a kid in the convent, Sister Cecilia was warm, gentle. Open. She told us stuff. About what we were doing, stories about the souls and demons, though she didn't present them in that way. She mentioned the demon, Irzelen, though not by name—but not demons, plural. She told us about her life before taking her vows.

"And Mother Lou—she was our mother superior before Agnes—was kind. Kind enough to let us call her Lou. Her real name—or chosen name; I was never sure how that worked—was Lucy. She was kind, but she was busy."

"Was Mother Agnes not kind?"

Fia puffed a laugh through her nose. "Agnes was . . . a general, hard-nosed and battle worn. We were her soldiers. Kind wasn't part of it." Annabel's face grew sad. "What? You disagree? She hasn't gotten any softer since I left."

"Reverend Mother is quite kind. She cares very deeply for all in her charge."

Fia twisted her lips and raised her eyebrows dismissively. "Maybe it's just me, then."

"Fia, have you tried talking to Mother Agnes?"

"About what?"

"These feelings you have. I know we've only just met, but I sense you are a strong, passionate woman, independent, fierce, but when it comes to the Reverend Mother, you are sad, hurt, and angry. And I think those feelings go very deep."

"It was tough growing up in a convent and being groomed from eight and nine years old to murder people. I know that's not really what I'm doing, but to a nine-year-old, 'shoot people in the spine' sounds a lot like murder."

"To a sixteen-year-old as well."

"Pardon?"

"You left the convent at sixteen, correct? And it was because you didn't want to murder people?"

"Yeah. Did I tell you—I mean, I've learned since then that that's not really what's happening, but boy was it scary at nine."

"And you blame Mother Agnes for that fear?"

"Why wouldn't I? My place in this world as a soldier, as a huntress, was all that ever mattered to her."

"Fia, did I tell you why I am here? Sister Theresa and I?" Fia considered the question, running through her previous conversations with the nun and, finding nothing, shook her head. "You are strong and powerful and a world-class hunter. We wanted to be near the best."

"What does that have to do with—"

"Mother Agnes? If you hadn't left an indelible mark on all the lives here, we may not have ever heard of you. You are important to Mother Agnes. Whether you are too stubborn to see it falls on your shoulders."

Fia let the nun's words hang between them without responding.

After a long moment, Annabel rose to her feet. "Dinner will be served in twenty minutes. Perhaps you should wash up. Arriving early is encouraged." With that, the nun flowed up the stairs. Fia watched her until she couldn't anymore.

Fia rose to her feet and headed back to the small bathroom that was next to the bedroom she was using. She washed her hands and ran them, still damp, through her greasy, unwashed hair. "You need a shower." It would have to wait.

She started to leave when a sound caught her attention. Looking up, she found a vent grate in the ceiling. From it, she could hear a woman's voice. The source was hushed and distant, coming through the ductwork, but Fia strained to listen anyway. She climbed up on the sink, once again grateful for her height, and stretched toward the vent.

"I don't care what you have to do." It was definitely a woman speaking, but her voice was low, muffled. She growled, receiving no response. "Just get it done."

TWENTY

ia scrambled down off the counter and out of the bath-room. She took the stairs to the nuns' quarters two at a time, hoping to find the source of the angry voice.

In the upstairs hallway, four doors lined the wall on her right, two on her left, and one at the end of the hallway: Agnes's room. All the doors were closed, blocking any hope for natural light. Every twenty feet, bronze sconces cast pools of yellow-orange light around them in a shallow circle. If anyone came out of these rooms, they had nowhere else to go. Whoever had been talking, Fia had them trapped.

She crept along the wall, pausing at each door to listen. She reached Agnes's door having heard nothing. Confused, she turned back, following the same path, pausing one more time at each door.

Silence.

What had she heard?

Realizing the ducts might have been pulling in a voice from somewhere else in the house, Fia returned to the lower level, defeated. She reentered the lower hallway just in time to see others filtering into the formal dining room. *Perfect timing.* She fell in line behind them and found a seat at the table. Seven children, four nuns, Fia, and Scott surrounded the table, waiting for Rebecca to bring dinner from the kitchen.

They had been waiting long enough for Fia to wonder what was wrong when Tianna pushed through the door carrying a cake pan pulling double duty as a casserole dish. She sat it in the middle of the table and reached for Fia's plate first. Rebecca came through the door next, carrying a punch bowl filled with mixed greens. A small variety of salad dressings had been waiting for them when they entered the room.

Rebecca set the bowl in front of Fia. "Guests may serve themselves first."

"Oh. Sure. Thank you." Fia fought the urge to scoop half the bowl onto her plate. For that matter, she really wished Tianna had given her twice as much of the lasagna. She was ravenous and hadn't realized it until the food arrived.

"I must apologize," Rebecca said, taking her seat as Tianna finished dishing out lasagna from the hot pan and the salad made its rounds. "I did not have the oven set high enough. Thankfully, Tianna came in and caught my error."

Fia furrowed her brow at the nun's explanation.

Fia, is something wrong?

The sound of Scott's voice broke through Fia's thoughts. She tried to suppress a startled expression, glancing in his direction to find him looking at her.

Apologies for intruding on your thoughts. You look pensive.

Fia decided to try sending a thought back to the angel

in her head, even though she wasn't sure what she was doing or if it would even work. Did he have to be set to receive her thoughts, like file sharing between phones?

Maybe a little. Just thinking about something I heard earlier.

Scott acknowledged her with a slight nod. *We should talk later.*

Out loud.

The priest smiled, his shoulders twitching with a silent chuckle. *Yes, out loud.*

Good. This hurts my head. Literally. It wasn't as bad to have Uhlpir's thoughts bouncing around inside her skull as Irzelen's—Uhlpir didn't seem to find it necessary to shout—but the divine invasion still made her head feel crowded.

Dinner conversation was sparse, just as Fia remembered it. There was a quick go-around-the-table at the beginning for the kids to share the best part of their day. "This was Sister Annabel's idea," Sister Cecilia had whispered at Fia's side. "Isn't it wonderful?"

When it was Kaleb's turn to speak, he looked at Fia. "I had a good conversation with our guest, Fia, earlier. I was feeling a little salty about something, and she made me feel better."

"I have enjoyed having Fia here as well," Mercy added. "I think we're learning some valuable tricks from her. And I'm glad she was able to improve Kaleb's mood."

"Ugh, stop it." Fia waved her hand dismissively at the two teens. "You're going to give me a big head."

After they had finished eating, Fia helped Kaleb and Mercy gather the dishes. "Please, let me do *something*," she had pleaded when Rebecca told her the teens needed to do it on their own. "I feel like I'm just sitting around on my—thumbs, letting everyone else wait on me."

"Very well. But they must do their share of the work. They *will* slack and let you do more than is fair."

"Deal." Fia turned to Kaleb and Mercy. "No slacking, okay?"

"Okay," they replied, nearly in unison.

The three of them carried their loads to the kitchen, managing to get it all in one trip. "You wash, I'll dry, Mercy puts away?" Fia said to Kaleb as they scraped leftover bits into the garbage and arranged the plates on the counter.

He agreed, and they set off on their chores.

"Are you allowed to talk while you do this?"

Mercy nodded. "As long as it doesn't distract from the job at hand."

"Of course. How could talking distract from washing— you know what, never mind. So, I'll be around for a little bit tomorrow morning, then again later. Is there anything else you want to learn? Tonight or in the morning?"

Both teens shrugged. "I think I speak for all of us," Mercy said, "when I say you have learned so much, it would be impossible for one of us to ask you to teach us anything specific. The better question is, is there anything you think we should know?"

"I'll think about it."

"That's all we can ask."

As they finished washing the dishes, Scott passed through the back door that led into the kitchen from the outside. "Fia, there you are! Would you have a minute to chat?"

"I think I do. Mercy, Kaleb, you two have this?"

They nodded again and Mercy stepped over to retrieve the towel from Fia's extended hand.

Fia waved a hand vaguely ahead of her. "Lead the way."

Scott paused, looking from the left to the right and back again. "Perhaps the library." He led Fia from the kitchen. "Upstairs," he added as they passed through the door, jerking his chin toward the stairs. He led her to a set of armchairs in a far corner of the library's upper level. "Tell me what is on your mind."

Fia shrugged, no longer certain she wanted to have this conversation. In the moment, Fia had thought Rebecca's story sounded suspicious, but the voice in the vent had still been fresh in her mind. Now, having had a while to think about it, she wanted more time to look around, maybe figure out where the voice might have been coming from, before bringing it up to anyone.

Instead, she decided to ask about the house. "Why are we here? I mean . . ." She waved her hand around her head. "Here. In this house. What happened to the convent?"

Scott took a deep breath. "The truth? We don't know."

"How's that?"

"There was a fire—arson or accident. It was started by a human, at any rate, nothing faulty in the structure itself."

"Arson?"

"Or an accident."

Fia narrowed her eyes. "Do you believe it was an accident?"

Scott didn't answer her, just continued with his story. "The fire appeared to have started in a remote part of the basement."

"Remote part of—I didn't know basements had *remote parts*. So, somewhere no one really went?"

Scott nodded. "It was a section that had been used, Agnes explained to me, as a possible fallout shelter in the 1950s."

"Oh, okay, I know where that was. We didn't spend a lot of time in the basement. There was that weird little space in the floor of Agnes's room, where we got our tattoos . . ."

"As I understand it, the basement was not commonly used at the time of the fire. It had fallen into disrepair and was mostly closed off to everyone."

"So, anyone could have gotten in there and set a fire without anyone really noticing." Scott nodded. "You talk like you weren't around, but you were."

"I was not living in the convent. In truth, I only moved in here shortly before the teens."

"Yeah, them. So, they were, what? Recruited? I thought this was a born-into kind of gig."

"Father Donovan was a hunter himself in his early years. He had seen potential in the four teens you have met and had been talking with Agnes regarding moving them in here even before the probability that the home he main-tained would close. In fact, that may have started while you were still in the convent."

Scott's face twisted thoughtfully. Fia guessed he was searching through his mental calendar to figure out if what he told her was accurate. "It was late to get them started, but he suspected something was happening behind the scenes that made it crucial to get new hunters on board sooner rather than later."

"He knew about the demons?"

"Not explicitly. It was more supposition, a feeling that the world we live in had been too quiet. I do not think he suspected a human element at play."

"You think he thought Irzelen was up to something." Another deep nod from the priest. "Tell me about this Father Donovan. Where is he now? What does he look like?

Have I seen him before? One of the rigid old priests that skulked around the convent?"

"The latter, perhaps, though I can't say for sure. He is fairly unremarkable as humans go. Balding since his twenties, no longer in the physical condition one needs to be to do the job you do."

So, old, fat, and bald. Sounds familiar. She chewed on that thought for a moment before another region of her brain rebutted. *Or like twenty other priests they could find for a police lineup.*

"So, someone burned down the convent, possibly on purpose, but you don't know who or how? Are there theories?"

"Some. Your compatriots had gone off on their own only recently. There was supposition that one of them had come back or potentially sent someone back to set the fire."

"What? No. What? I can't believe that. I hated that place, and even I wouldn't—put everyone in danger like that? That's not possible. What else?"

"Fia, I know it's hard to hear that these people with whom you spent your most formative years may have done something so malicious . . . there was fallout from your departure."

"Agnes punished them for me leaving."

"In a way, yes. But as I was told, there was a great deal of turmoil that was not punitive. There was a new, younger teen among them who required a great deal of attention, and there was the seed you planted. Did you tell any of them why you were leaving?"

"I didn't tell any of them *that* I was leaving. Meredith would have ratted me out, Terra would have wanted to come with me—"

"Aye, perhaps there is something in that. Terra. Why do you think she would have wanted to join you?"

"We never talked about it. Agnes could hear everything that went on there, like she had the place bugged. That's how I knew to look for the teens in the woods the first night I was here. That was the only place we ever felt like we were something other than soldier drones in this holy war Agnes was living in. We were told the severity, but it took being out in it, seeing the ruthless way one of those souls used their host to butcher people and then leave the host behind like a snake shedding its skin, for all of that to soak in."

"Was it a soul that made you pick up that crossbow, or was it Ted?"

"There are monsters in the world who have complete control of themselves and what they are doing. I can't stand on a rooftop and put a bolt through guys like Ted, as much as I wish I could."

"But someone else might have. Not a bolt, maybe, but dispatched him in the way you wish you could have."

Fia raised an eyebrow at this. "Did you have something—nope, don't tell me." She rubbed her hands over her face. "Who else was in the convent at the time of the fire?"

"No one but the nuns you knew, Agnes, Mother Lucy, Sister Cecilia, Sister Bernadette—Sister Rebecca had not yet taken her vows—and Levi and Callie."

"Someone endangered—Callie would have been an infant, right?" She felt the tips of her ears grow hot, the fever spreading into her cheeks. "Who would—Terra didn't do that."

"And I struggle to believe those inside the convent would have. That leaves us with a question, then, doesn't it?"

"One without an answer that I can see."

"At least not one we will ever find."

"I don't know about that."

"Fia, I must advise against rash behavior."

"Who's talking about anything rash? I certainly didn't suggest anything rash. And I might remind you, it's not polite to monkey around in a mortal's brain without permission."

"Plausible deniability."

"You got it."

The two of them sat in silence for several minutes before the priest rose to his feet. "I have some things to do in my office, if you don't have anything *else* you wanted to discuss?"

The emphasis he placed on *else* suggested he knew there was something else but he was going to let her bring it to his attention. She wondered if he knew what that something was or simply that there was something.

There were a lot of somethings.

"Nope, I think that's it. The fakir is supposed to be here in the morning? Do the teens know?"

"They do not. Just as you didn't know until you were led into the basement for your own tattoos."

"Yeah, why all the cloak and dagger? Does Agnes think she's protecting them—us—by not telling us things until the last minute? Or is it a control thing?" Scott didn't answer. "Okay, do you want me out of here before he shows up?"

"If you wanted to leave following breakfast to pick up Mr. Hawkins, that would probably be the most practical."

Fia groaned, though he was probably right. If she was up with the sun to have breakfast with the others, she would be ready to meet Max for lunch around noon, when normal humans ate lunch, turn around, and come back.

"Sounds good. I guess that's the plan, then. I'm going

to grab a quick shower. Do you think the teens will still be in the rec room for a while?"

"I believe they should be."

"Cool."

Later, after Fia was sure everyone in the house had gone to bed, she slipped out of the first-floor bedroom, leaving the door unlatched to stay as quiet as possible. She passed into the bathroom and climbed back up onto the counter beneath the vent she had heard the voice coming through.

It was possible the voice had been echoing from somewhere else in the house. Fia wanted to see if she could figure out where the ductwork went to figure out a possible source for the voice since she hadn't found anyone above the bathroom.

She had detoured through the garage on her way to the rec room after her talk with Scott and found a screwdriver that she hoped would fit the screws in the vent. Now she tried it, whispering a relieved thank you when it fit perfectly. She removed the cover from the vent and poked her phone up through the opening. With the flashlight on, she hit record on the video camera and slowly panned around the space above her head.

Once she had made a full circle, she pulled the phone back down and lowered herself to sit on the counter. As she played the video back, she was shocked by what she saw.

It was not a duct at all. At least, not in the way she had expected. Where she had expected to find an opening eighteen inches squared, she was actually looking at a space large enough for a grown man to crawl through. She stood again, this time with a measurement tool open on the phone.

It worked off the camera, measuring the space between the lens and the nearest object. She pulled it back out to look; the whole space was nearly three feet squared. There was a wall four feet from her toward the back of the house and twelve feet away in the opposite direction.

"It's a secret passage," she said quietly, not knowing where there might be another vent.

The vent wasn't big enough for her to crawl through; she was lucky she hadn't gotten her hand stuck in it. She replaced the cover and climbed down off the counter. Starting at the edge of the vent, she counted off roughly twelve feet, which took her to just inside the door of the bathroom. She looked up at the ceiling, trying to decide what to do next.

There was nowhere to go if the passage turned left here. It would dump someone out into the foyer. She stepped into the hallway and turned right, toward the kitchen, shining her light on the ceiling as she walked.

She passed into the kitchen, where she hadn't previously noticed the dropped ceiling. In the preparation area of the kitchen, the ceiling was higher . . . by close to three feet. She followed her path through the next door, into the hallway that would eventually lead her to the kids and Cecilia.

That's where she found what she was looking for.

A trapdoor, well concealed in the ceiling.

There was a switch on the wall below it. If Fia had even noticed it before, she would have written it off as a light switch. She considered flipping it to see what would happen, but without knowing how much noise it might make, she decided against it.

If the switch even controlled the trapdoor. She couldn't see any way to manually open it; it had to be electronic.

Satisfied she had figured out where the voice she heard had come from, Fia made her way quietly back to the bedroom. She wanted to know where the other end of the passage was but couldn't risk the noise of finding out. She'd investigate further in the daylight.

Fia woke with a groan to the alarm on her phone. She had had every intention of joining the others for breakfast before she headed back to the city, but now that the time had come, she wasn't so sure she really wanted to. She had just rolled over, burying her face in the pillow, when someone knocked firmly at the door.

"Fiammetta, if you are joining us for breakfast, please proceed to the dining room."

"Agnes," Fia muttered into the pillow. She drew herself up off the bed and dressed, before trudging across the hallway to the dining room.

She was, of course, the last to arrive. The others—nuns, teens, and small children combined—all looked bright and ready for the day. Fia looked around for coffee.

Finding none, she claimed the last seat at the table for herself.

"Would you like juice?" Sister Theresa offered, her dark eyes crinkling at the corners with her welcoming smile.

Fia rubbed her eyes with her fingers. "Please." She pushed the glass from her place setting in Theresa's direction. The nun filled it with pulpy orange juice and returned it to Fia, who indulged in a hearty gulp. "Maybe some water?" She motioned to the pitcher of water sitting on a credenza behind Theresa's chair.

"Of course."

Fia let Theresa pour the water into a second glass, feeling a little guilty for being waited on.

"Did you rest well, Fiammetta?" The tone of Agnes's voice gave away that she was asking more than just the surface question. Fia cocked an eyebrow.

"Okay. Not great." She decided to give the elder nun what she was looking for without giving her everything. "I did a little walking around; I hope I didn't bother anyone."

Agnes held Fia's gaze for a long moment. "It is the quiet. You have grown used to the sounds of the city."

Maybe she really isn't fishing, Fia thought.

"Did you find anything of interest in your midnight stroll?"

Or maybe she is.

"You just got up and walked around the house in the dark because you couldn't sleep?" Annabel asked.

Fia nodded. "I didn't want to wake anyone up if I opened a door too loudly or set off an alarm—is there an alarm in this place?"

"Maybe that's something you should have asked before traipsing around in a strange house in the dark." Annabel punctuated her statement with a bite of her breakfast. Fia thought the nun was accusing her of something.

Or maybe you want her to be accusing you of something. It would make it less uncomfortable to accuse her.

"You are absolutely right, Sister Annabel. I should have thought of that."

"There are no alarms," Agnes interjected. The conversation halted. Fia shoveled a forkful of eggs into her mouth.

After several moments of silence, Fia said, "After breakfast, I need to head back into the city to check on a couple things. I don't really get service on my cell phone up here." She looked pointedly at Agnes and the priest.

One of the teens whined, barely audible.

"We were hoping to spend some more time with you," Mercy said.

"I'll probably be back later." Fia thought for a moment, then amended her statement. "I will be back later. I just have something I have to take care of."

Agnes silenced any more potential protest from the teens. "Fiammetta did not sign up to train you. We cannot expect to monopolize her time. If she says she'll be back, we must trust she will return."

"Who are you trying to convince, them or yourself? Forget it. Yes, I will be back."

They finished the meal in silence. Fia helped clear the dishes, joining Kaleb in the kitchen to clean up. "Where's Sister Rebecca?"

"She said something about needing to run an errand of her own," Kaleb replied. "Honestly, I wasn't listening. I can wash dishes on my own."

"How did you get here? I mean, I got the official story. You were in a group home, and it had to close down. But I didn't get the story on how you ended up here, training to hunt? Did it just get dropped on you or . . . ?"

"Reverend Mother said you started your training around nine? I think we did too. We weren't learning about fugitive souls at that point, but they started giving us archery lessons."

"Was it just the four of you in the home?"

"And the twins."

"Hm, interesting."

"What?"

"Nothing, really. I just thought, all my life, that this was something you were born into. A *chosen one* situation. But it kind of sounds like maybe you guys were recruited."

"Yeah. Maybe. I don't know. That's the thing about being an orphan. You don't know much about your family. But I guess you know all about that." Fia nodded.

When they finished cleaning up from breakfast, Fia patted Kaleb on the back. "I'll be back later. I have to go talk to someone, and then I have to come back here for something." She laughed. "You don't know it yet, but you've got a big day ahead of you. It'll be fun, sort of. Different, anyway."

"What?"

"Nope. I'm not getting in the middle of it. Agnes wants it to be a secret, so I'm leaving it to be Agnes's secret. You get that, right?"

"Sure."

Fia left Kaleb in the kitchen, exiting the house through the front door. She climbed into the Scout and guided it back to the highway.

Twenty-One

She let the SUV carry her back to the city. The little thermometer on the dashboard clicked up one degree for practically every hundred feet she descended out of the mountains.

Back in town, she texted Max when she came to the first stoplight off the interstate. *Need a shower, then need to talk.*

She studied the words for a few seconds. *Don't worry. Not bad talk. Not pregnant.* She finished it off with a thumbs up and a wink, then waited for his typing bubble to disappear.

He replied first with a shocked, gasping emoji, followed by a string of emojis including a wave, a cucumber, a taco, lip print, and water droplets. He finished it off with a drunk face.

Everything, she replied, laughing. She thought she even felt a slight blush form at her cheekbones.

Yep.

See you in a bit.

Fia wasn't headed straight for her apartment, but she didn't think he needed all the details. And she liked the idea of him thinking of her in the shower.

Instead, she followed one-way streets to Zari's shop. She wanted to talk to her former mentor about what she had learned at the safe house.

Fia pulled up to the street side of the house, behind a car she assumed belonged to a customer in the shop. She was debating waiting until the customer came out when her decision was made for her. The same blonde woman who had been here previously, insisting Zari had a knife Zari didn't have, pushed through the glass door, this time with a paper sack looped over her wrist.

"Hm, I wonder what she found today."

Fia leaned forward, ducking below the steering wheel to watch the woman get in her car. Fia turned the key in the ignition, rolling the engine over, put the car in gear, took it back out of gear, and turned off the engine. She wanted to follow the woman, but she had other things to do. When the woman had pulled away from the curb, Fia climbed out of her own car and went inside.

Zari was positioned behind the checkout counter, finishing up from the sale. On the counter beside the cash register sat a plant Fia was certain had been much smaller the last time she had seen it. What she remembered as barely more than a sprout was now a pepper plant with a couple of small fruits ready to be picked.

Catching Fia studying the plant, Zari smiled. "I think he is ready to transplant." She lovingly caressed a leaf, as if presenting a child to Fia. "Would you like a cutting for your own garden?"

Fia snorted. "You know I have a miserably brown thumb, Zari."

"Ah, it has not gotten any better?" Fia raised her eyebrows in confirmation. "Best not to break your own heart, then, I suppose." Zari pulled one of the curved green fruits from the plant and offered it to Fia. "Try one. They are sweet. A little hot."

Fia took the pepper, turning it back and forth to examine it. It looked ordinary enough. Maybe the plant had been in a different part of the house before.

She sniffed at the fruit, not sure what she expected to learn, and took a hesitant bite from the tip. She had learned the hard way that she and the Haitian woman had drastically different ideas regarding the words *a little hot*. This time, however, she was relieved to find the pepper was in fact sweet, similar to a bell pepper, with just enough capsaicin to make her tongue tingle.

Zari laughed heartily at Fia's hesitation, crunching into her own pepper. "It is a hybrid. It is good, *oui*?"

"Yes."

"I know you worry when I tell you something is just a little hot. It is a shame your nuns did not properly teach you how to eat a chili pepper."

"I know how to eat a chili. I never learned how to deal with third-degree chemical burns in my mouth."

Zari laughed again. "What has brought you to my shop today, *chérie*?"

Fia gave Zari a quick run-through to catch Zari up on what she hadn't already heard, watching the expression on Zari's face as she outlined her fight with the thug, her conversation with Ariaz, and the strange snippet of conversation she had overheard through the vent.

"I didn't get a chance to investigate. I'm planning to look around more when I go back, but I think it's a secret passage between the floors."

Once she had finished her latest story, she waited for a response. Zari's face twisted with concern. "Please, Fiammetta, I urge you not to go looking for trouble. With what you know, I encourage you to keep your head low."

"I'll be fine, Zari. I won't do anything if I don't think it's safe. I have to take Max back up there later this afternoon. I'm actually supposed to be taking a shower right now so I can meet him for lunch."

"I will not pretend to understand any of that. You are taking him to get him tattooed?"

"I haven't mentioned it to him, but that's the plan. The teens are probably getting theirs right now, so it was a convenient time."

"You are taking him into the mountains to receive a blessed tattoo, and you have not talked it over with him first? Fiammetta—"

"I know. It was probably the wrong decision. But I weighed the options and decided it was better to spring it on him after having it set up than to offer it to him and not be able to follow through."

"Hm, I can see that. When do you need to go?"

Fia looked at her phone. "Probably now. I just wanted to touch base with you before I forgot everything that happened."

"You have had a full couple of days, that is for sure."

"Yeah." She let Zari pull her into an embrace.

"Please be careful, *chérie.*"

"I will."

When Fia reached her apartment building and started into the garage, her nerves lit on fire. She pulled back out, parking on the street. Retrieving a knife from the glove compartment, she walked back. Cold, panicked sweat soaked through the back of her shirt, accentuating the sound of her own heart pounding in her ears.

Was there really something here, or was she just still keyed up from her last encounter?

The garage attached to the apartments was small; for that, she was grateful. There weren't a lot of places to hide, and she was able to make a quick sweep of the ground level in a couple of minutes. She turned the knife so the blade was against her forearm and pushed the button to open the elevator door, flattening herself against the wall beside it. The car dinged, and the doors slid open.

Nothing happened.

No one jumped out; there wasn't a hail of bullets. Fia edged around the corner and peered in, feeling only a little foolish as she looked to all eight corners of the elevator car. She stepped in and pushed the button for level two, tucking herself into one of the front corners as the doors opened a second time. She waited a beat before depressing the "door open" button and stretching out of the car as far as her arm would allow. Seeing nothing unusual, she pulled back in and pressed three, her own level. The level where she would find her scooter. The level where she had watched an angel turn a condemned soul over to a demon.

This time, when the doors opened and she waited in the corner, a head slipped through the opening. Covered in the heavy black and white of a habit, the head leaned into the car, turning first to the left, away from Fia, then to the right, revealing a warm, tawny face and amber eyes.

"Rebecca! Jesus! You scared me half to death. What are you doing?"

"I was in the city, talking to administrators for one of

the high schools about the teens. I had a few minutes before I needed to head back, so I thought I'd pop in and surprise you. Where is your car?"

"Huh? I-I left it on the street. I had a weird feeling pulling in here. Obviously, less noticeable on foot than driving in, in a car."

"Probably just leftover anxiety from the attack," Rebecca assured.

"Yeah, how—how did you know—"

"Oh, uh, Father Scott told me. Told us."

"Sure, I guess he would. Hey, I've got some things to take care of. Mind if we put a pin in this surprise visit until later?"

The little nun's face fell, but she recovered quickly. "Of course. Yes, I'm sorry. I shouldn't have popped in on you. Want me to drive you back to your car?"

Fia looked over the woman's shoulder to the gold-colored car parked next to her scooter, in the Scout's space. "Nah, it will be fine where it is for no longer than I'm going to be here."

"Oh, you're leaving again?"

"Meeting Max for—well, honestly, not sure what I'm meeting him for. Lunch, I guess." She looked at the clock on her phone. Almost eleven thirty. She needed to get moving.

"Of course. I'll leave you to it, then."

Fia thought she heard disappointment in the young nun's voice, but she brushed it aside with a smile. "Thanks." She exited the elevator and turned away from Rebecca, heading toward the door leading to her apartment.

Her phone buzzed with an incoming text message.

Did you drown? Did you wash down the drain? Do you need help? Shower emoji. Eggplant emoji. From Max.

She sent him a quick response, fudging something about falling asleep.

Rain check?

She gave up and hit the call button. "No, no rain check," she said when he connected the call. "Just let me get dressed. Where are you?"

"Home." She realized she didn't know what that meant and asked him for clarification. "Oh, yeah, I guess we haven't talked about that. Southwest. Off Kentucky."

"Wow. I'm still not sure where that is. Want to meet somewhere on Sixteenth? In thirty?"

"I'll be there with bells on."

"I hope more than that."

"We'll see. What are you thinking? Coffee, lunch?"

Her stomach responded, loudly. Just as she had planned, she was ready for lunch after the early breakfast at the safe house. "Food, definitely. Your choice. I think it's your turn to pick."

"We're taking turns?"

"I mean, not on purpose."

"I'm kidding. You like Asian food? What about that build-your-own-bowl place?"

"Sure."

"Cool. See you in twenty-eight minutes."

"Reset the timer. I need the full thirty."

He groaned melodramatically before agreeing.

Fia smiled and hit the button to disconnect the call, suddenly wishing the nap hadn't been a lie. She stretched her neck and shoulders and headed out of the building.

Fia rounded the corner of the building where she had agreed to meet Max. He was waiting for her at a table on the patio. He stood when he saw her and greeted her with a warm embrace.

"How did your job go? Is that a normal question to ask a bounty hunter?"

She shrugged, remembering the white lie she had temporarily forgotten. "I guess. It's not an abnormal question. It went okay." She hoped he wouldn't press and force her to continue lying.

With a hand against the small of her back, he guided her to walk ahead of him into the restaurant. After ordering, they found a table away from the other patrons and put up their little flags to tell the server which orders belonged at their table.

"What did you want to talk about?" Max asked.

"Have you ever thought about getting a traditional tattoo?"

He held out his right arm, showing her a blue-and-red sparrow with heavy black lines on his wrist. "Like this or . . ." He pantomimed tapping on an invisible stick.

"The second," she answered.

"Oh. I hadn't. Until now. Do you know someone?"

"I do, in fact. Well, not the tattooist, exactly, but I know where you can get it done."

"That actually sounds—are you doing it too? That sounds really intimate. Are you sure?"

"No, I have mine already. There's a catch to all this, though."

"Okay?"

"It's free, but you don't get to pick what it is or where he puts it."

"Free ink and the experience of a traditional tattoo without having to travel to Asia—not that I wouldn't like to travel to Asia, but—" He rubbed his fingers together. "I think that's a catch I can live with."

A young man with red hair even brighter than Fia's brought out their bowls and took their flags.

"What brought this up?" Max asked after shoveling in a couple mouthfuls of noodles.

Fia sighed from deep in her gut. "A lot of things, actually, but ultimately, the last straw was the other night at the Lounge. If you're going to be part of this thing with me, you need to be protected like the rest of us."

"Protected?"

"The reason we go through the show of bringing in a fakir is there's a ritual that goes along with this. It's not just getting a tattoo; it's a blessed tattoo that prevents you from being possessed by one of the souls."

"What about that thing at the Lounge? What was that? Because that looked pretty intense, and I think I'd like to be protected from that."

Fia smiled, amused. "The souls are actually a bigger threat. The souls destroy their host. The demons can't harm humans."

"Demon? That's what that was? He dropped you seven feet to the pavement. That looked pretty harmful."

"I guess cuts and bruises are a gray area."

"Do you—do I get to know what the tattoo means? I know you said I don't get to pick it out, but . . ."

"This is a different guy from the one who did mine, and the guy who did mine didn't speak any English. But as it was translated to me, mine was chosen to represent Bel, a drake that was a familiar to King Nebuchadnezzar."

"I thought familiars were cats. Wait, familiar? So, Nebuchadnezzar was a witch."

"Yeah, I guess that's what that means."

"Witch? Wizard? What's the correct—"

"Does it—"

"I thought familiars were cats."

"Max?"

"Yeah?"

"Can you try to focus on me here?"

Pushing his bowl forward to the center of the table, he scooted to the edge of his seat. He rested his elbows on the table and his chin in his hands.

"Smart-ass," Fia muttered, suppressing a giggle. She refused to encourage him. "Now you made me forget what I was saying."

"Bel was a drake and a familiar to King Nebuchadnezzar. See? I was listening. What do you think the new guy will pick for me?"

"I don't know. I think they are a little psychic on top of everything else. The one who did mine just kind of waved his hands over me, mumbled something in whatever language he spoke—Sanskrit, maybe, or Aramaic; I really don't know—and then told Agnes—told me—that he had picked out this symbol"—she ducked her left shoulder toward him, indicating the first tattoo she had received at fifteen in a subbasement room of the convent—"because I have the soul of a dragon."

"I can see that."

"So? Are you down?"

"Absolutely. When do we go? Wait, *where* are we going?"

"There's a . . . well, a cabin—you'll see. Anyway, it's about an hour up into the mountains. And as soon as we're done here? Do you want me to follow you back to your place so you can drop off your car?"

"Your place is closer. Can we just leave it there?"

"If you're okay with that, I'm okay with it."

TWENTY-TWO

ia led Max into the safe house through the front door, looking around the giant open space for anyone who might be able to tell them what to do next. "You want the grand tour while I try to find someone to—"

"Fia. Hello," Sister Rebecca greeted them, coming in through the double doors at the back of the space. "Is this Max? Mother Agnes said you were bringing someone to meet with the fakir." The young nun extended a hand to Max. "I'm Sister Rebecca. I'll be joining you for your ritual, as the fakir doesn't speak any English."

"Oh, tattoo by committee. That's another one I've never done." He shook her hand. "I am Max, yes. It's a pleasure to meet you."

"If you'll follow me this way, Sahir is waiting for us in the garden."

"In the garden, huh?" Fia quipped. "Lucky. I got mine in a dark, dank basement." She took a step to follow Max and Rebecca.

"Fia, it is probably best if you stay—"

"Nope, I brought him. I'm sticking with him."

Rebecca pursed her lips and met Fia's eyes, her own set in a challenging stare. "It is better for the ritual if he is not distracted."

"You won't even know I'm there, but I'm not just throwing him to the wolves out there."

"Fia," Max interjected. "It's a tattoo, not—"

"No, Max, it's fine. Fia can join us," Rebecca acquiesced begrudgingly. "But please, do stay quiet."

"Right." Fia waved her hand for Rebecca to continue through the door.

They passed through the archway of trees that led to the cobblestone courtyard. Sahir was different, but a lot of the scene resembled Fia's memories. The Middle Eastern man was seated on an embroidered pillow, his legs crossed over one another. He was surrounded by tools, having already tattooed the teens earlier. One stone bowl was filled with ash, which would be mixed with water to create the ink for the tattoo. Another similar bowl contained a yellow-orange paste Fia guessed was the tincture to help with the ritual.

What had been used on her had been nearly black in the candlelight, a mixture of basil, cinnamon, and blueberries. She wondered what Sahir was using for his mixture.

A woven bowl held a bamboo rod, not quite a foot in length, and another rod of heavier wood. To the end of the bamboo, a thorn would be attached with leather straps, creating what Fia remembered looking like a comically oversized record-player arm. Each person would get a new thorn, just as with modern tattooing. Fia saw a small box in the same woven bowl and assumed the thorns were kept inside.

On the ground in front of Sahir was a woven mat weighted down in each corner by chunks of raw schorl, each a little larger than a chicken egg. Though still jagged and rough, the edges of the stones had been burnished smooth by years of handling, something Fia had seen in Zari's crystals as well.

Rebecca claimed a space on the ground next to the fakir and spoke softly to him in his native language, gesturing to Max, then to Fia. Fia picked up their names and guessed Rebecca was explaining who they were and which of them was getting the tattoo. The man spoke back to Rebecca less softly, his voice carrying the rasp of age.

Rebecca turned back to Max. "He asks that you strip out of your synthetic materials and lie on your back on the mat."

"Synthetic . . . ?" Max raised an eyebrow. Fia wondered if having Max strip out of his clothes was a part of Sahir's ritual specifically or if she hadn't been asked to because of her age.

Rebecca turned back to the fakir, exchanged a couple of sentences with him, and then replied to Max's question. "He says even the industrial dyes in your clothing can dampen your connection to the earth. Sahir's rituals are earth based, which is partly why he asked that we do them out here instead of indoors."

Max's cheeks flushed pink. "So? Strip? Everything?" Fia barked out a staccato laugh, covering it quickly with her hand. "You're enjoying this."

"A little," Fia confessed. She waved her hand over his body. "Let's go. Off with it."

"Fia, you promised," Rebecca scolded. "I must ask—"

"Sorry, Sister, his reaction just—I'll sit . . ." Fia stepped away to sit on the closest of the stone benches.

"*Eur*," Sahir said, the short word sounding even shorter

in what Fia thought was annoyance at Max's modest hesitation.

"Please, Max, remove your clothing and lie on the mat," Rebecca instructed.

"You could at least buy a guy a drink first," he muttered, pulling his shirt over his head. He handed it to Fia, kicked out of his shoes, and stripped from the waist down. Now fully nude, he eased himself onto the mat, lying on his back as he had been told.

The fakir muttered just above a whisper as he set to work. Rebecca translated some. Fia guessed the nun's knowledge of his language was scholarly and maybe didn't include his specific dialect. It was better than what Fia could do, so she set aside any judgment that Max wasn't getting the full play by play.

Sahir moved his hands over Max's body, not touching him, but with no more than an inch separating them. "Sahir is reading your energy, Max, to find the most appropriate guardian spirit for you. He wants to know about the lion tattoo on your chest."

"My birthday is in July. I'm a Leo."

Rebecca relayed the information, and after a moment of listening to Sahir, she spoke again to Max. "Astrology, he says, is linked to more than just where the sun was in the sky when you were born. The being to which you are linked—in your case, the lion—has roots in a realm far deeper than our own.

"For you, he has chosen the symbol of Narasimha. Each of these protective sigils is meant for the bearer alone. He has chosen your third chakra for its location because you are a wise protector." As Rebecca explained the eventual placement of the tattoo, Sahir pressed his fingers into the soft area below Max's sternum.

Fia considered what she was hearing. The fakir, after knowing Max for only five minutes, had picked up on his protective nature. She vaguely remembered something from her own ritual about Bel also being meant for a protector.

The truth was, she best remembered the rush that came from the secrecy of what they were doing, as if bringing in a Middle Eastern spiritualist to tattoo four fifteen-year-olds were the most dangerous thing anyone had ever done. She knew it was her teenaged brain overreacting, but in the moment, she had felt like she was getting away with something big.

Then there had been the rush of pain from that first tattoo on her skin. It was a rush she had been chasing ever since—at least, ever since she had gotten herself set up with a place to live and semi-regular meals.

But the rush of the experience had also done a good job of clouding the less exciting moments. While Fia knew who Bel was and why Jeevan, the man who had performed the ritual, had chosen it for her, she couldn't remember everything. She made a note to try to recover some of the missing details through hypnosis.

Later.

Right now, she was enjoying the visual of Max stretched out on the mat, his taut muscles fully exposed, and seeing his existing tattoos in full daylight for what she thought might be the first time. In addition to the lion clawing its way up the right side of Max's chest, as if scaling a cliff, his left side was adorned with orchids in shades of gray. She thought the juxtaposition of the ferocious lion and the delicate flowers was a perfect visual representation of Max's true nature.

Also, for what Fia thought might be the first time, she looked upon his naked flesh and felt something other than hunger. The lust was present, undoubtedly, but there was something stirring in her gut stronger than just a physical reaction to his sexual appeal.

Sahir dipped his fingers into the bowl filled with the yellow paste, spreading it over Max's torso, arms, pelvis, and into his groin. It reminded Fia of baby food, only thicker and grittier. She could see hints of a sparkle reflecting the sunlight overhead.

"It is a tincture of saffron, tarragon, turmeric, and sand from the desert near Sahir's home," Rebecca explained. "It will ground you, keep you connected to the earth as he works."

With deft, nimble fingers, Sahir wound leather laces around a thorn, securing it into a slit in the bamboo rod. He poured water from a glass jar over the ash in the second bowl and used his fingers to stir it into a paste as well. He dipped the tip of the thorn into the gray-black substance and, resting his hand on Max's stomach, touched the thorn to the unadorned section of pale skin.

With the first tap of the heavier stick against the bamboo, Max curled his fingers into the mat and ground his teeth.

Fia cringed involuntarily, memories of her own first moments, and every tattoo since, creeping into her brain. She knew Max was just as familiar with machine tattoos as she was, but this was a different kind of experience. The vibration of the machine and the speed with which the needle penetrated the skin would numb the nerves in the area being tattooed. This tap-tap-tap method with a single "needle" never fully pushed the recipient to that numb stage.

Eventually, if she remembered correctly, Max's brain would stop responding to the pain signals from his nerves, but the area would never fully go numb.

When the drawing was finished, Sahir spread more of the saffron tincture over the wound. He waved his hands over the fresh tattoo, humming and singing what Fia guessed—receiving no help from their translator—was a ritual blessing. His voice came out in chords rather than single notes, resonating through the trees as if he sang with the voices of a full choir.

After another minute or two, he waved his hands as though shooing Max away, saying something in the same short, brash tone he had used to ask Max, one last time, to strip.

"The ritual is finished," Rebecca explained.

Max lay frozen for another moment before climbing to his feet. "Can I clean—how do I clean this thing?"

"Gently. You may go clean off the tincture and blood, but treat it as I believe you would a machine tattoo. Let it rest awhile before cleaning it thoroughly." Rebecca then said something quietly to Sahir before finding her own feet. She helped Sahir to his feet and leaned down to gather his supplies. "Fia, you may show Max where he can clean up." The nun then led the fakir into the house through the kitchen, leaving Fia and Max alone in the garden.

Max reached out for the shirt Fia still clutched to her chest. She shook her head and let her eyes trace over him. "Can I just enjoy the view for a second?" She drew a circle in the air, urging him to turn his back to her. He obliged with a soft laugh. When he had turned the full circle and faced her again, she made the same gesture. "Again?"

He grabbed his shirt from her and pressed it to his own chest, above the tattoo. "Cut it out. I'm sticky, and I smell like Indian food. Just show me where I can wash this stuff off." He gathered up the rest of his clothes and looked at her, his face sober and reserved.

"Buzzkill. Come on." She waited for him to slip back into his shorts, then led him back into the foyer and down the dark hallway to the bathroom adjacent to the room she had stayed in. "In here. There are rags and towels—"

Max dropped his shoes to the tiled bathroom floor with enough of a thud, it cut Fia's sentence short. He tossed the rest of his clothes onto the floor in front of the sink and grabbed her butt with both hands, lifting her from the floor and carrying her into the room, kicking the door closed behind them.

TWENTY-THREE

Max Hawkins had lain awake as long as he thought he could. He couldn't believe how hard it was to sleep without the sounds of the city outside the window. It was too quiet up here.

He slipped out from beneath Fia's arm, which had fallen lightly over his waist, hoping not to disturb her. He gathered his clothes from the floor, where they had fallen the night before, slipped into his boxer shorts, and left the bedroom to finish dressing in the neighboring bathroom.

Finding a washcloth in one of the cabinets, he wet it in the sink. He dabbed it lightly against the angry red skin in the hollow beneath his sternum before lathering a fingertip's worth of hand soap on the hours-old tattoo. He gently wiped it clean, the whole procedure a well-rehearsed routine, and then searched the cabinets for lotion.

Finding none, he slipped into black jeans and a white t-shirt emblazoned with the image of a hair-metal band from the 1980s. He hung the wet cloth over a hook in the shower and left the bathroom.

Back in the hallway, he looked around, suddenly un-comfortable with the idea of roaming around as a stranger in a house full of kids. He was considering going back into the bedroom to wait for Fia to wake up when Rebecca rounded the corner.

"Max? You are awake early."

"Couldn't sleep. It's too quiet here."

"I imagine you are used to traffic sounds lulling you to sleep."

"Traffic, music from the neighbors, gunshots." He waited a beat for her to laugh. When her eyes widened instead and her jaw slacked, he backpedaled. "I was kidding. I don't have a lot of traffic in my neighborhood."

After a moment, the corners of the nun's mouth curled, and she chuckled softly. "Ah, sarcasm. Fia said you were funny. I should have known you were joking." She looked past him down the hall. "My apologies, Max, but I need to get started on breakfast."

"Oh. Wow, you eat early here. Is there anything I can do to help?"

"No. The teens take turns preparing meals. Mercy will be along. She may already be waiting for me."

"Please, Sister. I can't sleep. I've been awake, wide awake, for an hour already. And I didn't bring a book to read."

Rebecca chewed on his plea for a moment before giving in. "It is unusual, but you make a good case. Follow me."

Through the swinging restaurant-style door at the end of the hallway, Rebecca led Max into a restaurant-style kitchen occupied by a girl Max estimated to be about fourteen. She was busy pulling items out of a refrigerator Max thought could be used as a small apartment in more dire straits.

When she caught sight of Max, the girl jumped, squeaking in surprise, and the apples of her cheeks flushed pink.

Max extended a hand to her, smiling brightly. "I'm Max. You must be Mercy."

With a deep, shuddering breath, Mercy accepted his handshake. "Are you Fia's boyfriend?"

Now it was Max's turn to blush. "I—we haven't had—"

"Mercy, what were you planning for breakfast this morning?" Rebecca interrupted.

"Thank you," Max whispered.

"French toast with grilled bananas and those smoky sausage patties."

"Max has offered to help. Is there anything you want him to do?"

"Oh." Mercy took a quick inventory of her supplies.

"Mercy is quite the natural chef," Rebecca explained quietly. "To that end, however, she is not the best at delegating responsibilities. She is much more a do-it-herself kind of girl."

"I guess he could soak the bread?"

Max snapped to attention. "On it, boss."

Mercy giggled before a wave of embarrassment washed over her face. She turned her eyes away from Max and quietly pushed a glass dish toward him. In it were a loaf of bread and six eggs. "I haven't made the batter yet. Can you do that too?"

"I can!" He gathered up the gallon jug of milk from the other side of the teen and measured out a cup into the dish after removing the other things.

Mercy set about slicing bananas, arranging them on a cast-iron grate positioned over two of the eight burners.

Rebecca took it upon herself to arrange the sausage patties on a cookie sheet to go in the oven before taking a place in front of an iron griddle over two more of the burners, creating an assembly line with Max.

"So," Max said after he and Mercy had found a rhythm with the nun. "Tell me the story of Sister Rebecca."

"Not much to tell. I came here at fifteen. I took my vows at eighteen, and that's really it." She ended the sentence so abruptly, Max thought he could hear the period at the end of it.

"What can you tell me about Fia?" he asked, changing the subject.

"Nothing I am sure you don't already know. I am afraid I have not had much opportunity to chitchat with her."

"I guess getting blown up together has a way of making things like favorite color seem trivial."

"Likewise, you have fought demons at her side. I guess this is not a favorite-colors kind of world we are engaged in."

"Red," Mercy said after a moment of silence. "Fia's car is red. Her phone case is red."

"Her scooter is red," Max added. "Good catch, Mercy."

"Mine is green," Mercy added. "Xavier's is too. Tianna's is yellow. Kaleb's is purple, but he wants people to think it's blue because that's more masculine."

She returned her attention to her bananas, which were, by then, charred with the pattern of the grill pan. After she had removed them to a dish, she spoke again.

"What about you, Max?"

"Depends."

"On what?" Rebecca asked, her voice carrying a note of amused confusion.

"Color of what? I like black leather but white cars. Green for grass."

He left his quip to hang in the air, waiting for a response. After another long moment, Mercy laughed tentatively. "Green grass. That's funny."

"Thanks. You don't have to say so. One of the things Fia and I have connected on is a questionable sense of humor." He reconsidered Mercy's question. "I guess my favorite color is probably blue." He surveyed the kitchen and the state of breakfast. "If you don't have anything else for me to do, I'm going to go see if Fia's up."

"That would be fine, Max. Thank you for your help," Rebecca replied.

He turned and headed back to the bedroom.

Only half-awake, Fia reached her hand out across the bed, expecting to find warm flesh waiting for her. Instead, she found only sheets. She raised her shoulders off the pillow and looked around.

Heavy drapes over the windows cast the room in near-complete darkness, but there was enough light creeping through, she could see the glow of the white sheets to her side. "Where'd you go?" she muttered to no one.

She twisted herself into a seated position and swung her legs over the side of the bed. She flicked on the bedside lamp, which cast a soft orange glow over a small section of the room. "Well, that's less than helpful." She couldn't even use the flashlight on her phone until she found her phone in the dark.

She followed the edge of the bed into the deep shadows. As she fumbled naked through the dark room, the door eased open, letting in the scant light from the hallway.

"Mm," came a soft rumble from the doorway. "I was coming to check on you for breakfast, but my appetite may have changed."

Max pushed the door closed and crossed the room in two steps. He pushed Fia by her hips back the way she had come until the edge of the bed caught her legs, knocking them out from under her.

"Max!" She laughed as his hair tickled the inside of her thighs. "We—oh—Max, we can't. Breakfast."

With a shuddering sigh, she relaxed back into the mattress and succumbed to his firm kisses, tying her fingers in his hair. She grabbed at a pillow as he pressed his lips against her and covered her face with it. She pushed at the pillow until she had a mouthful and bit down hard enough, she thought she would break through the fabric. She felt a moan escape her chest, filling the pillow as her back arched to push herself harder into Max. He responded with a moan of his own.

And as quickly as it had started, it was over. Fia lay on the bed, panting, and Max spread his weight over her. He kissed her mouth softly, and she licked his lips.

"Breakfast is waiting for us," he whispered, pulling away. He used his own phone to shine a light around the room, finding her underwear tucked beneath the foot of the bed. He handed it to her and went to find the rest of her clothes.

Fia pulled a clean shirt from her bag, drew it over her head, and flipped off the light as Max reopened the door. He smiled wolfishly at her and gestured for her to leave ahead of him.

They crossed the hallway to the dining room, and Fia was grateful they weren't late. Though, if they had been, it would have been worth it.

"Good morning, Fia," Theresa greeted as they took two of the remaining chairs, leaving the others for Rebecca and Mercy.

Annabel raised an eyebrow at Max. "And who is this?"

"Sorry," Fia apologized. "Everyone, this is Max." She pointed to everyone around the table, rattling off names. "And I'm guessing it's Mercy's turn to cook? Mercy and Rebecca will be along soon."

Max nodded. "I met her already. It is a pleasure to meet everyone else."

"Oh?"

"How did you sleep, Max?" Cecilia asked.

"Not well, Sister. It is so quiet here. I didn't realize how much I'd grown to appreciate the noise of the city."

"I'm sorry to hear that."

"Thanks. I think the payoff will be worth it. A new tattoo and what looks like it's going to be a delicious breakfast. But don't judge too harshly. I helped. So if the French toast tastes like a shoe, please don't tell me. You'll hurt my feelings."

Rebecca and Mercy pushed through the door from the hallway, their arms loaded down with their meal. Max jumped up from his chair and carefully grabbed the syrup bottle dangling precariously from Mercy's pinkie.

"Thank you," the teen said, barely above a whisper.

"Of course." He placed the bottle on the table next to the platter of egg-battered bread, taking the tub of butter from her next, before returning to his chair.

"I am glad to finally meet you, Mister . . . ?"

Fia cringed at the curt tone in Agnes's voice, but Max didn't seem to notice.

"Max, please. Mr. Hawkins is my father." He took a

moment, then added, "I'm not even sure I've ever heard anyone call my dad *Mr. Hawkins.*"

"Very well, Max. We are glad you could join us for breakfast."

They had missed dinner the night before for the same reason Fia was currently wishing they had skipped breakfast too. She knew Max was taking Agnes's words at face value, but Fia couldn't help feeling a chill in them, as if the Reverend Mother knew why they had missed dinner and was passively scolding Fia for it.

"Did you get a tattoo too, Max?" Xavier asked.

"Too? You mean, all that production wasn't just for me? Well, now I'm sad."

"The fakir was here to tattoo the teens," Agnes responded. "Fia asked if we could include you in the ritual as well as long as he was here."

Fia shook her head. "He knows. He's kidding."

Max smiled. "Yes, Reverend Mother, Fia told me what was going on. I was—it was a terrible joke. I apologize."

Agnes huffed out a sound of disapproval, and the table fell silent for several long moments. Finally, Tianna broke the silence.

"Max, are you a hunter too?"

"No, but everything you are doing here fascinates me."

"I don't know that I agree with bringing in an outsider because he is *fascinated,*" Annabel asserted.

"If you are questioning Max's trustworthiness, then I must disagree," Rebecca said. "I apologize. I meant to say, I presume if Fia believes in him as an ally, we should trust her judgment. She is, after all, one of our own."

"Thank you, Sister," Max replied. "I think it's my turn to apologize, Sister Annabel. I will be honest, I kind of fell into Fia's—into your world. But I understand your hesitation to trust me. What you are involved in here—I understand it's dangerous and stealth is crucial to your survival. Fia, maybe after breakfast we should go back—"

"No, Max, please," Theresa spoke next. "I don't think that's what Sister Annabel meant. I for one would be more concerned with your safety than ours. You are correct; what we are doing is dangerous. Or rather, what Fia is doing. Most of what happens here is mundane. But being close to Fia could be more harrowing."

"I've seen a little of that already. That's what I meant when I said I fell into it." He looked to Fia.

"I mentioned I had a run-in with the demon, Irzelen. Max was around when that happened," Fia fudged, choosing to combine some of the details for simplicity's sake. "And the demons from the cave? He's had a run-in with one of them too. I'm no less concerned for his safety—fool me once, right? But as much as I hate to admit it, I think he's fine."

"Thanks," Max said, his voice betraying a hint of injury.

"That's not what I—you've proven yourself, despite my efforts not to let you. You're determined to be part of this thing, so I guess it's a good thing you can handle yourself."

They finished the meal quietly, with small, sparse conversations about the day's plans popping up at irregular intervals.

"Max, will you be staying for the day?" Theresa asked as everyone was finishing.

He looked from Theresa to Fia to Annabel. "I guess it's up to Fia. She drove."

"It's up to you. I dragged you up here. If you have something to do—"

"Not a thing. I wouldn't mind hanging out a little while. It's quiet up here, cool. And I hate to eat and run." He winked at Fia, his lips curling into a smirk. She felt her face grow pale, then bright pink.

"I guess we're staying, then," she said after a second of recovery.

TWENTY-FOUR

Outside the dining room, Max took a step to follow Rebecca and Mercy to the kitchen. Fia grabbed his hand and pulled back gently. "Do you really want to hang out here?"

"I do. It's nice to get out of the city for a while, and I'm meeting your family."

"They're not my family. I've known you longer than I've known most of the people here."

"Fia, that doesn't matter." She furrowed her brow. "Family is the people who will follow you into hell and never waver. I think these people are your family. Tell me about your beef with the Reverend Mother."

"No beef. Well, not on my end. I think she's still bitter about how I left."

"Fia?"

"Hm?"

"You ran away. On her watch. She probably got in trouble over it, don't you think? And she raised you. I'm sure having you sneak off in the dead of night stung a little."

"Her pride, maybe."

"Isn't pride one of the things nuns are supposed to give up? I mean, I realize things are a little unconventional here, but she's still a nun, right?"

"More than not, really. She was a regular nun before coming here. Or at least, that's the story I was always told."

Max tilted his head inquisitively. "That is the 'or so I was told' of someone who recently discovered something new."

"No. Not—I kind of always wondered what makes a nun from a traditional order give up rosaries and soup kitchens for grooming children to hunt condemned souls. How do you even find out something like this exists?"

"Isn't it all connected? I mean, I know the Church—capital *C*—looks down on things like exorcisms, but they still did them for a while. Isn't that kind of the same thing? The Reverend Mother seems like that kind of gal. Tough as nails, no bullshit."

Fia chewed on what he was saying. "It is, but it isn't. It's kind of Catholic adjacent. People like Agnes, and Theresa and Annabel, started out Catholic. Probably raised in that environment."

"I don't imagine too many become nuns after being raised atheist."

"But you learn things here that prove the Church—capital *C*—isn't completely on point. And then you run away in the middle of one of the worst winters in recent history and meet a hunter who was raised in Haiti and figure out that a lot of what you learned here wasn't completely on point either."

"How's that?"

"Zari." Max shook his head. "I didn't mention Zari?"

"If you did, I don't remember."

Fia gave Max a rundown of her time with Zari. "I think

she wants to meet you. She didn't say as much, but—I don't think she would not want to."

"Sounds good. When we get back?"

"Maybe. We'll see what happens."

"You're putting me off."

"No. We'll stop by Zari's when we get back to the city. Better? Commitment."

"A little. So, what do you want to do now?"

"Honestly, finish what we—what you started this morning. But we probably should . . ." Fia looked around, trying to find the rest of that sentence written on a wall somewhere. "Head out to the training grounds?"

Max's eyes traced over her body, pausing at her midsection, and he licked his lips. "I'm pretty sure *you* finished. But yeah, training grounds might be the best. Lead the way?"

As they walked, Max looped his arm around Fia's waist, pulling her close. She let him hold her like that for a few strides, then pulled away, lacing her fingers between his. They reached the yellow straw of the training grounds and found the teens already running what looked like a modified obstacle course on the gymnastics equipment.

"Fia! Max! I am so glad you decided to join us," Theresa said with a bright smile.

Fia smiled back. "Is there anything we can do to help?"

Theresa forfeited one of the two stopwatches she held and nudged Annabel, encouraging her to give up one as well. "If you want to help us time them. This one is Mercy's." She placed it in Fia's hand. "And that one is Tianna's." She gestured to the one Annabel had handed to Max. "They are running a circuit. Uneven bars, up and over, across the parallel bars, back across the balance beam, stop at each target, set up, load, shoot, then run through the whole thing over again two more times. They just started."

"Do we stop when they get to the last target?" Fia asked, reading the labels on the watch buttons. When she found the stop button, she pointed it out on the watch Max held too. He gave her a thumbs up and turned his attention back to Tianna.

"They'll tag in here." Theresa slapped her hand on a post. "That's the official end of the course."

"Is this what they were doing when Mercy fell?" Fia asked, her eyes tracking the small girl through the maze. Theresa nodded.

They watched each of the teens run through their circuit. Fia guessed they had staggered their starts so they wouldn't collide in any of the obstacles. On his second time through, Kaleb's foot slipped off the balance beam, and before he could correct himself, he had toppled to the ground. Xavier caught up to him, and with a quick glance from his peer to the timekeepers, he jumped onto the beam and ran across, leaving Kaleb to gather himself off the ground.

Fia felt a pang of sympathy watching Kaleb climb onto the rail and walk, rather than run, across to the other end. She thought she had talked him out of pursuing feelings for Xavier, but she also knew that was easier said than done. She looked at Max, at the deep hollows of his cheeks beneath his sharp cheekbones, at the hard line of his jaw, tracing her eyes over his full lips and dark eyes. His warm-brown hair fell over his shoulders in soft waves that glinted red and gold in the sun.

Definitely easier said than done.

She turned her attention back to Mercy as the small girl started her third and final circuit. "Is Mercy just naturally good at everything?" Fia asked Theresa quietly.

"I understand she's a lot like you."

"Might explain things."

"Excuse me?"

"Agnes—Mother Agnes seems a little harsh on Mercy. If she reminds her of me, that would explain that."

"Fia, I think you should take some time while you are here to talk with the Reverend Mother. I think you believe there is hostility where there is none."

"Maybe."

Maybe I should. At least try. Fia didn't have high expectations for any heart-to-heart with Agnes, but this chat seemed to be a popular idea, so she decided she would try.

Mercy reached the pole and jerked down hard on a rope Fia hadn't noticed. The clang of the brass bell at the top startled Fia, and she jabbed her finger down on the stop button on the watch. Mercy leaned in to look at the time on the watch, and Theresa did the same from Fia's other side.

"Good job, Mercy. Two seconds off your last time. And that was with an amateur timekeeper." Theresa offered Fia a smile and a playful wink. "Grab a drink and have a seat while the others finish."

Tianna came in a breath later, and the three of them— Theresa, Tianna, and Max—ran through the same steps, with Theresa sending Tianna to sit with Mercy.

When everyone was finished, Kaleb struck out angrily, kicking the shed hard enough to make the steel side ring out.

"Kaleb," Annabel scolded. "There is no call for that."

"He's embarrassed," Fia whispered to the nun.

"I understand that, Fia, but that is no reason to act out in aggression."

"Hey, don't turn that venom on me. I just know what—"

"Fia, please stay out of it. I appreciate your experience, but these kids are our responsibility, not yours."

Fia raised her hands in surrender. "Yeah, fine. Whatever." She moved to a bench a few feet away.

Max sat next to her. "Hey, you okay?"

"Fine."

"You sound fine."

"I can't talk about it. It's between Kaleb and me. I just don't think Annabel should come down on him like that without knowing what's going on." She got up and took a step toward the kids. "I'll be right back; stay here?"

Max pointed a finger down at the ground between his feet.

Fia crossed over to where the teens were recovering. "Hey, that was pretty cool. You kids do that all the time?"

"Once a week," Mercy answered, climbing to her feet and taking a step around Fia.

"I'm impressed." Fia caught Kaleb's attention and mouthed to him, *"You okay?"*

He rolled his eyes toward Xavier and shrugged dismissively.

"Hey, Fia," Mercy called from the shed door. "Could you show us how you take down a target?" The smallest of the teens was wheeling a cart out of the shed, a man-sized dummy strapped to it.

"I don't know that I have any tricks—"

"We just want to see you in action. And we can't go on a real hunt with you, so this is the next best thing."

Fia studied the ballistic gel sculpture and flashed on her memories of shooting a similar one as a child.

Breathe. Inhale. Exhale. Inhale. Squeeze, don't pull.

The string twanged softly as it released, sending the

metal projectile zipping through the air. "Again!" Another perfect shot, another rap on the knuckles from Sister Agnes. As ordered, Fia went again to retrieve her bolt and repair the target.

Except there was nothing to repair.

How could this be possible? Fia had left the bow exactly as it had been after her last perfect hit. This one should have at least been close. She carried the bolt back to the nun, who she found holding the crossbow. Her face revealed nothing. The child wasn't sure Sister Agnes even had emotions—save anger—let alone knew how to express them properly.

"What did you learn, Fiammetta?"

"I learned that if I leave my weapon unattended, a vindictive nun will monkey with my shot."

The sound that followed was sharp and crisp, and her cheek burned. "Set it up again and mind your arc."

Fia shuddered free of the memory and told Mercy to set the dummy up near the targets.

She climbed to the crow's nest and gathered the weapon that waited there for her. "Can everyone see me?"

A chorus of affirmatives echoed back to her. She lined up her shot and squeezed the trigger. The bolt tore through the sticky yellow-orange substance, sticking in the top edge of the target behind it.

"If you can," she called out, "try to shoot your targets in the back. There is a lot of room between the front of the throat and what you're trying to hit that could cause things to go wrong. But that's not always possible, so work with what you've got?"

Fia felt like she was just spitting words into the air without any real plan. Of course it was better to shoot into the back of the neck. Of course there would be times that wasn't possible. Of course Theresa—and possibly Annabel—had already told them all of this.

I never said I wanted to be a teacher anyway.

"Another thing to remember is that you are very rarely going to get a target to stand still and expose their spine for you. I'm sure you've heard all this before, but more often than not, you're going to be aiming for a moving target. Not someone at a dead run, but the natural movements of daily life. You need to be able to plan ahead and shoot at where they're going to be, not where they are."

Fia examined the dummy and the cart it was standing on. "Mercy, do you feel comfortable trying to move him around while Tianna comes up here and takes a shot?"

Mercy gave the cart a tug and then dove with the reflexes of a cat to grab the dummy before it could fall face-first into the dirt.

Fia laughed. "Okay, bad idea." She climbed back to the ground and crossed to the dummy. The wheels on the cart were designed for forward and backward movement only, not all directions, and she didn't think it would move easily on the uneven ground anyway. "Hey, Sisters. Theresa, Annabel, do you have a padded suit in the shed? Like one of those dog-training suits?"

Sister Annabel beckoned for Fia to follow her. "Are you sure about this?"

"Do they get a lot of training shooting at something in motion?"

"Probably not as much as they should."

"Then I'm sure. I'll be fine."

The two women worked to outfit Fia from head to knee in two inches of heavy foam rubber. She left her lower legs free to be able to move more easily and penguin-waddled back out to the shooting range.

Max growled from his seat on the bench. "That's hot."

Fia laughed. "You know it." She stood in front of the dummy and urged the teens into the crow's nest. "I want each of you to take a turn trying to hit me. Anywhere, but preferably in the neck."

Obediently, they climbed up the ladder, but at the top, they stalled. All four of them stared hesitantly at the weapon Fia had left behind. "C'mon, guys, someone take the shot. This padding is hot." No one moved. "I'll be fine!"

"I'll do it," Mercy said finally. She stepped up to the crossbow, pushing her peers out of the way.

Fia watched her set up the shot, doing her best to dance in place despite the several pounds of extra weight she was carrying. She watched the teen inhale, exhale, and inhale again—something Fia did herself—preparing to take a shot. One deep-gut breath before squeezing the trigger. It helped to ground and calm her.

When Fia saw Mercy's finger move to squeeze the trigger, she dove, bending at the waist—the best she could under the circumstances—and completely ducking the projectile. It sunk into the ballistic gel with a soft sound.

"Hey!" Mercy shouted. "That wasn't fair. You didn't tell me you were going to duck."

"Is that how you've been running these drills? Are you going to scold a target for bending to tie his shoe? Tianna, your turn."

"What happens if something like that goes wrong on a real hunt?" Theresa asked, quizzing Fia for the teens' benefit.

"If you can recover and try again, do it. If you can't, cut your losses and save your butt. I'm not going to sugarcoat things, kids. Shit's going to go wrong. You're going to miss targets. You're going to panic and not know what to do to fix the problem. You're going to try, and you're going to make a bigger mess than you already had. Take a deep breath and move on. Most of this job is split-second, one-chance moments. A lot of thinking on your toes. You have to figure out how to adjust and adapt in the moment. I can't tell you what to do in every situation you encounter. Tianna?"

The other three teens ran through the same drill, Fia throwing a different curve at each of them. Xavier came closest to hitting her, his bolt grazing across her shoulder blades as she turned sideways away from him.

"Max," Fia called out. "Do you want to try?"

"I don't know anything about shooting a crossbow."

"I meant try the suit, but hey . . ." She waved her hand to the crow's nest.

The muscles of Max's face worked as he contemplated his choices. With a shrug, he crossed the field to the ladder.

"I didn't mean it," Fia said.

"No, I think I want to try. I haven't experienced soul-crushing embarrassment in front of a woman in a while. I'm probably due."

Fia chuckled with a shrug. "Whatever finds your lost remote."

She watched him approach the weapon, looking a little lost. Xavier stepped forward to help, but Max waved him off.

"I'll figure it out. How hard can it be? People in zombie movies find these things lying in the streets and start picking off monsters without any training. I can too."

The teens each looked appalled and shocked at his declaration. Fia laughed.

"Max, cut it out. They're not used to your humor. He's kidding."

Max took the bolt from Xavier's hand and, after some fumbling and prodding, was able to load the weapon without any real help from the teens.

On the ground, Fia let him get positioned to watch her through the bow's scope before attempting jumping jacks. They were clumsy, but she was leaving the ground and flapping her arms, so she called it a success. He raised his head to look at her and then returned to the scope.

Fia started dancing, shuffling her feet to the left, then the right, hopping in place and doing it all over facing a different direction, imitating—poorly—one of the line dances she had seen in the bars.

The bolt hit her shoulder solidly, its nose embedding in the foam deeply enough to make Fia stop moving and stare at it before it fell to the ground.

"You hit me!" she shouted. "I can't believe you shot me!"

Max laughed. "I can't believe I did either." He scurried down off the platform, back to the ground. "I shot you!"

"Yeah, I was there when it happened." She picked the bolt up off the ground and handed it to him. "Souvenir?"

Max's face was glowing like a child's. He accepted the projectile from her, looked it over for a moment, and then handed it back to her. "Nah, I'm good. I shot you."

"Beginner's luck." The edges of Fia's ears were growing hot.

"I shot—"

"Max!"

He shrank back, still grinning. "Sorry. Hey, I think I want to try some more. Do you think it would be okay if I hung out here and shot at the targets?"

"Don't ask me; ask the nuns. If you want to, though, it would be perfect timing. I keep getting pushed to go talk to Agnes."

"I think you should."

"Yeah."

A swarm of locusts came to life in Fia's gut, swirling around, buzzing, making her feel nauseated. The idea of confronting her former mentor made her feel like a helpless child who had broken her mother's favorite vase doing something she had already been told not to do.

"Someone help me out of this thing? Hey, Theresa," she called, taking a few steps toward the nun. "Do you mind if Max hangs out out here with you guys, maybe does a few shooting drills? He wants to learn, and I'm apparently going to go talk to Agnes."

"Yes, absolutely. Max can stay," Theresa replied, unfastening the buckles and straps to pull Fia free of the padding. "I don't mind letting him try his hand at them. He, too, seems to be a bit of a natural."

"Cool." Fia stood still, her feet refusing to move her body back toward the house.

"Fia," Max said, his voice gentle and soft. "You'll be okay." He looped an arm around her and kissed the top of her head before pushing her in the direction she needed to go.

Twenty-Five

Back in the house, Fia stood in the foyer, frozen. Not only did she not know what she was going to say to Agnes, she didn't know which direction to go to find the elder nun. She didn't have to wonder long, however. The stern woman stepped out of the shadows of the upstairs hallway to descend the stairs, stopping short when she saw Fia.

"Fiammetta. I thought you were out with the teens."

"Had to go to the bathroom," Fia lied, losing her nerve.

"Ah." Agnes regarded her only briefly before continuing down the stairs and crossing the space toward the library.

Say something.

Fia watched silently as the mother superior disappeared into the cavernous library and turned to make her lie a truth.

In the bathroom, she stared at the redheaded woman in the mirror. "Nope." She shook her head. "Can't do it. She looks at me and sees an impudent teenager who turned her back on everything. I don't doubt she caught hell for me running away. But after that settled down, she was probably glad to see me gone. Insubordinate troublemaker, good to get me out of her hair." Fia stared at her reflection awhile longer and shook her head again. "Nope."

She stepped back out into the hallway and looked around, checking the time on her phone. Nine thirty. Lunch would be in an hour and a half. She had a little time to check out that secret passage.

The kitchen was dark—as dark as it could be with all its shiny, light-colored surfaces—and she pushed through the second door into the living quarters and listened. Children made sounds, even when they were being quiet, but she heard nothing. She made her way slowly down the hall and around the corner, listening as she walked. She didn't know for sure where Cecilia and the children were—or Rebecca or Scott, for that matter—and didn't want to get caught nosing around somewhere she wasn't supposed to be.

But she wanted to find out about that passage.

She waited below the trapdoor for several seconds, giving anyone who might catch her a chance to come out of one of the rooms. When no one appeared, she flipped the switch on the wall, and with a groan, the ceiling opened, and a ladder rolled down to meet her. With another quick look around, she climbed up the ladder into the crawl space.

There was another switch up here, which she guessed would retract the ladder and door. She flipped it, to the expected results, and set off through the space. It ran perpendicular to the hallway she had come in from, above the bedroom shared by the younger kids. As she crawled, little motion-sensing lights came on around her, and she marveled at this hidden space. She wondered what it had been intended for as she reached the corner outside the hall bathroom.

She crawled until she found the air vent where she had heard the woman's low, angry voice, then on past it to the end of the passage. When she reached the wall, she looked around for another switch or something to indicate how she was supposed to get out of here. There was nothing in the floor, though she hadn't really expected there to be. She felt along the ceiling of the space, where she found a small knob that resembled a cabinet door's. She turned it.

With a click, she pushed up on the surface and found herself in a different kind of darkness. Where she had had a little light from the small lamps in the crawl space, there was only a sliver of light creeping into this new darkness from beneath a door. She pushed the door the rest of the way open until it fell against the wall.

"Sh," she hissed at the inanimate object and pulled herself up out of the space. She peered through the slats in the louvered door to try to determine if the room on the other side was occupied but couldn't see more than a few feet of the space.

From what she could see, it was barren. Someone used the room, but they were scant on material possessions and creature comforts. Not that Fia had expected rock posters on the walls or sequined pillows, but this looked like a college dorm room before the occupant had arrived.

Seeing no one in the room, Fia pushed gently against the lightweight door, knowing she couldn't see the whole space. She peeked out and found the coast was clear. She closed the trapdoor and stepped out into the room. She considered snooping but decided that might be more risk than she needed to bring on herself. Instead, she eased her way through the door into the upstairs hallway. Her final concern was running into Agnes on her way back to the office.

Finding herself outside the first door at the top of the

stairs, Fia darted back down to the foyer, just in time to find Agnes returning from her business in the library.

"Fiammetta? You are right where I left you."

"Back again, Reverend Mother. On my way back out to the hunters." She ducked her head and aimed for the doors.

"I am glad I caught you. I would like to talk to you about something. Could you join me in my office?"

"Um . . . sure." Fia motioned for Agnes to lead the way up the stairs.

They had just stepped through the door into Agnes's office when Sister Cecilia came up behind them, guiding Levi ahead of her. "Reverend Mother, I have—Levi has something he needs to tell you."

Agnes looked from the boy to Fia and back again before speaking. "Fiammetta, I apologize. Could you let me speak with Levi first? I can come out to find you later. I would still like to speak with you."

"Sure."

Fia turned and left the office, and Sister Cecilia pushed the door closed behind her, though not enough to latch it. Fia hung back a moment, scouting out an escape should she need it. She tried the knob on the neighboring door, finding it unlocked. Nudging it open, she gave herself room to duck inside if she needed to. Then she pressed herself against the wall opposite the opening of Agnes's office door to listen to the conversation in Agnes's office.

Levi's small voice was in the middle of a story. "She asked me about the red-haired lady. Asked if I knew who she was."

"And what did you tell her?" Fia was surprised by the soft, gentle tone of Agnes's voice as she spoke with the child.

"I'm sorry, Reverend Mother. I lied to her. I didn't like

the way she talked to me. She scared me, and I told her I didn't know a red-haired lady. Did I do something bad?"

"Goodness, no, Levi," Cecilia cooed. "Can you tell Mother Agnes what the lady looked like?"

"Tall, like you"—Fia guessed he was pointing at Agnes—"and had white hair, and she talked funny. Like from another county."

The lady from Zari's shop?

Fia had heard all she needed. She pulled the door closed on the other room and proceeded toward the stairs.

What she didn't know was what to do with the information.

She thought about the woman asking Zari for the quartz blade. Nothing about that sounded positive. Maybe she should head back to the city, find out what the woman had been able to buy from Zari. Reaching the foyer for the third time, she had taken a step toward the back doors to go tell Max she needed to go when someone clamped a hand down on her arm.

She wheeled around to find Scott looming over her. "Oh, okay, I could stand a minute with you." She nudged him back toward the hallway.

"Fia, is something wrong?"

"I'm not sure. Something weird is going on around here."

"Oh?"

She quickly relayed what she had seen and heard over the previous few days, cherry-picking the details she was ready to share. She left out her journey through the crawl space and only briefly touched on her inspection of the bar Mercy had fallen from. She also chose to omit listening in on Agnes's conversation with Levi.

"Were you leaving?" he asked.

"I was thinking about it. I think there might be something Zari could help me with. I was going out to see if Max wanted to come too or if he wanted to stay here. He shot me and got all giddy over his beginner's luck, so he's out shooting with the kids."

"He—"

"I was running a drill with the kids and asked Max if he wanted to try. I meant try the padded suit to get them to shoot at him, but he took it the other direction and tried shooting me in the suit. He was actually the only one out of the five who managed to shoot me."

Scott laughed, a heavy belly laugh.

"It's not funny."

"It's a little funny."

"Anyway," she said, annoyed. "I was going to see if he wanted to stay here and shoot and have lunch with everyone else while I bounced back to the city to talk to Zari. Or if he just wanted to pack it in and go with me."

Scott's expression darkened. "Fia, I was coming to find you to ask that you stay here for the night. I am not sure it's safe for you in the city right now."

"Do you know . . . ?"

"About Levi's encounter with the woman at the museum? Yes. And I think you are safer here, at least for tonight."

Fia chewed on the information. Maybe whatever the woman had bought at Zari's shop on the second day had been a ruse. Maybe what she had really been shopping for was Fia. She still wasn't sure she was ready to share that encounter with Scott.

"Yeah, if you think so. We'll stay."

"Thank you."

"Sure. I guess I'll head back out to the training grounds. Unless you need me for something else?"

He waved a hand toward the door, and she turned to go.

TWENTY-SIX

Max and Fia spent most of the afternoon on the training grounds with the teens. Annabel had left after lunch to go into the city—"I am helping with an outreach center, in addition to my duties here," she had explained—leaving Theresa alone to mind the teens for another afternoon.

They came back in to give Kaleb time to clean up before helping Rebecca with dinner. "I think I'm going to jump in the shower too," Fia offered, giving Max a wink.

He furrowed his brow, suddenly unsure about taking her up on her suggestion. After the day they had had outside, he almost felt uncomfortable being so brazenly intimate with her. He really did feel like he was staying in her family's home.

"I'll wait until you're finished," he said, offering her a chaste kiss on the cheek.

She narrowed her eyes in confusion before shrugging. "Have it your way." She started for the bedroom to get what she needed before the shower.

"If you would like, Max, there are also showers in the community bathrooms up and downstairs," Theresa offered after Fia had closed herself in the bathroom.

"Maybe I will." He grabbed what he needed from the bedroom and followed Sister Theresa through the kitchen. She showed him to a locker-room-style bathroom.

"This is where the boys shower. There are towels in here." She showed him a linen closet just inside the door. "Help yourself to anything you need that doesn't have a name on it."

"Thank you, Sister."

Once he had finished, he realized he never had found lotion for his tattoo. He opened a couple of cupboard doors for a quick look, finding a familiar white bottle in the third one. He gently spread the unscented, oil-free cream over his still-angry skin and dressed in the clean clothes he had brought. He ran a comb through his hair and repacked his toiletry bag.

Pushing open the two-way door to leave, he nearly collided with Rebecca. "Sister! Hello. I'm sorry. I didn't expect anyone to be out here."

"I just wanted to make sure you were getting along all right in here."

"On my way out. Can I help with dinner?"

"Oh. I guess. If you would like to."

"I would love to."

Rebecca waved a hand for him to join her on the way back to the kitchen. They found Kaleb pulling things from the refrigerator, a similar scene to the one Max had witnessed before breakfast.

"Kaleb," Rebecca said. "Would you like to take a night off?"

Kaleb's brow furrowed, as if he thought Rebecca was trying to trap him.

"Just between us, you have my word," Rebecca added. "I would just like some time to talk with Max. I will come and get you before we are finished so you can help me serve and no one will know the difference."

"Are you sure?"

"It is completely up to you, but I promise I will not say anything to anyone if you want to relax in the recreation room. Or out behind the garden."

Kaleb removed his apron and nearly ran for the back door of the kitchen before the nun could change her mind.

"You wanted to talk to me?" Max asked when he and Rebecca were alone.

"Please don't worry. I thought we could talk about you and about you and Fia."

"Oh. What do you want to know?"

"Tell me something about you. I know you are a musician, quite skilled as I understand it."

"I didn't realize Fia had talked about me. That's kind of exciting. What can I do?"

Rebecca pushed a bowl of potatoes toward him, placing a vegetable peeler in his hand. "I'm not sure what Kaleb had in mind, but I think we'll mash those. Mashed potatoes seem to go over well. Do you like gravy on your potatoes?" Max nodded. "Or garlic and sour cream mixed in?"

"Either sounds great." He started peeling the potatoes. "I am a drummer. I've been playing since I was about seven. I don't know about skilled, but it's the only thing I really know how to do."

"I understand you were out at the training grounds shooting with the teens. Theresa suggested you were a natural in that area. Perhaps you would want to join our fight?"

"I can't say I haven't thought about it. I'm not sure it's what I was made for. And I have a career up and running. I actually have to leave again. Tomorrow night, I think. Another week on the road."

"Oh? That is exciting. Does Fia know?"

"She should. I know I told her."

"That is exciting."

"It is, now that I've got the first leg behind me. Before that, it was overwhelming." He pushed the bowl of peeled potatoes back toward Rebecca, looking for a place to put the peels.

"We compost all vegetable matter." Rebecca opened a door that Max had originally thought was a small dishwasher. "In here."

He shoveled the potato peels into the bin. "What's next?"

She pointed to a cabinet near the enormous refrigerator. "Pots and pans are in there. Grab one and start the potatoes?"

"So, what brought you here, Sister Rebecca?" Max asked as he grabbed a pot from the cabinet. "You mentioned you came here when you were fifteen and took your vows at eighteen?"

"I did. My father was—my father is a minister. I was falling in with an unsavory crowd. He shipped me out here to get me away from them and back on the right track."

"Wow. I didn't know people really did that anymore. Ship girls off to convents." He looked around. "Convent?"

"This space is not, not technically. But when I first came here, I did live in the convent. The same one where Fia grew up."

"What happened there?"

"Fire. Luckily, only the structure was harmed."

"Oh, that's terrible. Were the kids there?"

"Only Levi and Callie. Levi was born there. Callie was orphaned and left with us."

"Levi was born in the convent?" He ran through a quick calculation. "He's what? Eight? Did Fia know his mother?"

Rebecca fell quiet, focusing on the steaks she was battering for several moments. "No, she didn't. She had left by the time . . ."

"Rebecca? Are you okay?"

She took a deep breath. "Yes, my apologies. Sometimes the memories are hard."

Max left her statement hanging on the air, not sure what to say. She suddenly seemed sad. He didn't know if he should ask why, but he wasn't sure where to take the conversation instead. He didn't have to wonder long.

"No one else knows about Levi. Only Mother Agnes and Sister Cecilia." He let her take her time saying whatever it was she needed to say. "Max, has anyone ever told you you're easy to talk to? I think maybe that's why Fia is so fond of you. You are—you are comforting."

Max shrugged, feeling self-conscious. "I have heard that once or twice."

"I have to warn you about something. I think it is also why Mercy—"

Max sighed. "It comes with the territory. She's about the right age."

"Right age?"

"I have already run into a few girls in their early teens who are looking to grow up faster than they should, in a way they shouldn't. Mercy is about the right age. Don't worry; that's not me."

"Oh, I am not worried. I simply wanted you to be aware."

With the potatoes started, Max decided to press on. "What about Levi? What does no one else know? I'll tell you what I told Fia when we first started hanging out: it might feel good to get it off your chest. But I think I already know."

Rebecca turned to face him. Her eyes were wide, surprised and pleading. "Max, please don't say anything. The only reason I was allowed to stay with him was under the condition he never find out."

"Levi is . . ." Max lowered his voice to a whisper. "Levi is your son." Rebecca nodded. "Damn, Sister, that's a lot to carry."

She drew a floured hand across her cheek. "Could you put some paper towels in that basket for me?"

"Sure."

After her shower, Fia had gone searching for Mother Agnes. She wasn't looking forward to the conversation, but she thought she might as well get it over with. She didn't even know what Agnes wanted to talk to her about, but her instincts told her to be wary.

She found Father Scott instead.

"Fia, I am glad to see you elected to stay."

"I was coming back."

"I understand that. I just wanted you to know I appreciated you taking my advice."

"Do you know any more about the woman who talked to Levi?"

"We don't. He doesn't remember much more. Would you like to try talking to him?"

"I'm not very good with kids."

"You've been great with the teens."

"They think I'm cool." She held up her left arm, showing off her tattoos.

"It's your choice, but I think you might be able to help Levi tap into a memory he doesn't know he has. Through hypnosis?"

"I call it hypnosis, but it's really just a heightened focus."

"Could you help him?"

"I can try."

"Now?"

"Lead the way."

Scott guided Fia into the library. In the lower level, he pushed into one of the classrooms, where they found Sister Cecilia waiting with Levi on a pair of cushions on the floor. Fia's core tightened as she took a seat beside them. In the time she had spent in the house, she had met the younger kids but not spent any real time with them. She really didn't know anything about how to deal with kids.

"Hi, Levi," she greeted him softly.

"Hi."

"Father Scott wanted to me to try a little memory trick with you, see if you could remember anything else about the lady who talked to you."

"Okay." He scooted on his cushion to face her. "What do I gotta do?"

Fia walked Levi through the first few steps, focusing his breathing to calm his mind and heart. "Tell me everything you could see in the museum. What were you looking at when the lady approached you?"

"We were looking at old weapons, arrowheads and knives. From the first people who lived here."

"Where did the woman come from?"

"Behind me. She knew my name was Levi and asked me if I lived . . ." He hesitated, long enough for Fia to wonder if she had lost his attention.

"Where, Levi? Where did she ask if you lived?"

"In a cabin."

"She asked if you lived in a cabin?"

"And she asked if I knew the red-haired lady. I think she meant the new lady that started coming around. Mother Agnes and the other sisters know her, so I think she's okay. I told the lady no." His eyes popped open, wet with tears. "I'm sorry I lied. I know I shouldn't ever lie, but I think she was a bad lady."

"I think she was too, Levi. Sometimes it's okay to lie to bad people."

"Fiammetta, we discourage the children—"

"I apologize, Sister Cecilia. I know that's true under normal circumstances, but don't you think it's also important for them to learn to trust their instincts? Levi may never be trained as a hunter, but he is still connected to them—to us—and apparently susceptible to dangerous people."

Sister Cecilia offered Fia a deep, respectful nod. "You may have a point, Fiammetta. I will let you continue."

"Levi, do you remember anything else? Sounds, smells? Did she have a smell you can remember?"

"No, I'm sorry, Fia."

"Don't apologize, Levi. You did fine. What did she look like?"

"Short white hair; tall, like Mother Agnes; white. I don't remember much else."

"Thank you, Levi. Fia, can I talk to you outside?" Father Scott reached for her hand to help her off the floor.

"Thank you, Levi." Out in the main space of the library, Fia turned to Scott. "What's up?"

"You know the woman." It wasn't a question.

"I don't know her; I've seen her. That's what I was going to see Zari about. She was in Zari's shop a few days ago looking for a quartz blade, which Zari didn't have, and then I saw her again a couple days later coming out of the shop having purchased something. But now I wonder if, the second time, she wasn't looking for me."

"Fia, I would like you to stay here until we figure out what is going on, until we are able to assess this threat more deeply."

"I can't. I have to take Max back to the city tomorrow. He has a rehearsal."

"Fia, I—"

"Scott, I know you're worried. But remember who you're talking to. I've been on my own for a long time. I don't think this threat on my life is new; I think we're just finding out about it. Irzelen said those demons were summoned because of me. No one just decided a month ago to summon a small army of demons. This has been in the works, maybe for years. I appreciate the concern, but I'll be fine."

Scott set his jaw and crossed his arms over his chest. "I cannot force you to stay. But I encourage it. One of the sisters can take Max—"

"I brought him here; I'll take him home. I can handle myself. I'll keep my head down and hide out in the condo. I'll come back up here as soon as I can." She studied his face for a long moment. "I promise. I'll be fine."

She pushed around him, ending the conversation, and headed back up the stairs. She headed for the kitchen, hoping to find Rebecca.

Outside the kitchen door, she heard Rebecca's voice asking someone to put paper towels in a basket. Expecting a response from one of the teens, she was surprised to hear Max's heavy baritone instead. She pushed through the door to find Max lining a wire basket with paper towels and Rebecca removing what looked like country-fried steaks from a deep fryer.

"Fia!" Max stepped around the nun and gathered Fia into a firm embrace. "How was your shower?"

"Lonely. Is it just the two of you in here?"

"Please don't say anything," Rebecca replied. "I asked Kaleb to take the night off and let me get to know Max a little better."

"Oh." Fia studied the situation, gauging what she had walked in on. "Can I help you two with anything?"

"I think we're pretty much finished. Someone needs to mash the potatoes," Rebecca answered.

Fia stepped around Max and headed for a utensil drawer. "I can do that." She found a manual potato masher in one of the drawers and stepped up to the pot of potatoes. "Do you add anything?"

"We had talked about sour cream and garlic," Max answered. "But you weren't asking me." He stepped back, tucking his chin into his chest.

Rebecca chuckled. "Do you think sour cream with the steaks and gravy?"

"Butter," Fia said, sticking her head in the refrigerator. She reemerged with a stick of butter and a jug of milk.

"I'm going to go get Kaleb," Rebecca announced, removing her apron, as Fia started working on the potatoes.

After she had disappeared through the back door, Max stepped in close behind Fia, wrapping his arms around her waist and kissing the back of her neck. "I'm sorry about earlier. I just felt weird about jumping in the shower with you after spending a day with nuns and impressionable teens."

"I get it. I guess I felt a little weird about it too. But you owe me." She turned her head to kiss his mouth. "So, what did you two talk about?"

Twenty-Seven

After dinner, Mercy asked if Max and Fia would be joining them in the rec room. "Oh, I don't . . ." Max looked to Fia.

Fia took in the hesitant expression on Max's face and shook her head. "I actually wanted to spend some time with the adults tonight. I think Annabel wanted to get to know Max a little better."

Mercy's face fell, but she recovered quickly. "Okay, we'll be in there for a while if you want to come in when you're finished." She turned and retreated toward the rec room.

"Rebecca thinks Mercy might have a crush on me," Max whispered after Mercy was out of sight.

"I can't say I blame her."

"Fia, that's—she's fourteen."

Fia laughed. "I didn't say I was going to encourage it. But I have a little crush on you too, so I can see the appeal. And I suppose, for a fourteen-year-old, having a bona fide rock star staying in her house—it's probably a little over-whelming. Not to mention a man who isn't a priest or—" Fia stopped herself before saying too much. "Someone she sees every day."

"You have—did Annabel really want to get to know me?"

"You looked desperate. I guess now I know why. Though I don't think Annabel wouldn't want to get to know you better. Should we go find her?"

"Why not?"

They headed toward the foyer in time to catch the nun headed up the stairs. "Sister Annabel," Fia called out. "Are you busy?"

Annabel leaned her lightly freckled face over the railing. "Fia, I—" She looked up the stairs in the direction she had been going. "No, I'm not busy. What do you need?" She turned and started back down the stairs to meet them.

"I don't need anything. Max and I wanted to talk to you. Just to get to know you. We've spent a little time with the others, but not much with you."

"Oh. Oh, I guess I have a little time. Would you like to sit in the library? Or there is still some daylight in the garden."

Fia waved to the door. "Garden sounds nice."

The three of them made their way out to the garden. Max looked around. "I didn't get a chance to look around the last time I was out here. It's pretty."

"Sister Rebecca does most of the tending. She teaches the children, but I think she enjoys doing most of the work herself. We get most of the produce we use, especially in the summer months, from this garden."

"How long have you been here, Sister?" Max asked.

Fia suddenly realized why she had wanted him to come out here with her. He was an outsider. He could get away with asking questions she didn't feel like she could.

"I guess it's been about eight months," Annabel replied.

"And you came here because you wanted to work with the hunters?"

"Sister Theresa and I did. We had had a little experience with the possessed in Las Cruces. When the space opened up here, we asked to be transferred. We had hoped we would get the chance to meet Fia. We were disappointed—or I was, at least—when we were told that was unlikely."

"You have a reputation?" Max asked Fia.

"I guess so. Which, no offense, Sister, is a little alarming, considering how I work."

"How's that?"

"I fly as far under the radar as possible. I guess I don't do much as far as using a fake name or anything like that, but hell, I had a mortgage on my condo so no one would get weird about a twenty-one-year-old kid buying a million-dollar condo in cash."

Beside her, Max choked. "I guess I shouldn't be surprised, in that neighborhood," he muttered.

"Sorry, I didn't mean—I was just pointing out that I try to keep pretty low-key. So the fact that you knew about me—I guess it's a little spooky to have a reputation when I've been trying so hard not to."

Annabel remained silent for the span of a couple of Fia's breaths. "I would like to know about you, Max. I don't believe Fia had mentioned a boyfriend at all, and then you showed up to get marked with the hunters. How long have you and Fia been together?"

"About . . . what? Six weeks? Three, if you don't consider the time I was on tour."

"Three—only three weeks. That is quite impressive. It seems they have been an intense three weeks, then?"

"They have been—interesting."

"I understand the risks involved with being part of this world," Fia cut in. "Max, whether he meant to be or not, is part of it now. More than anything, I wanted to avoid finding his information in one of Father Scott's packages. If he is marked, he can't be possessed. I wish I could mark the whole city."

The words hung on the air until Max changed the subject. "Sister Annabel, did you always want to do this? I don't mean—" He waved his arm at the house. "But take your vows, become a nun? Was that an aspiration in your childhood?"

"In a way, yes. I attended a Catholic school. The nuns there were very important to me. I would not say I had the best childhood, so I looked forward to the refuge school provided for me."

"What happened to you? I mean, as a kid?" Fia asked, now genuinely interested.

"It wasn't bad in the way most people expect. My family was influential, wealthy. I spent most of my time with house-keepers and nannies. And they cared for me, but the nuns— the nuns cared about me. I was impressionable, and they made an impression. I think, in a way, the modesty and minimalistic lifestyle were appealing after the lavishness I was accustomed to."

Annabel turned her attention to her watch—the same modest, no-frills sport watch as the others wore. "I apologize for cutting this short. I have to get to my quarters. It is past prayer time."

"Oh, right, sorry," Fia said, embarrassed. "You could have just said—"

"Nonsense. I have enjoyed talking with you, Fia. As I have mentioned before, you were a bit of an idol to me."

"You did mention something like that, yes."

The three of them stood. Fia grabbed Max's hand as Annabel turned toward the house. "I think we'll stay out here, enjoy what's left of the sun," Fia said with a smile.

"Very well." The nun offered them a shallow bow and left them alone.

"Is something wrong?" Max asked after Annabel was out of sight.

Fia put her finger to her lips and shook her head. She pulled out her phone and typed furiously into a text message. *I don't know who I can trust.* She motioned for him to look at his phone, then beckoned for him to follow her. She led him through the trees to the clearing, then on past it.

"I think we can talk out here."

"How do you know you can trust me?"

Fia leveled her eyes at Max. "Call it instinct; call it blind faith. Let's just say the cards are in your favor. I know I've got you and Scott. Agnes and Cecilia are wild cards. My history tells me to trust them, but the evidence suggests they could be at the top of the list."

"Evidence?"

"Max, there's something I didn't tell you. There are probably a lot of things I haven't told you, but not intentionally. There's just a lot—that night at your show, when you found me lying on the pavement? I had seen that guy before."

"Right, the phoenix—"

"No. I mean yes, but also while you were gone. He cornered me in a garage on a job."

"Okay. I hate to say this, Fia, but I didn't see any *guy.*

There was that bird and—shit, I don't even know what else I saw."

"No, I know, that's what I'm trying—I'm trying not to sound crazy. Because I feel crazy. He's—all of this started because a demon guard in Hell set his prisoners loose, sending them back here to the mortal world. That guy—that thing—that was him, the demon. He calls himself Irzelen—or we do, I'm not sure—and he told me that the zombies—that guy who was attacking people outside Kate's bar? Those things are demons too. They were summoned by a human who doesn't know what they're doing. Because of me. Irzelen wanted me to—the only plausible way to break the bond between demon and summoner is to kill the summoner. Irzelen wants his demons back, and he wants me to get them."

"Why doesn't he just—"

"Divine law? Apparently, demons and angels risk losing their immortality if they harm a mortal—"

"He dropped you from seven feet in the air—"

"Either way, I've been recruited. I guess it's mutually beneficial."

"He wants you to kill someone. That doesn't sound beneficial."

"Getting rid of the demons does. Anyway, I don't know who it is. But the worst part is, Agnes and Cecilia have known me longer than anyone. Who else would summon demons to deal with me?"

Max studied her face for a moment. "How do you know you can trust the demon? A demon, Fia—you are letting a demon turn you against people who are fighting the same fight you are."

"Just one person."

"But you don't know which one person."

"No. I don't." She buried her face in her hands. "I don't, and it's making me suspect everyone—except you and Scott—"

"You said that. You didn't say why."

"Scott—there's just something about him. Also not my secret to tell. But you—Zari has warned me all along not to take the cards seriously, but there was a card, and I knew right away it was telling me to trust you."

"Cards?"

"Tarot. Zari reads tarot cards. She read for me and told me someone close to me was stabbing me in the back and if I didn't take care of it, it would all end in flames."

"Fia." He pulled her into his chest. "Fia, you can't base your decisions on tarot cards."

"I'm not. I mean, I am, but the cards supported what the demon said, and I don't see a reason for the demon to lie to me."

"To get you to do his dirty work?"

"I don't think it's that. I just really don't think it's that."

"Okay, Fia, I trust you. So what do we do?"

She raised her hands in defeat. "I don't even know. I've just been watching, listening, but I'm not making sense of what I'm hearing. I overheard a conversation before I came back to town to get you."

"You were here? I thought you were on a job."

"I was ducking you, okay. I knew you wouldn't let me keep my distance, and I didn't know if I could, so I ducked you. I was afraid if you were close, you'd get in trouble. That demon—those demons showed up at your gig."

"Demons? Plural? I thought you said just one."

"I technically didn't specify, but I led one—like that dude from the bar—out the back door. That's where Irzelen found me."

"Maybe we should get back. Before someone wonders where we went."

"Maybe. Max, I should never have come back here."

"Doesn't sound like you had much choice."

"Maybe not. But if someone here is—I walked in here with a target on my back. Did I make it bigger? Or easier? And have I put everyone else in danger by being here?"

"You came back here before you knew, right?" Max asked. Fia shrugged. "Just saying, you couldn't have done things any differently."

She stared silently into his eyes for a long moment before motioning him back to the house. "Let's head back." She looped her arm through his, resting her head on his shoulder as they walked.

TWENTY-EIGHT

The following morning, Fia eased the Scout into the little parking lot outside what looked like the shell of a Mexican restaurant. The side windows had been bricked over, their arches left behind, and the new brick had been painted to match the orange-sherbet color of the rest of the exterior. Decorative tile mosaics had been removed, their ghosts still visible beneath the same paint.

Two large bay windows had been left at the front, flanking a heavy, ornate oak door. A gold plate on the door was the only visible indication that they were in the right place. *Hacienda Studios.*

Clever, Fia thought, pulling up parallel to the front of the building. Max stayed firmly planted in the passenger seat. Fia watched him for a moment.

"Is everything okay?"

Max laughed mirthlessly. "Everything is weird."

"I guess I can give you that."

"No, Fia, that's not—this—" He waved his hand at the studio building. "This is everything I have ever wanted since

I was ten years old and really grasped that it could be everything I ever wanted. Everything, Fia. Do you understand that? But the last couple of days, I've been part of a whole different world, and while I wouldn't give up music for anything, I'm now trying to figure out whether I could take out zombies with my drumsticks. And yes, I know that thing at the bar wasn't a zombie, but you know what I mean."

"Rock-star soul hunter."

"Something."

"Max, I'm glad you—maybe *enjoyed* isn't the right word—felt like you fit in. I think you did too. I am also scared to death that you're going to get hurt or killed or worse."

"What's worse?" It was a genuine question, Fia realized, based on all he had learned over the few days in the mountains.

She shrugged. "I don't want to find out. Do you?"

"Probably not."

They sat quietly for another moment before Fia spoke again. "You're going to be late."

"I know. But I'm not ready to leave you. You've made me soft, Fia Drake."

"You already were soft."

"Hey!" Max made a big deal of pouting as Fia reached across him and pushed his door open.

"Don't make your band hate me for making you late to rehearsal."

"A drummer is never early or late."

"Max!"

"I'm going. I'm going." He turned in his seat to face her, drawing her close with one hand against the side of her neck. He pressed a firm, hungry kiss to her mouth.

"When should I be back?" she asked once he had released her.

"What do you mean?"

"Are you going to have one of them bring you to get your car?"

"Fia? We're—I'm not going home." Fia felt a wave of confusion pass over her. Max must have been able to read it on her face. "We've got four more shows on the road. I know I told you."

Fia felt her guts twist as confusion turned to guilt. He had told her. Maybe more than once. And she had forgotten. Fever touched the tips of her ears and flushed through her cheeks.

"Shit, Max, I'm so sorry. I forgot."

He waved a hand dismissively, looking away from her. "It's not a big deal. I'll be back in a week." He reached up, cradling her jaw in both hands. "Come with us. I mean, not with us, but follow us. Meet us in Albuquerque tomorrow night."

She thought about it.

She thought about it seriously for a moment.

Someone here was looking for her. Scott wanted her at the safe house, but wouldn't following Max's band on the road be just as safe?

The *cha-ching* of an antique cash register rang out from her pocket. Someone had put something in her drop box. She couldn't leave with a bounty on the line. Even if it was just for a couple of days.

"I can't. That sound was a new job."

Max nodded sadly, kissed her again, and climbed out of the SUV. He turned and made his way into the building without turning to look back at her. When he was gone, she slammed her palms against the steering wheel, scolding herself for forgetting something so important to Max.

It's not going to be a demon that hurts him worse than death. It's going to be you.

She pulled the SUV back out into the traffic of the main drag and headed for the drop box.

Three hundred bounties.

Of course, she hadn't kept an exact running total, but at the rate of one and a half per month, every month for seven years, it was a fair estimate. There had been a few she had lost and a few times she had taken down three in four weeks, but it averaged out.

She hadn't perched, legs dangling precariously over the edge, on three hundred ledges of three hundred roofs, the way she sat now, but she thought half that was a safe wager. She had seen angles and views of this city most people would never imagine, let alone experience for themselves.

Today, she was having trouble focusing on the city stretched out below her. Voices in her head—the echoes of several very long days—nearly drowned out the sounds of traffic she normally found so relaxing.

I'm not going home. We've got four more shows on the road. I know I told you.

Max had been hurt. He should have been hurt she had forgotten. He had every right to be. What she hated more was how much his pain had hurt her.

He, too, seems to be a bit of a natural.

She had thought about what Theresa had said over and over since Max had joked about stabbing monsters with his sticks. From what Fia had seen, he had taken to the cross-bow quickly. She had already considered letting him in on a hunt, even before taking him to the safe house. Maybe all this was an indication she should.

Distracted by the attack coming from within her memories, Fia almost missed the reason she was on the roof in the first place.

She had initially cursed Scott for waiting until she was in the city to deliver her next bounty when he could have simply handed it to her over breakfast at the safe house, especially after the fuss he had made over her safety.

But when she had opened the envelope, something felt different. The cash was there, just as it always was, but this was more of what she had gotten while she thought Scott was dead. Barely any information, no real surveillance. And judging from the timeline of his crimes, she had barely any time to catch the host before the soul abandoned him and moved on.

What she did know was that her target, Thad Osterman, was an intern for one of the city's celebrity ambulance chasers, the kind with a face made for the side of a bus. Thad Osterman was also playing taxi for the fugitive soul of a true lady killer. By the time Fia had picked up the envelope, he had picked up three women in three bars and strangled them in nearby alleys.

He was currently trolling downtown bars looking for a fourth victim.

Strange movement at street level caught Fia's attention, drawing her out of her mind. The man whose face had been in her bounty packet was staggering drunkenly away from a bar, half led, half dragged by a fit-looking woman, abnormally tall, with snowy-white hair in a short bob that exposed her long neck. Fia guessed from her physique, visible even at this distance, that she could probably take care of herself.

In normal circumstances.

These were not normal circumstances.

Fia had learned firsthand that while the souls did not endow their hosts with immeasurable super strength, they did get a lot, as well as an unimaginable tolerance for pain and a fair amount of speed and agility. She didn't think she could get to the street in time to save the woman; she would have to try to hit Thad Osterman from here.

She climbed down off the ledge and readied her bow. Looking at the pair through her scope, she gasped.

This wasn't just any stout-looking platinum blonde. This was the woman from Zari's shop. The woman Fia suspected had cornered Levi in the museum. Fia looked over the lens at the pair, then back through the lens. Her heart pounded in her ears as she wondered what this woman was doing with her bounty.

As she watched, the blonde woman turned, nudging the drunk man into an alley. Except Thad Osterman, Fia's bounty, was more than just faking drunk to get the woman to leave with him. He showed distinct signs of being drugged.

Half a block down the alley, a priest stood concealed from the street. Fia turned her scope toward him as soon as she noticed this. It was the same man she had seen looking paranoid as he crossed the threshold into Armando Ariaz's inner office. Older, midfifties or early sixties, close-cropped white hair with flushed cheeks and a potbelly.

The blonde woman led her captive to stand in front of the priest.

Fia looked up over the top of her scope, hoping she

could see details without the magnification, but the distance was too great. She put her eye back against the glass and continued watching.

Two more men came out of the shadows as the blonde woman propped Thad Osterman against the wall. Each of them took hold of one of his arms, and the woman drew a knife from her belt.

Fia's head bounced frantically between looking through the scope and trying to see with her naked eye. She didn't need psychic abilities to know what was coming. She herself was preparing to do a similar job, but when she was finished, the soul would be contained and sent back to the underworld. She had doubts that it would stay there, but that wasn't Fia's immediate concern.

Guaranteed, though, this woman facing Thad Osterman with her knife drawn had no intention of sending the soul back to Hell. Fia's heart raced as she watched the scene unfold. The priest was making gestures, chanting something Fia couldn't hear from this distance. Out on the street, a pair of women, wrapped lovingly in each other's arms, were moving toward the scene, unaware of what they were approaching.

The woman took a step closer to Thad Osterman, her long, thin blade glinting in the streetlight. She had gotten the quartz blade she had wanted Zari to sell her. Not from Zari, Fia was certain, but from somewhere.

In a flash, the blade severed Thad Osterman's throat, spilling blood down his chest and spraying it across her face. Unperturbed, the blonde woman stood motionless as the two men let the host crumple to the pavement.

On the street, one of the women lurched, diving at her partner. She pushed the other woman into an inset doorway, hands closing furiously around her throat.

In the alley, the piranha demons descended on the corpse, devouring it in a ravenous blur as the four humans watched.

Elsewhere on the street, also seemingly unprovoked, two men started throwing punches—hard, driving punches meant to break bones—until they drove one another to the pavement. The one with the upper hand grabbed the other by the sides of his head and slammed his skull into the asphalt.

Fia made a snap decision. She flipped the switch on the collar and hurled it over the side of the building, aiming for the escalating chaos below. She ducked below her perch, scrambling as low as she could toward the Scout parked at the back of the level, near the exit. She drove it down to the next level and pulled as close as she could to the open edge, climbing out to peek through. Here, she felt a little more protected.

On the street, the screaming had stopped. In fact, everything had stopped. Twenty or twenty-five people lay motionless, unconscious, on the sidewalk, including the four who had caused the ruckus, as an angel assessed the situation. Fia guessed that when he had arrived, the soul was gone.

Or worse, it had already inhabited a new host.

The angel stepped diligently around each of the bodies. At each, he lifted their heads from the ground and peeled open their eyelids, looking into their eyes. Satisfied—or maybe not—with one, he returned them gingerly to the ground and moved on to the next. After he had checked each body, he picked the collar up out of the middle of the street and glittered out of existence.

Once his shimmer was completely gone, the people strewn where they had fallen began to regain consciousness.

Bewildered, they clambered to their feet, looking around for some explanation of what had happened.

Fia wondered as well.

She guessed the angel hadn't found the soul in any of them. So where did it go? She slid down the concrete half wall, drew her knees to her chest, and buried her head in her hands, rubbing hard enough at her temples to expect bruises to form. "Well, that was a disaster," she scolded herself aloud, grateful for the empty space. She let a few seconds pass before finding her feet again, driving one of them into the wall with an animal shriek.

She didn't even care if the people at street level heard her. What difference would it make now? Their night had already gotten weird; what was one more screaming woman? She climbed into the SUV, wishing there was another way out of the garage besides through the crowd.

Considering the whole mission a disaster, Fia wound the red SUV up and down one-way streets with her windows down and radio up, letting the city night cleanse her mind. She wasn't going anywhere, just driving, running away from the chaos that had just unfolded before her. Late night on the radio was practically all music, several songs playing in a row before a commercial interrupted the flow. There was no disc jockey to distract from heavy drums and intricate guitar solos, screaming singers and throbbing bass lines.

She would eventually need to make her way back into the mountains, clean out the bunker, and burn the remnants of Thad Osterman in the pit outside. But for now, she just wanted to drive.

Fia combed through her memories, trying to find the itinerary for Max's mini tour. They had started in Albuquerque. She thought the next stop was a small town in

Oklahoma, before circling up through Kansas and back home. By the time she had wound her way to the avenue that would eventually meet back up with the interstate east of the city, she thought she could be in central Kansas in plenty time to see him.

Skin to skin. For years, Fia had used someone else's flesh to decompress, to reconnect with her own humanity. Flesh with only a first name, sometimes not even that much.

Max Hawkins was somewhere between the panhandle of Oklahoma and the middle of Kansas, with a *last* name—worse, with a story she was learning—and with warm, inviting skin she wanted to feel against her own. With her mind made up, she turned the wheel toward the best route east; the interstate ran right through the town where she would find him.

As she drove, the city grew smaller; the lights, less bright. Soon, she was past the streetlamps and storefront signs, and the silver blue of moonlit cheatgrass and wildflowers stretched as far as she could see. At this time of the night, there was virtually no one on the road, and she could open up and drive. She eased her way around a lonely eighteen-wheeler, and everything ahead was clear.

She thought she should feel foolish for what she was doing, but she only felt determined. No longer was she running from the nightmare scene she had left downtown or the burden of her mantle. She would return to all that darkness after spending some time in Max's light.

She hadn't lied; she really had reached a point of not trusting anyone but Max and Scott. And Zari. The three people who had proven there was no reason not to trust them.

Fia pressed on the gas pedal, watching the needle on the

speedometer climb above the limit posted on the sign she blew past. Soon, the headlights of the semi were a distant memory, and she was alone on the interstate.

She was nearly to the state line when her headlights caught a void in the horizon. She swerved into the left lane and slammed on the breaks, coming to a stop a few feet from the demon.

Irzelen stood waiting for her in full demon form in the middle of the eastbound interstate. She left her headlights on him and slowly stepped out of the vehicle, leaving the door open behind her.

"How does that divine-law thing work if you cause that semi behind me to wreck trying not to hit you?"

"He would not."

"Oh, okay, so you're just out here for my benefit? He's not that far behind me."

"He will not catch up to you while I am here."

Thinking back to the scene on the street, Fia stepped back to the SUV and glanced in at the navigation panel. An analog clock sat among the other gauges and dials, and she focused on the thin red line of the second hand. It had stopped moving. She flipped on her hazard lights—just in case—cut the engine, and closed the door.

"Next question: what happens to me when you guys stop time like this? Because I'm pretty sure this is the second time it's happened to me—*today*—and I'm wondering if I should be concerned about premature aging. Or never aging beyond this point. Because I'll be honest, I get that you guys are attached to it, but as a mortal, I'm not excited about the prospect of immortality."

The demon's yellow-gold gemstone eyes glinted against the moonlight, trained on her, burning into her. After a long moment, his voice rattled its way through her skull. *"Are you finished, mortal?"*

"Mortal? What happened to my name?"

Flesh ripped and bones cracked, and soon the space was occupied by the human form she had originally encountered in the parking garage with the still-living corpse of one of her bounties wasting away at her feet.

"Are you any closer to retrieving my property?"

"Maybe thinking of them as property is what made it so easy for this human to usurp them from you."

In a blink, he was on her, his thick, heavy hand on her throat. "I could crush your throat, and you would never even know what happened."

"And then you would lose your wings, or whatever happens when you become mortal—except you don't look like a mortal. Even in this suit, you look superhuman. I guess you would fit in with the basketball players, maybe football."

Irzelen squeezed in response, and Fia coughed involuntarily. She was ready for someone to punch her in the gut, hit her in the head with a two-by-four—anything but strangle her. She reached up and clawed at his wrist, wishing she didn't keep her fingernails cut to the quick.

As her vision began to darken at the edges, he let go, backing away a step. He loomed over her, waiting for her to catch her breath before speaking again.

"You have a job to complete. Are you any closer to finishing?"

"No. I'm not. You've got me running around inside my own head, blaming everyone who looks at me weird, questioning everyone—"

"You are not questioning your practitioner. Or your lover."

"Ick. No. Are you saying I should?" He remained silent. "Hey, you left this up to me. You didn't offer me anything in the way of clues. I'm just flying by the seat of my pants out here, looking for someone who hates me enough to summon a whole army of demons to deal with me. I appreciate the urgency. I'm not any more excited about those things roaming my streets than you are. But I'm doing the best I can. And I'm not going to let you drag Zari or Max into it. I've absolved them. I need to be able to trust someone."

"Aye, perhaps you are correct. I sent you to do this job because of your reputation—"

"There's that word again."

"I beg your pardon?"

"Nothing. Never mind. It's not your problem. What do you mean, because of my reputation?"

"Had I not thought you possessed the proper skill and lack of mercy to dispatch this summoner, I would likely have let the demons devour you."

"Let?"

"I would not have warned you."

"Swell. I guess a thank-you is in order."

"Do not thank me. You have a job, and I suggest you complete it. Your time is running out."

"Do you know something I should know?"

His silence in response made Fia shiver despite the heat from the asphalt. After a long moment, he simply repeated his previous threat. He punctuated it with a shift, resuming his demon form. In a manner similar to the angels, he shimmered out of view, and Fia was alone, standing in the middle of the interstate.

It took her a second to realize she was going to need to move. Irzelen might have been holding time for the duration of their conversation, but now that he was gone, that tractor trailer would be bearing down on her any minute. She climbed back into the SUV and started the engine.

She continued the way she had been going, now more determined than ever to find Max and the rest of the band.

Twenty-Nine

Fia reached Hays, Kansas, shortly after dawn. By the time she had taken a quick tour around the small town to find where Wyldfire might be playing, she was ready for breakfast and a nap. She found a small motel that looked locally owned, hoping that would mean they wouldn't be full and she could get into a room immediately. Once she had secured a room, she walked across the parking lot to the adjoining diner.

Of course, Max was excited to see her. Once the band had finished loading out, he told the others he would leave with Fia and meet up with them the following day to pick up his gear from the trailer. Fia took her time driving them back, following the sun west. By the time she pulled into the studio parking lot, shadows stretched their fingers across it, reaching to devour her car. Max punched a code into a panel next to the studio door, and the two of them made their way through the shadows.

"Looks like no one's here," he said, leading her to a

bank of steel cabinets at the back of the building. "Want a tour?"

Fia cocked an eyebrow. "Is that okay?"

Max shrugged. "It's not *not* okay." He tried the handle on a door close to the cabinets and found it locked. "All right, maybe it's not okay. Anyway, this is where we recorded our album. We play in there, and the mixing boards and stuff are in there." He pointed to another door not far from the first.

"And all my stuff is in here. At least, I hope it is." He pulled out his keys and used a small silver one to unlock one of the cabinets. Inside was a collection of round black cases, some hard leather like her guitar case, others soft and made of nylon. He started pulling them out one by one, looking at each before setting them on the ground beside him.

Fia reached for a small hard case, and Max shook his head. "That's not mine. Mine all have a blue star stamped by the latch. It's embroidered on the soft cases."

"Clever." She picked up another case. Finding the blue star, she moved it out of the pile, grabbed another, and carried both to the parking lot. She propped the door open with a rock before she got too far and couldn't get back in.

With ten cases loaded into the back of the Scout, Max locked everything back up, double-checked it, and climbed back into the SUV.

"How do we get—"

Fia was interrupted by her phone. *Scott.* "Hang on." She tapped the green button to connect the call.

Scott began speaking as soon as she did, not giving her a chance to speak. "Fia, I need you to come to the safe house."

"Now?"

"As soon as possible, please. Is Max with you? I know he was out of town . . ."

Fia looked over at Max, sitting in the passenger seat. She didn't like the sound of Scott's voice. He sounded almost panicked. She put the phone on speaker and held it out where Max could hear too.

"Yeah, he's here. What—"

"I think it might be best if you bring him with you when you come."

"What's wrong?"

"I think I would prefer to tell you in person."

Max turned to Fia, his brow furrowed, but remained quiet.

"We need to drop something off in the Tech Center first—"

"We can leave it at your apartment," Max offered. "I'm fine with that if you are. It's more on the way."

"As soon as possible, Fia, please," Scott pleaded. His tone prickled her skin.

"Yeah, sure. We'll be there in about an hour."

She disconnected the call and turned wide eyes to Max. "I don't like the sound of *that*."

"He sounded pretty freaked," Max agreed.

"Yeah. I guess we're headed back into the mountains."

When they pulled the Scout into the large clearing outside the safe house, Scott was waiting for them under the open garage door. Fia noticed the large green van was missing from the collection of cars and wondered if that had anything to do with Scott's panicked demeanor.

He beckoned them to follow him and led them through the garage, through the kitchen, and out the back door. To the right of the door was a small opening barely large enough for an average adult to squeeze through and a set of concrete stairs leading belowground. At the bottom, they reached a steel door and, beyond that, an unfinished basement area.

The floor was concrete, and the walls were bare drywall. Floor joists and insulation were visible overhead, and one lonely bulb in the center of the joists illuminated a small portion of the floor. Seven folding chairs had been arranged in a circle around the pool of light; four of them were occupied by the nuns—save for Cecilia—and three sat open, awaiting Fia's arrival with Max.

Along the back wall, across from the entrance they came in by, was another steel door, this one with a heavy padlock on the latch. To the left of it was a pegboard lined with weapons: crossbows in a variety of sizes and complexity, the two-handed sword Rebecca favored, a katana, and a collection of daggers.

"What's going on?" Fia asked as the three of them claimed their seats. "Where is Cecilia?"

"That is part of why we are here," Agnes replied. "Sister Cecilia has taken the young children to another location."

"Because of the lady at the museum?"

"More has developed in the interim. Kaleb called us from school. A man approached him during his meal break. Sister Theresa should tell you more; she is the one who took the call."

"The school security intervened," Theresa said, picking up the story. "But not before the man could ask about you and our location."

"Did someone go get them?" Fia asked. "It doesn't seem safe to leave them—"

"Father Donovan picked them up immediately follow-ing—"

"Father Donovan?" Fia turned wide eyes to Scott, before remembering she hadn't told her handler about the unexceptional but twitchy priest she had seen with Armando Ariaz.

For that matter, she hadn't had a chance to tell Scott what had happened before she took off to meet up with Max. She made a note to come back to it and continued questioning the decision to have this priest, who may or may not be working for the bad guys, pick the hunters up from their schools.

"Are they coming back here? How long ago did he pick them up? Shouldn't they be back by now?"

"Fia, they are not coming back here," Rebecca replied. "Father Donovan has been instructed to take them to an undisclosed location. Only when we are sure the threat is neutralized will it be safe to contact him—as well as Sister Cecilia and the younger children—to bring them back here."

Fia nodded, feeling panic wash through her, a panic that was amplified by the stress in Rebecca's voice. *She's not happy about this decision either.*

"Okay, so we have four hunters-in-training on their way to . . . somewhere, with someone who may be a black hat, and the only way to find them is to hope the black hat answers the phone when we call. Solid plan."

"Fia, what do you mean, *black hat?*" Annabel asked.

You tell me, Sister, Fia thought, with enough venom, she was certain everyone would be able to hear it. Aloud, she said, "I am not positive, but based on the description I got from Father Scott, Father Donovan may have a connection to the demons."

"From the cave?" Rebecca asked.

"Yeah. I don't think I ever got that full story out, what with Annabel's snake, but the head demon, Irzelen, suggested those demons were summoned to *take care* of me—in *The Godfather* sense, not the kindly nurse sense."

"Summoned?" Theresa asked, her eyes wide. "By whom?"

Fia shrugged, grateful no one had noticed the barb she had thrown at Annabel for being so intimate with the creature in the garden.

"Really don't know. I don't *trust* Irzelen, but I also question what motive he would have for lying to me. He said he can't track the summoner because the demons have left a shadow on them. I don't pretend to fully understand everything he said, other than he's bound by his own cultural laws that he can't intentionally harm me—or any human—without risking the loss of his immortality. He kind of recruited me to handle his problem, which he claimed was also my problem."

"And you believe him?" Rebecca challenged.

"I do. Call it instinct, but I don't think there is any reason for him to lie about this. I get the feeling if it weren't for these demons being abducted from Hell—the underworld—he would be completely disconnected from anything humanity did, ever. I don't think he honestly cares about humans at all, positively or negatively. I think he's disdainfully indifferent."

"So you think Father Donovan has had something to do with summoning these demons?" Annabel asked, returning to the original topic.

"I know that hinky priest, Armando Ariaz, has something to do with the demons, and I think Father Donovan has had something to do with Ariaz."

And you.

Of course, if Father Donovan was still involved in the teens' lives, it would make sense for Annabel to be associating with him. But not for him to be associating with Ariaz. Fia sighed, trying to make her head stop spiraling around the dozen or more theories she was developing in the moment.

Fia looked around the circle at the faces staring back at her. Desperate to get the attention off herself and the bombs she had just dropped, she dove back in.

"Okay, we don't know where the hunters are, which means the blonde woman shouldn't either. Or the man who approached Kaleb. Did he say anything else about the man? A description?"

Theresa shook her head. "Not much I took as useful. He said the man was large. Tall and broad, the kind where his shoulders extend from his jaw—"

Fia groaned. "I was afraid of that."

"Pardon? Do you know this man?"

Fia shook her head. "If it's who I think it is, I don't know him, but he works for Ariaz. Hired muscle of some kind."

"Why does a priest need muscle?" Max asked, speaking, Fia thought, for the first time since they had pulled off the interstate, maybe even since they had left the city.

Fia put her hands in the air, defeated. "The same reason he needs demons? Beats the hell out of me." She pressed her hands into her forehead and ran them back through her hair. "What now? The kids are—hopefully—safe. Are we just hunkering down here? Because I don't love that idea."

"Fia," Scott said, "I asked you and Max to come here to ensure your safety. Two people now have approached the children to inquire about you. You think the woman was also looking for you in your friend's shop. I think it is best—"

"No offense, but it's best if I go hunt down these creeps

and—I am not going to simply sit here on my ass, waiting to find out if or when someone is going to do something. I am taking the fight to them. I've had run-ins with Ariaz; he knows what's coming. Well,"—she patted her thigh—"not exactly what's coming, but I think I scared him the last time I was there."

Rebecca shifted in her seat. She cleared her throat before speaking, her voice strained and angry. "I think Fia's right. I think we should take the fight—"

"Sister Rebecca." Agnes cut the younger nun off before she could finish her thought. "We discussed this."

Fia raised an eyebrow. "Discussed what?"

Neither woman replied. They stared into one another's eyes, locked in a silent battle. From the expressions on the faces of the other two nuns, Fia deduced it was a battle only Agnes and Rebecca understood.

She tried again. "Discussed what? I don't think this is—"

"Fiammetta, this is between—"

"I should have been the one to take the children," Rebecca blurted. "Reverend Mother knows that, but she sent Cecilia instead, and now I don't know—"

She bit her lip, interrupting herself, and turned her face away from the circle. She released a deep, shuddering sigh before returning her attention to the circle. "I should have been the one to take the children."

Silence enveloped the room for a long moment before Annabel broke it. "Rebecca? You know they are safe with Sister Cecilia. Everything is going to be okay."

"With all due respect, Sister Annabel, you don't understand any of what is going on." Rebecca growled, standing up from her chair. She crossed to the weapons and pulled down her sword. "Fia, I'm coming with you."

Agnes was the next to find her feet. "Sister Rebecca, please sit down. No one is going anywhere. We are going to stay here, where we are—"

"Where we're what?" Fia interrupted, standing to join the others. "Safe? If we were safe, there would be nine more of us here than there are now."

She turned to Rebecca. Fia was ready for a fight, but Rebecca was not. Rebecca was angry, and anger, Fia had learned, was the fastest path to terrible decisions. She couldn't take Rebecca into the city to confront Ariaz. She tried to defuse the situation, crossing the room to grip the nun by the shoulder.

"I don't think we're safe here, but maybe the others are right. Maybe we should wait, see what happens."

Rebecca turned deep brown eyes to Fia. They were edged in tears but flashed wildly. "If you're not going, I'll go. I'm not afraid of this Ariaz."

"Rebecca, do you know who he is?" Annabel asked, joining them. The others followed behind her, closing a circle around Rebecca.

Rebecca froze for a moment, studying Annabel's face. "Are you accusing me of something?"

Annabel raised her hands and took a step backward. "No, not at all. But how can you not fear him if you don't know him. Fia has met him; she knows the kind of threat he may pose. I would venture that Fia would be able to obtain and maintain the upper hand, should it come to physical combat—"

"Oh, if I go down there, it's going to get physical," Fia announced. "There is no question of that. Which is why I think, maybe, we should stay put for a little while." She reached for Rebecca's sword.

Rebecca raised the sword as Fia advanced. "No, Fia. My mind is made up. I'm going, with or without—"

In a moment, Scott had Rebecca off her feet, dangling a few inches above the ground, his arms tight around her torso, pinning her arms to her sides. Agnes stepped between Fia and Rebecca, wrenching the sword from the younger woman's grip.

"Sister Rebecca, I think it might be best if you spent a little time in your quarters, focusing on your calming rituals. Should this threat come to us directly, you will be of no use to us in your current condition." Agnes nodded to Scott, who gently returned Rebecca to her feet.

"Are you calm? If I let you go, are you going to stay calm?"

Rebecca snarled before responding. "Yes, sir."

"I think it might be beneficial for all of us to take a little time," Annabel added. "If there truly is something coming, cooler heads will be important."

"That is an excellent point, Sister Annabel," Agnes agreed. "We should all retire to our quarters. We can reconvene for dinner." To punctuate her statement, the elder nun turned and peeled off from the group.

Fia glanced at her phone. An hour until dinner. With everyone in their rooms. She looked at Max from the corner of her eye. He was the wild card, but she was certain she could figure that out.

THIRTY

Outside the bedroom, Fia pressed a hand against Max's chest. "Wait here? I have something I need to ask Scott, then I'll be in."

Max nodded and pulled her close. He kissed her forehead and released her. "I'll be waiting." He gave her a sly wink and disappeared into the room, closing the door behind him.

Fia had no intention of asking Scott anything, but it was an easy lie. Instead, she returned to the kitchen and cut through to the garage, hoping this path would keep her from running into anyone she might otherwise encounter on her way to the front door. She exited through the side door, grateful she didn't have to figure out what to do with the bay doors; she hadn't thought that far ahead.

She crossed the driveway to where she had left the Scout. She opened the back hatch, pulling out the guitar case that held her crossbow, closed the hatch, and headed back to the driver's door. She opened the door, and keeping her attention focused on the house to make sure she was still moving unnoticed, she reached to put the guitar case in the passenger seat.

She jumped when she finally saw him.

Max sat straight in the passenger seat, his eyes on the trees ahead. He didn't look at her and didn't even flinch when she nearly sat the case in his lap.

"If you're going," he said quietly, "I'm coming too."

Fia studied his profile for a long moment. His sharp square jaw was set slightly forward, his full lips turned down in a frown.

She rubbed her hands against her forehead. Then she put the case in the back seat and climbed into the front. Max strapped on his seat belt and reached to close the door he had left open after following her.

"Damn it, Max, I don't want anyone to come with me. I don't know how this is going to end, and I'd rather have everyone here, as far from me as they can get."

"You're going to have to physically remove me from this car."

Until we get where we're going, and then I'll have to handcuff you to the steering wheel.

He wasn't going to let her go alone, and she wasn't going to let him watch her murder a man. She slammed her open palms against the steering wheel and climbed out of the car, dragging the case out of the back and slamming the door.

Max climbed out after her and gestured for her to walk ahead of him.

Back inside, Scott stood in the center of the foyer, his arms crossed over his chest. "I'm glad you decided to stay, Fia."

She narrowed her eyes and, for half a second, considered lying and telling him she was just going out to get her weapon. But she guessed he would know, the same way he had known she was leaving. Max hadn't had time to tell him and sneak out the front.

"Yeah." She turned to face Max, who was standing close enough to touch her but with his hands shoved deep in his pockets. "Give me a minute? I really do want to run something by Father Scott."

Max hesitated, meeting her eyes with his own narrowed suspiciously.

"We won't leave the foyer," Scott offered reassuringly.

"Fine." Max reached out and took the guitar case from Fia's hand and headed toward the bedroom.

When he was gone, Scott spoke again. "What's wrong?"

"Two nights ago—Jesus, that was only two nights ago—I had a job that went . . . way sideways."

"Oh?"

She quickly told him the story of Thad Osterman and the blonde woman who murdered him. "So, it kind of looked like the angel didn't find the soul to turn over to the little demon—by the way, that was kind of mind-blowing to learn. Your angsty angel, the one I met in the park, just handed the soul—I guess it was the soul; it was like a puff—well, you know. And the little demon just—" She made a sucking noise through her lips, imitating drinking from a straw. "Then the whole thing was over."

Lines of concern cut through Scott's weary but youthful face. "Mortals—" He scratched his head, more out of worry than confusion. "You should not have seen that."

"I guessed as much. But I would wager there has been a lot I shouldn't have seen over the years." Scott cocked an eyebrow and bobbed his head in a gesture Fia took to mean she was probably right. "What's the plan? What do we think is coming? Are you worried about that priest?"

"You do not know for sure that it has been Father Donovan you have seen? Why did you not express this concern previously?"

That was a fair question. "I wasn't sure," she said with a shrug. "I thought maybe I'd get a chance to confront him directly. Or ask Ariaz who he was."

"Why would you rely on information from an enemy over asking me?"

"Your judgment is clouded. I've learned over the years, if you want dirt on the allies, you get it from the enemy. Is there some reason he would be involved with Ariaz that isn't nefarious?"

"Not officially. I must say, Fia, I have no reason to doubt Father Donovan's commitment to our cause or the hunters. However, your claims have me concerned that there may be something more . . ."

She waited a beat for him to finish. When he didn't, she pressed. "More?"

"More sinister. I am concerned that Donovan has been working against his will."

"What kind of leverage would someone have against a priest?"

"He has a family, a sister for certain. I believe his mother is also still alive. His sister has children. It is also possible Ariaz is simply threatening Donovan's life. I don't believe there is any chance he could expose Donovan for any sort of impropriety."

"He had the kids in that house." Fia left the statement hanging, letting Scott glean what he would from it.

After a moment, Scott chuckled, a mirthless sound. "I see where you're going. It would be unfounded, though no less damaging should it be said to the right people." He sighed, pulling a breath from deep in his core. "I think, for the moment, it would be best if we take Sister Annabel's suggestion and retire to our quarters until dinner. Before that, could you come to the office with me? I want to give you something."

She followed him down the dark hallway, through the kitchen, and into the hallway where the children should have been. It hadn't been riotous before, but now it was eerily quiet. Like a power outage. The deafening absence of sound that was virtually imperceptible when present.

In the office, the priest opened a cabinet and pulled from it two short crystal rocks glasses and a crystal decanter filled with an amber-brown liquid. He rested it all on the desk and poured from the decanter, holding one of the glasses out to Fia, keeping the second for himself.

"Fia, I want you to decompress. Annabel was not wrong in saying we will need clear heads to deal with anything that might be coming. I would like you to share what you have seen with the others over dinner, what you know of the blonde woman."

"Should I tell them about Donovan?"

Scott took a sip from the glass, considering her question.

"There's nothing they can do about it," she added. "If he's got the teens somewhere, we can't get hold of them."

"I think they should know. The younger children are with Cecilia, and I believe the teens have enough training behind them, they will be safe."

Fia sipped from her glass, letting the warm whiskey wash over the tightness in her throat and chest. "Can I take this to Max?"

"Peace offering?"

"Peace offering, liquid courage, all of the above."

Scott retrieved a third glass from the cabinet and

handed it and the decanter to Fia. "With my blessing. Go, do what you need to, to get your minds off what is happening."

Fia finished the drink in her glass and left the room, heading back to Max.

When she reached the bedroom, she tapped lightly on the door. "Max? Are you in there?"

He opened the door, his handsome face twisted in an angry grimace. "You told me to wait here. Where else did you expect me to go?"

"Max, I'm sorry. I didn't mean—I was pretty sure I was headed to—I didn't want anyone else involved if I got myself in a position to have to kill that priest." She held up her offering. "Truce?"

Max's face softened. "Okay, that's fair." He stepped out of her way, letting her into the room. He took the glasses and whiskey from her. "Crystal, huh?"

"It's good stuff too."

"I would hope so." He poured a drink for each of them. "Should I have one by myself, to catch up?"

"That's up to you."

He responded by draining the glass and refilling it. He handed the other to her and tapped his own against it.

"Scott . . . may have just told me that we—you and I need to—well, the word he used was *decompress*."

"Did your priest just tell you to get laid?"

"Yeah. Yeah, he did."

Max finished his second glass and set it on the dark wood top of the dresser. He took Fia's from her, placing it next to his, and pulled her close. The room was dark, despite the red evening sun outside. Streaks of light striped the room, and Max stood in one of them. His dark eyes burned into hers, even in the scant light.

With her hands on his hips, she pushed him back toward the bed. He took one step back, then countered, stepping into her. He reached around her, pushing his hands between her thighs and lifting her off the ground. He wrapped her legs around his waist and carried her to the bed.

He laid her on her back across the wide four-poster bed and stripped her from the waist down. She raised her torso to finish removing her clothes. His eyes traced over her body, pausing briefly at key points along the path: her breasts, her stomach, her hips, and then finally the garter sheath on her right thigh. He unfastened the strap and laid the weapon to the side, where he had gently placed her clothes as they came off her body.

Fia reached up and unfastened Max's jeans, rubbing her hands back over the flesh of his hips as she pushed down on the garment. He stripped off his shirt, revealing the deeply chiseled muscles of his abdomen and the black and gray of his gallery of tattoos, the newest shining the darkest black of them all. He climbed onto the bed, slipping free of the remainder of his clothes, and laid his weight upon her. He pressed deep kisses into her mouth as she clawed at his back, urging him deeper and chewing softly at his lower lip.

She moaned into his mouth as he rolled his hips gently, his body heavy on top of her. She savored the security of his strength as he pressed it into her.

He lifted her up by her back, rolling them both and giving her the advantage. She raised up on top of him, exposing her body for him. He traced his long, slender fingers over her skin as she lowered herself over him again. He drew abstract patterns, raising gooseflesh over her entire body and making her nerves quiver as her muscles tightened. She took a deep, slow breath and another and another, filling her lungs, as he watched her breasts heave and fall.

She lay back down, pressing her torso against his. He rested his hands firmly against her buttocks, guiding her, forward and back.

She gripped his hips with her thighs and pulled him back the way they had come, pulling his weight back on top of her. He lifted himself free from her grip, hovering over her, and the look in his eyes made her shiver. She took one more deep breath into her lungs and held it, digging her fingers into his back and pulling him down.

When they had finished, he rolled onto his back, pulling her to lie against him.

THIRTY-ONE

They fell asleep across the width of the bed, wrapped in each other, and woke only when Agnes's voice rasped through the door. "Fiammetta, we are gathering in the kitchen for the evening meal. Please join us."

Fia groaned, not wanting to shatter the calm of the moment. Max replied with one of his own before lifting her off his chest. "We should go."

Fia grumbled unintelligibly and redressed, pausing briefly to savor the view as Max dressed with his back to her. The flowered pattern that covered his left side reached delicate fingers of vine around to his back. Words she couldn't quite make out scrolled around his right arm from the inside of his bicep in an elaborate black script. On his right shoulder sat a bass clef the size of her hand.

Max turned back to her, pulling his shirt over his hair and his hair from the collar. He pulled a rubber band from his pocket and tied the brown waves back at the base of his neck. He flashed her a grin and waved at the shirt in her hand. She looked down to see what he was waving at, having gotten completely lost in watching him.

Dressed, they proceeded to the kitchen. As Max reached to push the door open for Fia to go ahead of him, a scream ripped through the house. They exchanged startled glances and hurried to the foyer. Mother Agnes was already on the third riser up to the second floor by the time they got there. Rebecca and Scott had come out of the kitchen behind them, and the four of them ascended behind Agnes.

Fia. She felt the electric tingle of the divine invading her thoughts. *I smell blood. Lots of it.*

They crested the stairs, and now Fia could smell the blood too. The scent of hot pennies filled her lungs and nose, permeating so deeply, she could taste it too. She worked at the saliva in her mouth, trying to wash away the taste.

The first door at the top of the stairs was open—the only one in the hallway that was. Once across the threshold, Agnes gasped, stopping short quickly enough, Fia nearly collided with her. The curtains—the same blackout curtains that covered the windows in the downstairs bedroom—were open wide, the late sun through the trees casting long shadows over the scene.

Sister Annabel was on her knees on the floor beside the bed, her hands clenched in prayer. In them, she held her rosary. Sister Theresa lay on her side on the bed, facing the wall, still in her robes. If not for the red stain beneath her head and shoulders, Fia would have thought she was asleep. Her veil lay at her feet on the bed, revealing a short crop of black hair to Fia for the first time.

"Annabel!" Fia scrambled to pull the woman to her feet. Annabel turned her ashen face to Fia's, responding dumbfoundedly to the sound of her own name. "Annabel, what the hell happened in here?"

"I-I don't know. I was coming out to meet everyone in the kitchen and knocked on Sister Theresa's door. But it wasn't latched, and when I knocked . . ." She looked back at Theresa.

Fia followed Annabel's gaze to the body of her fallen sister. She stepped closer to inspect it. "Annabel, did you touch anything when you came in?"

Annabel's voice came out in a gasping stutter. "N-no. I couldn't think—I just collapsed. There's so much blood, and the smell—"

Fia felt a pang of sympathy for the young nun. Fia was used to death: the sight, the smells, the feeling in the air. She guessed this must be Annabel's first real exposure to it.

Fia looked over Theresa's body as best she could without moving or touching it too much. It looked, Fia thought, like Theresa had taken the opportunity for rest to heart, lying down for a nap while she waited for dinner. Someone had slipped in quietly—it didn't look like Theresa had even stirred at the intrusion—and cut her throat. It had been fast and efficient; that much Fia could see.

She turned back to the others. Five faces stared back at her, frozen in various stages of shock. "We should call the—"

Before she could finish, there was a crash in the foyer. It was a deliberate sound, the sound of crystal shattering on stone. The faces staring back at Fia turned toward the sound, and Fia moved toward the door. Max put up a hand to stop her. "Watch out," she said and pushed him aside, stepping out into the hall.

She was greeted by a booming female voice calling out

her name, thick with a Scandinavian accent. "Fiammetta Drake, my master requests your presence."

Fia headed for the stairs, stopping on the second step down. "Master? Aren't we being a little melodramatic?" *When in doubt, belittle your opponent.*

"Come with us, Fiammetta, and no one else has to get hurt."

"Fiammetta is so formal. I assume the ultimate goal is to kill me, which is pretty intimate, really. Fia will do just fine." She took a deep breath, hoping she sounded more confident than she felt.

She took another step down on the stairs and felt a presence behind her. It wasn't the electric tingle of the angel, but it did set her nerves on fire. She didn't have to turn to know who it was.

"Stay back," she hissed through clenched teeth, moving her lips as little as possible. She wanted to let this intruder think she was alone for as long as possible. She took another step down the stairs, assessing the situation as she descended.

There were ten—eleven including the ringmaster, the blonde woman. From where Fia stood, the woman appeared unarmed, but Fia couldn't believe that was the case. She considered the small knife in the sheath on her thigh, suddenly wishing she had her little 9mm. She had never shot anyone with it, but she felt, in this moment, as though she had brought the proverbial knife to a gun fight. Despite the broad man behind the blonde—Ariaz's thug—slapping ol' Lou against his palm like a caricature, Fia couldn't imagine the blonde lady wasn't packing real heat.

She decided to lay on the bravado as thick as she could, maybe figure out Blondie's game. "I don't know what you think you're going to find here, but it's just me. Nobody here but me and the chipmunks."

And the nun you murdered.

"Now, now. Fia, was it? What would Mother Agnes think of such a bald-faced lie? Maybe I should ask her. Mother Superior? Do you hear the lies your prodigy is trying to pass off out here?"

Fia chose to keep up the story. It was just her, no one else in the house. If she kept the woman talking, there would be less shooting.

She hoped.

"There really isn't anyone else here. We found out you were coming, and they took off. Kansas, I think. Maybe New Mexico. They left me here."

"You want me to believe they left you here as sacrifice?"

"I insisted. You were coming for me, right? You asked an obedient little boy if he knew me. Even he was able to sniff you out, to know it was okay to lie to you. Told us everything. I told Agnes and Scott to get the kids and get out of here."

The woman's face shifted, and for a second, Fia thought she might be buying the story. "Your Father McGregor is far too protective of you for that, I think. No, they are here, somewhere. I might even wager there, at the top of the stairs. In the hallway, just out of sight?"

Fia shook her head. She had no way of knowing what was going on behind her, but she hoped she could stall long enough for the others to work out some kind of defense. As far as she knew, her knife was the only weapon among them.

"All alone. He knows I can handle myself. It took some talking, but I convinced him that getting the kids away was more important."

"Ah, the kids. There are small ones, no, and teens? A

young group of new hunters. Tell me, how is the girl? She took a nasty spill. You say they are gone? With Father McGregor? I thought my companion here told me the fat priest took them."

She turned to face Muscle and his bat. "*Gå og se*," she said to him with a wave toward the stairs.

He dropped the bat against his shoulder and started in Fia's direction. Not wanting another run at the lout, Fia laughed. "Too afraid to come up yourself? You gotta send a scout to see if the little girl is bluffing?"

The woman reached out one long, muscular arm and clapped a hand on the man's shoulder. "We'll all go." She spoke only to him but loud enough, it echoed through the foyer.

With the blonde woman leading, the small platoon rounded the bottom of the staircase. Fia took a spare second to steal a glance over her shoulder. She *was* alone. The others had retreated into the shadows somewhere, supporting her story. She thought about the secret passage, hoping they had too.

The blonde woman was visibly shocked to see no one standing behind her foe. A slight, unassuming redhead with dragon-scale scars stood alone at the top of the dark staircase. With nothing but the knife on her thigh, Fia was able to hold her hands up, unarmed, vulnerable.

"Where are your soldiers, Miss Drake?"

"I told you. Kansas. Maybe Nebraska. I really don't know. We loaded everyone on a bus, and I told them to drive until they needed to stop for gas and flip a coin if they had to change direction."

Blondie took a step up the stairs, watching her feet, looking for traps. As she did, the squad behind her fell into two lines, side by side, but a step out of sync. Fia guessed that when they reached the stairs, they would be staggered, one on each step, but spanning the width.

The blonde woman raised her hand to bring them to a halt behind her. "You appear to be unarmed, Miss Drake. I am struggling to believe, if you knew we were coming, that you would greet us without defense."

"Would you believe I just got out of the shower?" The woman's face remained still, unresponsive. "No?" Fia searched frantically for another stall when a slight movement caught her attention.

At the bottom of the stairs, Mother Agnes moved silently, as if floating above the floorboards, and swiftly pressed a cloth over the nose and mouth of a woman at the rear. She pulled the woman's body back into her own chest, pinning her arms to her side and used her own height to leverage the woman off her feet.

It took two of Fia's pounding heartbeats for the woman to wilt into Agnes's grasp, then the nun passed the limp figure off to Scott, who picked her up like she weighed no more than a sack of groceries.

One down, ten to go.

Agnes met Fia's gaze and held up her little pistol bow, giving Fia a nod. Fia hoped that meant Agnes was telling her to engage if she could.

Agnes moved silently up a step and pressed the nose of her weapon into the soft side of the neck of the next person in line, covering his mouth with her other hand.

Before Fia could process what had happened, there was a soft thump as the bolt from Agnes's bow hit the wall on the other side. Impressing Fia with her grace and speed, the nun was out of sight by the time the blonde woman turned to see what had happened.

Without time to wonder why Agnes had left the first

soldier alive, Fia took the stairs two at a time to wrap her arm around the blonde woman's neck. With deft precision, Fia removed the knife from its sheath inside the fake cargo pocket of her pants and pressed the tip into the woman's back.

"Get her!" The woman's voice was strained as she screamed against the pressure from Fia's inner elbow. Her dwindling army started up the stairs to rescue their commander from a captor barely half her size.

Fia pushed harder on the knife. "Tell them to stand down, or I'll put this through your spine."

The woman growled, an animalistic sound emanating from deep in her broad chest, but said nothing in her own defense. She had come here prepared to die for her cause. With a jerk, she flipped Fia over her back. She had misjudged Fia's size, however, and the momentum of throwing her little foe pitched the blonde woman forward too.

The women toppled down, taking Muscle with them as they went. A woman standing behind him had enough time to react, but she foolishly tried to stop their descent instead of moving out of the way, and they gathered her into their expanding human snowball.

The four of them hit the landing with a collective groan. Something crunched on impact, and Fia realized the woman who had tried to stop their momentum had been trapped beneath the big man. Once he was able to find his feet, he reached down to help the woman find hers, and pain twisted across her face as she breathed.

Broken ribs, Fia thought, scrambling back away from the pile as the two ahead and five behind closed in on her. She tripped over the body Agnes had left behind and landed firmly on her butt.

Another bolt came from above, ripping through the

neck of another of the blonde woman's platoon. As the body fell down the stairs, Fia looked up to see Annabel looking down on her before the young nun slipped back into the darkness.

Three down, eight to go. All standing above her.

Ariaz's thug lifted his bat, preparing to swing it with maximum force, something Fia did not want measured. Before he could swing, the woman with the broken ribs cried out behind him. She had dragged herself to her feet to rejoin the fray but hadn't stayed on them long. On her knees on the stairs, her body twitched and jerked, and Fia saw coiled wire extending out of her back to a little black futuristic stun gun Rebecca had gripped in her hand.

The writhing woman was enough of a distraction, drawing the eyes of the intruders away from Fia. She crawled up a couple of steps to get behind them. Once on her feet, she bounded for where she had last seen Annabel. She needed something with a longer reach than her dagger.

"Here," Annabel whispered from the doorway to Theresa's room. She held out a bow similar to the one Agnes had used. Fia accepted it gratefully, and when she turned back to the stairs, she found the horde had followed her. The blonde woman was still leading the charge.

Fia let the woman advance on her, allowing her to get within point-blank range. When there was no room for error, Fia squeezed the trigger, sending the crayon-sized shaft of metal tearing through the woman's midsection with enough force, Muscle reeled backward when it then struck him in the shoulder, nearly toppling him off the stairs.

The blonde woman fell to her knees at Fia's feet. Fia took two steps down, hoping for a better angle for what she planned next. She put a sneakered foot against the woman's chest and pressed back until the woman lay on her back along the stairs. Fia dug in with her heel, and the woman clawed uselessly at her ankle, trying to lift her foot.

"You can kill everyone here, you stupid little bitch," the woman spat. "But we'll never be gone. There will always be new children to join us, to fight for the True Ones."

Fia glared down at the woman for another beat. This woman was a woman. No malevolent soul, no veiled demon. Just a mortal, human woman.

If you are not able to convince them to forfeit their control of the demons, you may be forced to kill them.

Fia reached down, pressing her knee into the woman's chest. She touched the tip of her knife to the soft area behind the woman's jaw, applying enough pressure to draw a drop of blood. "Your devotion to Irzelen"—she pressed harder on the knife—"only makes him hate you. Most humans are little more than pests to him. *You* disgust him. He would kill you himself if he could."

The woman responded by spitting on Fia's cheek. Without another word, Fia dropped the knife, gripped the sides of the woman's head, and slammed her head against the hardwood beneath it. The woman's eyes rolled around like marbles in her head.

"Annabel!" Fia called, reaching for her knife. "Watch her."

As she stood, the stairs beneath her shook with the weight of something heavy being dropped on them with a *whump*. She turned to see Muscle lying facedown, his bat on the stairs above him, only one step down from where Fia stood.

Max hovered over him, his knee in the middle of the man's back, his hands on the hilt of a knife completely obscured in the man's neck. Max pulled the knife from its target and met Fia's eyes, returning to his feet. His whiskey eyes shone black, and tears threatened the edges of them. The deep angles of his handsome face were dark with shadows that she didn't think had anything to do with the lack of light. She moved toward him, down to the next step. He threw the knife to the ground beside the body, stepped over it, and retreated back down the stairs.

While Fia had attended to the group's commander, the two nuns and priest had dispatched the remaining six soldiers. The first two downed women—the one Agnes had drugged and the one Rebecca had stunned—were nowhere to be seen, nor were either of the two bodies. Scott was busy with one man, wrapping his wrists in a plastic zip tie, and stepped quickly out of the way as Max stormed past him, Fia a few steps behind.

Fia caught up to Max on the granite floor of the foyer, grabbing his arm on the backswing. He jerked it away from her, turning to face her. His eyes blazed into hers, and he ground his teeth.

"Don't touch me."

She staggered back a step. "Max? What's—"

"What's wrong? Really, Fia, that's the question? You lied to me, left me stranded here, pushed me out of the way—"

"Max, I didn't know—I wasn't pushing *you* out of the way. I just needed to get through. And I didn't leave you stranded—"

"Because I followed you. You lied to me, Fia, so you could leave without anyone wondering where you were going until you were gone. So you could do something stupid. You still don't see anything wrong with it."

"This is my responsibility, Max. It's my job to take care—"

"Of everyone. Except yourself. You're reckless, Fia, but

that's not even why I'm mad. And I'm not even mad. I'm worried—"

"It's not your place to worry about me, Max."

"You don't get to make that decision. You brought me into this place, into this war, made me care about these people, bond with them. And then you can't even trust us to fight beside you. To protect you when you need it. And Fia, you need it sometimes." He waved a hand wildly toward the stairs. "You were busy with Heidi up there and about got your head caved in."

He backed away another couple of steps. "I need some—I need to go."

Fia reached for him. "Max, stop."

"No. Fia, I have given you the benefit of the doubt because you have been alone for a long time. You are adjusting to having a team again. And I understand that, but I need some room to breathe. Don't follow me." He turned from her to cross the granite floor.

"Fine," she snapped. "Go, then."

She turned her back and met several pairs of eyes staring back at her. Her face burned, something between rage and embarrassment. She had nowhere to go, nowhere she could get away from their piercing stares.

Scott stepped up next to her. "He's right, you know."

She shot him a glare, shocked. "Whose side are you on?"

"Oddly, yours."

She flinched as Max slammed the door behind him. She ground her own teeth and snarled at the faces staring back at her. "What are you all looking at?" She took long, deliberate strides back toward the stairs, climbing toward Max's felled victim. "Someone gonna help me get this out of here?"

THIRTY-TWO

Rebecca's voice was calm, soothing. "Fia, if you want to go after Max, we can—"

"Mind your own business, huh?" The small nun recoiled as if Fia had struck her.

Mother Agnes was the next to speak. "Fiammetta, perhaps Sister Rebecca has a point. We are a long way from the city; at least take him home."

"He made his bed. He can use it to fly back to the city for all I care." She locked eyes with the Reverend Mother before looking suggestively at the corpse she was still clutching by the collar of his shirt. "What are we going to do with these bodies?"

Scott stepped between Fia and the elder nun, throwing the man over his shoulder with tellingly little effort. "Everyone left alive is a prisoner. Move them to the basement."

"You mean, the basement where the pointy things are?"

Annabel spoke next, her crossbow still trained on the blonde woman, who had regained consciousness. "There is a cell in the basement. The back half."

"Perfect. Because every house filled with nuns and children should have a prison cell." Fia rolled her eyes and started up the stairs to meet Annabel. Propelled by anger and grief, she grabbed the wounded Scandinavian woman by her upper arm and hauled her to her feet. The momentum nearly knocked them both down the stairs. Fia jabbed the handle of her knife into the woman's back. "March."

"Do you think she's going to be okay?" Annabel whispered behind Fia after they'd reached the bottom of the stairs.

Fia wheeled around to find Annabel leaning toward Rebecca. "I'm fine," she growled. "There is work to be done. If you're not going to help, get out of the way." She grabbed the man Scott had zip-tied on her way by and half dragged him behind her as she urged the woman forward. Rebecca fell in line behind her, guiding two more prisoners toward the kitchen.

In the basement, Fia leaned on the steel door of the cell, waiting for Rebecca to secure the prisoners. Fia pushed the door closed after the nun had reemerged, clicking the lock for added security.

"What are we going to do with them now?" Rebecca asked, her voice overly gentle. It sounded to Fia like she was trying to keep herself safe from Fia's wrath.

"I'd take them deeper into the mountains, put a steak in each of their pockets, and let nature take care of the rest. But I imagine Scott and Agnes will want to interrogate them. Or some shit."

She watched Rebecca's face, expecting the woman to be appalled by the suggestion of throwing human beings to the lions, but if she was bothered by it, it did not show. Fia sighed deeply, exhausted from what felt like a seventy-two-hour day. She grew even more exhausted when she realized it hadn't even been twelve hours since Scott had called them back to the house.

"C'mon. Let's go see what's going on upstairs." She led the way out of the basement but turned back when she realized she was alone.

"Just making sure," Rebecca responded, waving a hand over the door.

"Yeah. Right. Can't be too careful."

Back in the foyer, Scott was coming in from the garden. "All the bodies have been moved to the shed," he said quietly.

"All?" Fia turned her eyes toward the upper floor. "Even—"

"Fiammetta, if you would like to catch up with Mr. Hawkins—"

"Leave it alone, Agnes." Fia looked down the hall toward the room they had shared. "Is there an empty room upstairs?"

"There is. But Fiammetta—"

"Show me. Where's Annabel?"

"Sister Annabel insisted on tending to the deceased. She is with them in the garden shed," Scott replied.

Fia thought for a moment, unsure what to do with her next question. "Is that safe? Do we know she wasn't responsible for all this? We've been trying to catch a mole, then she conveniently finds Theresa's body when no one else was around, after *she* made the suggestion we spend an hour alone."

"She deserves our trust, Fiammetta."

"She might deserve your trust. I don't know that she has mine anymore. What about Theresa? You didn't take her out to the shed?"

"I moved Sister Theresa's body to a respectable location. She will be attended to in the morning."

Fia met Scott's white-blue eyes, studying his face to figure out what he might have meant by "respectable location." Unable to determine anything from the blank expression on his flushed face, she nudged Rebecca toward the stairs.

"Where's this empty room?"

She caught her own eyes in the rearview mirror of the stolen car. She didn't realize she was crying until she saw the tears glistening against the red and green looking back at her.

Over her shoulder, he lay stretched across the mustard-yellow upholstery of the car's back seat, bleeding from where a bullet had ripped through his chest. She could hear the sucking sound of the air passing through the hole in his lung and pleaded for him to stay with her.

"Max, please, please stay with me, Max. I'm going to get you help." She punched uselessly at the dashboard, her plaintive pleas escalating to a shriek. "I can't lose you too."

Fia woke before the sun had reached its full morning light. In the gray-blue haze of predawn, she slipped into her sneakers, having slept in her clothes. She had only slept about three hours, but after several nightmares kept her from truly resting, she didn't think she wanted to try anymore. She slid open the door of the small bedroom she had occupied in exchange for not going back to the oversize bed she had shared with Max and, keeping close to the wall to avoid creaking floorboards, made her way to the stairs.

She had left the keys to the Scout in the other bedroom. She ducked into the room, grabbed them off the chest of drawers inside the door, and ducked back out, not wanting to look around.

She crossed through the kitchen and headed for the basement. Belowground, she checked the door on the prison cell where five of their attackers had spent the last few hours. Everything was still locked up tight. Her chest heaved with a deep sigh, though she wasn't sure if that was from relief or exhaustion.

Back upstairs, she looked around the foyer of the safe house. She wasn't coming back here. She had decided that before she even went to bed. She had even considered leaving Denver, leaving Colorado.

When the going gets tough, the tough get going. She was certain there was still a target on her back and demons aimed at it. The only way to find out who had put it there was to get it as far from this place as she could. She pushed her way out the heavy front door and headed for her car, which was parked on the far side of the driveway.

As she pulled away from the house, she wondered if the guy who had made her first fake ID was still in the business.

Thirty-Three

Fia pulled the Scout into the garage attached to her condo, winding up the ramps to the top level. She paused as she crested the last ramp; where she expected to find only a glittery red scooter, she also found the white car Max had left.

She didn't know where she was going. She only knew she needed to take the target on her back and get it as far away from people like Max—and Zari—as possible.

Her gut twisted with a pang of guilt at the idea of leaving Zari again. But the blonde woman had connected the dots, used Zari to stalk Fia. It was only a matter of time before someone else made the same connection. And they might not be as subtle as the blonde had been.

Fia stopped her SUV behind Max's car, left the engine running, and climbed out. Crossing to the scooter, she wheeled it around so the nose faced out away from the wall. From a storage closet at the end of the space where she usually parked the SUV, she produced a small loading ramp, which she leaned against the wall behind the scooter. Maneuvering the Scout, she lined the tailgate up with the nose of the scooter. She pushed the scooter up the ramp into the back of the SUV, collapsed the ramp, and shoved it in beside the scooter.

She slammed the tailgate closed, harder than she meant to, and climbed back into the driver's seat.

Back down at street level, Fia paused at the exit, checking the street for traffic. Facing her on the left was an old blue pickup truck. In the driver's seat was a kid; Fia guessed he was no more than sixteen, maybe seventeen.

His eyes locked with hers through the glass. He set his jaw, and she watched as he tightened his grip on the steering wheel. His engine roared, and Fia had the space of a breath to react before the truck lurched forward.

She slammed her foot down on the gas pedal, wrenching the steering wheel to the right, away from the impact. Metal screamed as a spray of glass from both side windows filled the cabin. The scene through the windshield splintered as jagged fractures snaked across the glass. Fia's vision flashed between blinding white and hazy gray.

Through the pounding in her skull and ringing in her ears, Fia barely registered the sound of her passenger door opening. She felt the pinch of a hypodermic needle in her right bicep, and the gray haze deepened to black.

RAGE AND RELEASE

Fia Drake, Soul Hunter Series
Book Three

Coming Fall 2021

Acknowledgments

I would like to express my gratitude to my Patreon community, whose support helps to make this series possible.

Founding Legacies
Patricia Harris
Redbird Stormcrow

Concrete and Chords
Glenda Pearl Kilgore

Mortar and Monitors
Caroline Barnette
Robin Stevens

Thank you to Jacob Staley for helping me to name Mitchell Wylde and his band, Wyldfire, and for offering a male perspective on all things Max.

Thank you to my reader group, the Fia Drake Faction, for your support and occasional input.

Thank you to my Zeta Pis, who continually show me the meaning of poise, purpose, and power and who remind me to live joyously every day. You are my measure of strong women.

Cover Art by Adam E. Mathews (Instagram @atomichdr)

About the Author

What began with a princess captured by a pirate and rescued by a dragon has developed into D. Gabrielle Jensen's lifelong fascination with stories of the unexpected and unexplored. She has dabbled across many styles and genres, but whether through startling, staccato works of pulp horror or the dirt and grime of urban fantasy, she always finds her way back to speculative fiction.

An award-winning bestseller, D. is built from drumbeats and hot asphalt. Even as an imaginative child in the rural mountains of Colorado, she felt pulled to the chaos and clamor of The City—any city, every city. With this in mind, she aims to infuse her work with mortar and music. Her favorite views of any city are from the rooftops and the side streets. She strives to show the beauty of both in her stories, urging readers to walk the streets with her as she introduces them not only to powerful heroines and antiheroines but to the buskers, bartenders, and baristas who make up the fabric of every city.

If writing be her first love, music is the trusted friend D. turns to when that love forgets her birthday. She can sing along with new songs before they've finished playing and set up a drum kit blindfolded. She can't remember a time when she didn't know how to play her parents' vinyl records. She has one Spotify playlist (out of many) that can run for two full days without repeat and an active hatred for paperless concert tickets. She works that love of music into her writing through allusions to lyrics in imagery, characters named after songs and musicians, and behind-the-scenes playlists. She will even write to a metronome if she needs to give a scene just the right cadence.

D. loves things that begin with the letter *C*—coffee, cats, cities, conversation, concerts—and things that don't—airports, humans, macrophotography, urban decay, macrophotography of urban decay, and the beauty of flaw. She encourages everyone to join her across social media and on Patreon. Strike up a conversation. What are you waiting for?

www.patreon.com/writerdgabrielle

www.instagram.com/writerdgabrielle

www.facebook.com/writerdgabrielle

www.twitter.com/writerdgabriele